<u>Dedication</u>

This really isn't the kind of novel that anyone would be pleased to have dedicated to them. It's a sordid story, about horrid people, so I can't possibly dedicate it to my wonderful innocent son Christian, or to any of the amazing friends and family who have offered their help and advice while writing this. If this were a very different type of book, then I would dedicate it to all of you.

The Six Steps
To Marrying a Superstar

The day I proposed: Saturday 26th November 2010

I was wearing my best and most fashionable tailored suit, sitting confidently in a straight backed chair in a busy restaurant, waiting for my date, the girl of my dreams to breeze in through the doors. When she entered, all heads turned, and the gentle clamour of the restaurant transformed into excited whispers, all directed at my woman. I knew the power she had on others; I knew that as soon as the rest of the 'normal people' in the restaurant went home, they would recount it to their friends and relatives.

The woman, my woman, was the one and only Elisha Cicero: the Oscar winning actress and model. Without a doubt, all the other men sitting around me would have had sexual fantasies about this woman at some point in their lives. For them, these fantasies would never be fulfilled – this was as close as they would ever get. That night, they would dream they were me, the man she loved.

The story is quite clear cut: on the 26th November 2010, I, Shaun Valfierno, proposed to Elisha, and the following year she became my wife. The envy of the nation, all eyes were on me and I appeared beside her in countless glossy magazines. I grew rich, and made love to her every night of the week. Most importantly, I was happy, and she was happy.

Did I love her?

Fuck no, of course not. I'm not that kind of man.

Just remember this:

1. I never treated her badly.
2. I rarely cheated on her.
3. I could make her come like a dog on heat.

3

Don't get me wrong – I loved having her as my wife. She was, after all, my dream woman. Over the years I'd had my own fair share of unfulfilled fantasies about this girl, and during our engagement the long hard struggle to ensnare her was never far from my mind. My blood, sweat and tears went into catching Elisha, and at the time, I would have dragged her to the altar kicking and screaming if that's what circumstances required. It wouldn't even have mattered if I couldn't stand the sight of her: love was not a prerequisite for my marriage.

Like so many before me, I could have sat on my hands forever and waited, gained nought but a lonely life of bachelordom. Instead, I chose to own my life. I climbed the branches and plucked the best girl from the top of the tree before roasting her. Step by step, one foot in front of the other, I never took my eye off the prize.

They say that there are six degrees of separation. Everyone on this earth is linked with everybody else by a maximum of six people. Although it was a wholly conscious decision to make my way up the social ladder so as to meet Elisha on a level playing field, it is only now that I realise I have whored and manipulated my way through the people separating me from her. The steps taken to reach her, the people who helped me along the way to my marriage, are as follows:

Step 1: Polly Edant
Step 2: Terry Taylor
Step 3: Scarlett Smith
Step 4: Charlie Ekells
Step 5: Damien Woland
Step 6: Elisha Cicero

What ensues is an account of my interactions with these people. It is the story of my success:

Step 1: Polly Edant

<u>Thursday 16th August 2007</u>

I first set eyes on Elisha in an art gallery. Strictly speaking this isn't the kind of place I usually attend, but Polly, a friend from my university days had come up to visit. She lived around two hours' travel away in Dover, but it so happened that my place was only two doors down from the North London office in which she was having a job interview.

Islington is a beautiful place to live, much underrated by those who have their hearts set on the very centre of the city. It is a stone's throw from Angel and the trendy Upper Street, and boasts a fairly large array of Victorian Architecture still in peak condition. The spacious one-bedroomed flats around there were not as expensive as the obnoxiously overpriced squalid studios in the more popular parts of Chelsea, Kensington and Mayfair. I was happy where I was, and in fact, was beginning to consider re-mortgaging to get a buy-to-let in the same area. The homes in Islington were always appreciating in value; by 2007, I had personally made £100k in equity on my flat. Aged twenty-seven, I was old enough to earn the money to afford London-life, but young enough to still enjoy it.

I hadn't seen Polly for four years but we still spared time in our hectic lives for the occasional email to each other. When I found out where her interview was, I was more than happy to invite her up to stay over. In fact, due to our relationship at university, I'd been looking forward to it. The plan was for her to come up on Thursday, we could go for a few drinks and she could then prepare for her 12:00 interview on the Friday morning. Unfortunately, Polly wasn't half as attractive as I remembered; nor did we have quite as many things to talk about as we used to.

At university she had been fun, flirty, and sexy. She was one of those girls that couldn't say no to a kiss, and more often than not answered with an affirmative and overtly satisfying passionate yes to something a little more than a kiss. When she confirmed that she was coming up to stay, I imagined a return to the old days – a fun night out drinking and a frolic or two under the bedcovers. Unfortunately, she appeared to me in a dull grey suit, utterly devoid of colour, with a personality to match.

Here is the general gist of every conversation we had that day:

Me: "So Polly, what have you been doing for four years?"

Polly: "Stand at the mirror and make myself look miserable, I do it at least twelve times a day."

Completely stuck for anything else to do, and wishing that I hadn't asked her to stay, I took Polly to the Tate Modern. I hate modern art, I really hate it, and I can't see how an infantile blob of nothing ever manages to attract paying customers. That particular visit did nothing to dispel my feelings; in fact, the first instalment we saw confirmed them beyond reasonable doubt. In the big and otherwise quite enthralling entrance hall, some wanky artist had decided to build a giant teapot and let people slide down the spout into a make-shift café where you could drink a polystyrene cup of lukewarm tea. It wasn't as if I could even be arsed to wait around and get a drink of tea, the queue would have taken about three hours, so filled was it with equally uninspired arty types trying to convince themselves that the 'piece' would somehow seem a lot better if they had a go on it. I think Polly was tempted to stand in line for the spout-slide, but there was no chance that I was going to wait around for three hours trying to pretend that I was interested in anything that she had to say, so I ushered her into the main foyer and into the rest of the God-forsaken gallery.

At some point, the trip began to blur into a vague sense of meaningless colour. So bored was I with both the company and the exhibits, that at first I didn't even notice Elisha. She was walking barely five metres in front of me; in such plain clothes that not even the Paparazzi would have recognised her. It was strange, at that moment in time I wasn't just a man watching a movie, I was a man watching a movie star. She was in the UK promoting the DVD release of her Oscar winning performance in the film adaptation of *'A Better Class of Enemy'.* Her face was currently plastered on all the billboards amongst the tunnels of the Underground. She should have been untouchable; in no circumstances would someone expect to see her bumbling about on her own in the Tate Modern. Even in such plain clothes, she was amazing and I couldn't take my eyes off of her. I undressed her, took away the baggy jeans and long grey coat, and I imagined her with wide eyes and my cock inside her. I thought of her with an O shaped mouth, and sweat all over her forehead. She was something I wanted to be with, she was something that drove me wild, and before my thoughts formed fully, before I worked up the courage to approach her, she was gone. I immediately left Polly's side and tried to find her, but she had disappeared, vanished into that vast and magical place of nothing where every famous person goes when not in the public eye. I was the only one that saw her, and my eyes continued to roam and search for her after she was gone, a fleeting glance of beauty and then an almost unbearable return to the horrendous Polly and her miserable soulless droopy breasts.

Five hours later, after a prolonged visit to the pub, Polly opened up her legs for me. I had treated her like shit all day, barely talking to her, and she still wanted it. It was too easy. There was something slightly desperate and pathetic about her, but I was drunk and it was a better option than going to sleep. After ten minutes, it was all over. Polly lay beside me, silent, naked, and with a rancid look on her face. I knew that she hadn't really enjoyed it and as I examined her features, I was overwhelmed with guilt. I didn't know why I felt bad. I hadn't done anything wrong, but I still had memories of that raunchy girl from Uni. All of a sudden it grew too much to bear, so I got out of bed and left the room. To settle my nerves I made myself a glass of Bloody Mary, lay back on my black leather sofa, and mulled over the day. After cleansing myself of the guilt from sleeping with Polly with an easily forgettable yet all-encompassing excuse, I began to ponder on Elisha Cicero: how close I had been to her, and how I was sure that she must have noticed me too. I pondered over what could have happened if I had been five footsteps ahead, five footsteps closer to her, would it have been possible that we could have talked? Could I have flirted with her, and maybe even had my wicked way with her? That night there were only half formed ideas in my head, nothing concrete, and to tell you the truth, for a good many weeks after that night I did not think of Elisha all that much. I was too wrapped up in the dilemma that presented itself a few seconds later.

"Don't tell Terry" said a quiet voice behind me (Polly feeling guilty for cheating on her boyfriend).

Another rush of guilt overcame me. Who was Terry? Was he someone that I was supposed to know? As far as I could remember, I had never met anyone called Terry. I racked my mind, trying to think....Terry..., no, I was certain that I knew nobody with that name.

"Okay" I shrugged, happy in the knowledge that I could tell everyone that I had ever met exactly what had happened, and how rubbish it had been.

Polly took this as an invitation to sit down next to me and cry on my shoulder. I rolled my eyes, wondering when she would go home.

"What happened to you?" she said.

I barely had time to register what she was saying, and my head was in mid-recoil when she continued.

"You used to be a nice guy, now you're just a fucking loser."

What? *Me??*

"Go fuck yourself Shaun." She stood up, walked into the bedroom and slammed the door.

What the hell was going on? Had the world gone mad? How could a desperate, wobbly-thighed bicycle with no personality call *me* a loser?

"What a freak." I mumbled to no one in particular, after which, I sat on the sofa and fumed into the twilight hours

When I woke up the next day, Polly had gone.

September 2007

Four weeks later, drunk and vaguely disorderly, I had my epiphany. It was a very cold night, storm clouds lay to the South, while I suffered in a slight drizzle. It was the type of light rain that inexplicably makes one incredibly wet. I sang the 'Sloop John B'; ever so slightly slurring so that all the words seemed to interconnect. It had been a great night out. It started, as most very good nights start – as a quiet drink after work:

"Just one" coaxed Guy; I screwed up my face, and considered whether it would be wise to go on a viewing with a stinking hangover the next day.

At the time I was the No.1 salesman in *Fisher & Irving Estate Agents*. Naturally, I was a popular man amongst my clients and considered part of the clique by my workmates so was never short on invites to the pub. Alas, the bane of every salesman, very few of the people I came into contact did I actually want to spend any time with.   I knew my workmates felt exactly the same way about me – a bi-product of the healthy competition in our office. With my clients there was a pretence at friendship, but that is all it was: pretence.   In reality I was only providing a highly priced service. I made them money and I did it with a smile; it was a logical way to conduct my business. My vendors would drop me like a loaf of mouldy bread if I ever failed to live up to my promises – there was rarely any loyalty client-side. Occasionally someone cropped up who actually did like me, but I classed them all as one breed: *colleagues* and they could never be any more than that. Guy was one of those rare breed of colleagues who I could almost count on as a friend.

I knew we wouldn't stop at one, no matter how much we promised ourselves; no matter how much we meant it, we knew that one would lead to two, and two would lead to three and so on...

"Only one, mind you." I replied, my famous last words.

We started in the Rosy Queen, a quietish pub where you could generally find a seat during the week. For a good few hours we talked shop, complaining at the stupidity of our applicants and the general arrogance of everyone that lived in Chelsea. As our pint glasses were emptied, and filled, then emptied again, our conversation turned to our favourite beers.

I drink Guinness. I feel that Guinness is a drink that marks me as different from other people. No matter where you are, and who you are with, you can always begin a conversation with a fellow Guinness drinker, or if push comes to shove, with a lager drinker genuinely puzzled why anyone would drink the alcoholic equivalent of a Sunday Roast.

I have a few set replies to the lager drinker's uncomprehending stare, which vary in accordance to how drunk I am, and which I proceeded to work through with Guy:

Stage 1 (still relatively sober): I go into an in depth discussion that my Dad always drunk Guinness, and that I have always drunk it.

Stage 2 (a little bit tipsy): I go into great detail describing how bloated I feel when I drink lager, and can't stand it. Guinness goes down so smooth, like velvet.

Stage 3 (drunk and arrogant): I tell them with glee "I only drink Guinness because St. Patrick was an Englishman!"

Stage 4 (too far gone to even care): I belch in their face and tell them to fuck off.

Now, I'm not a man to belch in a colleague's face, but you must take it for granted that stages 1-3 were all covered over a period of two hours. If I'm honest, Stage 3 probably lasted the longest: I kept repeating that same sentence over and over again, finding it slightly funnier every time I said it.

Before we knew it, it was midnight and we ambled into a night club. It was one of those faceless, vaguely familiar places that I will never be able to find or name again. Some people feel a little bit funny going drinking while wearing a suit. Not me, I look good in a suit. Guy on the other hand took off his jacket and tie, making himself look like a badly dressed schoolboy.

We hit the dance floor immediately, I'm a terrible dancer, but when I'm that drunk I don't really care. I made a bee-line towards a glamorous harem of off-duty receptionists whose tight-grey skirts cupped their firm backsides and made my mouth water. Edging my way ever closer, I eyed up my potential targets, looking for an opportunity to make my move. Being an awful dancer has never really affected my chances with women. As long as you show that you don't care, and remain confident, it always seems to work.

Getting a girl to agree to get into my bed has always been unchallenging. Lesser mortals envy my talents with women, my effortless ability to reduce them to slaves of lust. I rarely exaggerated my conquests. I was able to seduce the most unlikely individuals so the truth was always juicy enough without the need for embellishment.

To illustrate my case in point, one example of my prowess took place during my first successful job interview after university. Although Samantha, my interviewer, was ten years my senior, I could tell she was hot for me the moment I walked through the door. It was in the way her mouth parted when I looked into her eyes, and how her bum wriggled when she crossed her legs. She had dark auburn hair, and pale, almost translucent skin; she was beautiful. Around half-way through the interview, in the middle of asking her about her own hobbies, I couldn't help myself – I reached my hand out and gently began to stroke her inner thigh. She stopped speaking mid-sentence and, blushing, opened her legs wider. I pulled her up off the chair and pushed her back against the door. Dropping to my knees, I pulled down her pants, and ate her cunt out right there, my head inside her grey skirt. Anyone could have walked in on us, but neither she, nor I, cared in the slightest. We never spoke of the incident again (she was married, as it turned out), but I could tell that she thought of it fondly.

People used to shake their heads in exasperation when I relayed this tale. Most men in the same situation would have had their hand slapped away and been told to leave. I, on the other hand, got my end away and was given a job offer too.

I can't wholly explain why I was so good with women, but it may have had something to do with the following:

(i)   Perception – I had a natural instinct that allowed me to understand someone's needs and desires, and like a predator, how to exploit them. This is also what made me a successful salesman.

(ii)   Vanity – I didn't just look after myself, I chiselled myself to perfection. I had no grey hairs, and my hairline was not even considering receding. I watched what I ate, and had a regular exercise regime. Due to my long working hours I could rarely make time for the gym; I preferred to keep fit with a morning routine and a rigorous amount of running. During the weekend I always enjoyed getting over to one of the many large parks that North London had to offer, but in the evenings when I got back from work and it was dark, I ran through the streets. I especially relished the feeling of jogging in poor weather. I felt a great sense of peace running in the rain, in the dark, through the streets of Islington. The frustrations of the working day would roll off my back into the stratosphere. Over the years I had become a flawless example of masculinity. Similarly, the clothes I wore were well tailored to suit my physique, and I ensured I was well groomed at all times; I always wore the same signature designer fragrance; I shaved every morning, plucked my eyebrows every Monday, and cut my hair twice a month, without fail.

(iii)   Research – I always found out as much as I could about the woman I was trying to seduce, be this on Facebook (a recent development which had made my investigations remarkably easy), Google, or if it was the first time I met them, simply by asking questions about their life. If you know their history, and their motivations in life, it makes manipulating them all that much easier; besides, everyone loves to talk about themselves.

(iv)   Adaptability – I wasn't one to go for cheesy chat-up lines; I charmed women in other ways. It was partly about making them laugh and partly about a self-deprecating humour that forced them to continually tell me how great I was. Something about this worked, and after telling me how great, or funny I was a few times, they seemed to come to believe it. More than that though, dependent upon what popped up in my research I was able to change myself to suit their needs. If they wanted someone who loved animals, I would invent a regular donation to the RSPCA. If they needed a family-man, I would reminisce about imaginary good times with my nieces and nephews. If they just wanted a fuck, quite simply, I would unleash the beast. On the other hand, someone who looked as good as I did could never pass as a choir-boy; underlying all of my accomplishments at adaptability and changing my mask, deep down, I was something else. Women looked into my dark brown eyes and saw danger staring back at them. They were helplessly drawn to me, yearning for the unknown.

(v) Affection – I didn't just sleep with any old pair of legs that came my way. There were always moments before my dick got wet, that I genuinely felt true affection for my conquests. Seconds before I came, I could have quite happily told them I loved them, and I would have been telling the truth. Before I bedded them, I usually felt optimistic that our relationship *might g*o somewhere; that those feelings *could c*ontinue beyond the bedroom. I don't think that it would be inaccurate to say that while I was seducing them, women could sense my own genuine curiosity and cautious hope that I could end up loving them permanently. Dangerous and affectionate, it's a good combination. It was only after our climax that I decided I didn't want to see them again, my motivation would vanish, and I would realise it had all amounted to nothing.

But that evening in the nightclub, I was off form, and something akin to disgust arose from out of my subconscious. This was too easy and so unfulfilling. Perhaps something of Polly's parting words had unsettled my mind, but I soon realised that tight backsides or not, I wasn't at all interested in any of the women before me.

I turned away and began to make my way towards the bar. Someone grabbed my hand from behind, and pulled me back. The room swayed and I realised that it was one of the receptionists I had been dancing with. She had peeled away from her tribe in the hope I would choose her. A pleading look in her eyes begged me to stay, but I shook my hand free and moved on. I had no idea where Guy had now moved away to, but my head was swimming and I needed to get out of the club. Staggering past the bouncers and the crowd of people queuing to get inside, I made my way to the nearest bus stop where a large sign was flashing the destination: '*Highbury and Islington'*. I had no idea where I was, but the flashing red letters told me that a bus would be coming in five minutes to take me home. Night buses being what they are, it didn't actually arrive for forty five minutes, by which time the last vestiges of my final few shots of absinthe had taken their toll on my brain. I stumbled onto the bus and swiped my Oyster card. It took roughly an hour, and I had to struggle incredibly hard not to:

- A. Vomit
- B. Piss myself
- C. Fall asleep
- D. Fall asleep then vomit and piss myself

I focused on the road, avoiding direct eye contact with the bunch of crazies surrounding me, until we finally pulled up outside my closest bus stop, a good ten minutes walk from my flat. This was when the drizzle began to fall, and after relieving myself down the closest dark alleyway, I began to sing '*The Sloop John B'*. It is strange to think that on that evening I would make a decision that would begin a course of events that would change my life forever, that in my inebriated state of mind, I was able to formulate a plan which no sober person could have ever realistically thought feasible. I was mulling over the girl who had been so desperate for me to stay dancing with her, I thought of Polly who had so easily succumbed to my advances despite my having acted like a complete arsehole, and I also thought of Elisha Cicero. How close I was to her, how easily it would have been to strike up a conversation with her. It occurred to me that I could theoretically charm any girl into my bed. If I could talk to them, look into their eyes and share a little joke, they would sleep with me. Even someone like Elisha Cicero would succumb to me. All I needed was a fair chance to talk to her.

But how?

I'd have to chat with her as one in the same social circle – otherwise she may not give me the time I'd need to close her down. I decided that I would have to somehow enter her group of friends. The celebrity world is certainly not impenetrable; theoretically all it should take is a friend in the right place inviting you to all the right events. Then, if you play your cards right – Bob's-your-uncle – you can continue to move on up through the ranks of stardom.

As this was all going through my mind, I rounded a corner and bumped into a woman I recognised called Jessica Fernly. She was a well-known celebrity, being the third runner up of *Soma Holiday* 2005.

Soma Holiday was a reality show and the main talking point of every summer. It was beyond a shadow of a doubt my favourite television programme. To my most fiercely masculine companions, my fandom of such a show was a source of contempt, but I would bet money that they all watched it too. It followed the lives of twenty people locked in a house with copious amounts of alcohol. It was a source of sex, intrigue, and unimaginably larger than life characters. Over the summer months when it was filmed, one could not even hope to avoid an addiction to the program.

In my drunken haze, I thought that it was fate – could this have been my chance to make a celebrity acquaintance? Jessica Fernly's career had recently reached the pinnacle of tabloid success when it was rumoured that she was having an affair with a footballer. She was cuddled up to a man who was most certainly not her husband. I didn't recognise him, but I don't like football, so was unable to verify for certain whether the tabloid rumours were accurate.

I made a snap decision to try my luck with her. Perhaps she'd take a liking to me? Unfortunately, when I say that I 'bumped' into Jessica Fernly, it wasn't a turn of phrase – I literally stumbled and barged into her with my shoulder.

"Excuse me!" I said with my hand rested on her elbow. I must have looked a little dishevelled. She glared at me like she was seeing a worm.

"Are you Jessica Fernly?" I smiled at her and swayed a bit.

"Fuck off." She spat at me.

I think I muttered something slurred about parties, and not wanting an autograph, but her boyfriend started pushing me and threatening to hit me if I didn't leave her alone. I decided to oblige – I didn't think it was worth getting a punch in the face. As ill-fortune would have it, they were walking the same way I was. I continued behind them feeling increasingly more uncomfortable – they kept turning around and scowling, as if I was following them on purpose. Finally they veered off down a side street and, with a sigh of relief, I continued on my way home.

September 13th 2007

The day that Northern Rock collapsed, I woke up fully clothed on my sofa with a half-eaten bacon and egg sandwich balanced precariously on my knee. How that sandwich had stayed there all night, I will never know. However, I had my terrible hangover to contend with, so such mysterious happenings were not awarded much thought. I stumbled into the kitchen, letting the sandwich fall to the floor, and poured myself a glass of cold water from my Britta filter. My head was a smouldering sphere of pain, and a rhythm of nausea seemed to intensify with each heartbeat. I got the tube into work – my car, used for ferrying applicants to their potential homes, was still at the office. I was a good half our late through the doors, and with my breath reeking like the bottom of a public toilet, I was hardly in any fit state to sell houses.

Plastered across the News were forecasts of doom and gloom and the end of the world. I'm not an economist, but from what I understand, the long and short of it all was this: The banks decided to lend out a shit load of money to a lot of incredibly dodgy people without even asking for reliable collateral. They were surprised when, amazingly, all this money didn't come back. When the banks realised all their equity had been flittered away into smoke, they panicked and decided they needed to keep hold of what little money they had left. They didn't even want to lend to other banks as they didn't know how much money everyone else had lost. So when Northern Rock stuck out its hand asking for a loan, nobody would help. In short, Northern Rock was fucked. Although I was aware that there was a chance it would cause us trouble, it didn't really register as being that important at the time. Clearly, there were murmurings around the office, especially from the applicants, but we were so used to a booming market that it didn't dent our confidence, not even remotely. We were so sure that the London property market would stand strong. Little did we know that Northern Rock was only the beginning, the losses would come, and continue growing until our entire economy collapsed. Back in September 2007, for me at least, I thought it to be a minor blip in the face of a prosperous future in the dazzling world of London property. The streets were still going to be paved with gold.

The painful reality of working with a diabolical hangover took up all of my attention; in the light of day and the company of a wealthy pair of newlyweds hunting for a three bedroomed flat with panoramic views of the river, my plan, hatched only the night before, was completely forgotten. Likely as not, it would have remained that way, were it not for the fact that there was a two-page article on Jessica Fernly's illicit affair in my weekly delivery of *A-List Magazine*.

A-List, the celebrity news magazine was a dirty little secret of mine. I had a monthly subscription and was fascinated by the stories of intrigue and scandal. My favourite pages were those stories with illustrated paparazzi pictures of arrogant C-listers getting drunk and shouting abuse at each other. I also liked to read stories with titles like '*Trouble in Paradise?*' when it speculated, without any evidence whatsoever, on the ins and outs of a well-known couple's domestic problems. I'm not entirely sure where this less than masculine pastime came from. I know my mother loves to read this kind of magazine, to my father's disdain. I also had a brief relationship with a girl who regularly absorbed a few hundred glossy pages in any particular week, and for two months, my flat was filled with old copies. It was only after we broke up that I realized how much I enjoyed reading them. I always found it much too embarrassing going into the shop to buy them. If I was ever going to read on a regular basis, I had to have the magazine delivered to my front door. My reading habits were always a great source of mirth and ridicule to my friends, but that didn't bother me in the slightest.

During a much needed toilet break, I thumbed through the pages, and the memories from the previous evening came flooding back. I mused over the idea, looked at it from afar through the eyes of a sober and rational human being. It seemed completely half baked.

Still, I ploughed through my day, praying that I wouldn't be sick in front of any of our clients.

By the evening, I had almost dismissed the idea completely. When I arrived home at 9:00 pm, I was ready for sleep. Fate had other things in store for me that night, and the first in a series of events that would culminate in my eventual courtship of Elisha Cicero came crashing into my life.

Being early autumn, it was beginning to get dark by the time I got home. My feet were dragging on the floor as I walked wearily up the concrete steps, and began to search my pockets for my keys. All of a sudden, a figure leapt out of the darkness at me, shouting. I was so surprised that I jumped backwards, lost my footing and fell down the steps. I twisted my ankle and hit my head. Looking up from the cold hard pavement, I realised that it was Polly who had pounced at me. Her eyes were red from hours of crying, and my obvious pain had somehow caused her condition to deteriorate – she was openly sobbing, a yellow rivulet of snot streamed out of her nose. I slowly got to my feet and hobbled up to my front door without speaking or showing any real sign that I knew she was there. I wasn't badly hurt, but I was still extremely pissed that she had frightened me in my already delicate state. What was she doing there anyway? I'd thought I would never have to see her again.

"Shaun, can I speak to you please?" she wept. I opened the door without saying anything, and for one brief and glorious moment, I was tempted to slam the door in her face. In the end, my middle class upbringing got the better of me, and it just felt too rude, too embarrassing to leave a hysterical girl calling after me in the doorway, so, although it was the last thing I wanted, I left the door open for her, and she slunk in after me.

"What do you want, Polly?"

"I'm sorry about the other night!" She ran at me and began to kiss me. Once again, I was filled with that vague sense of pity for this girl who had been so full of life. To my utter horror, I began to feel aroused, and was soon kissing her back. This time was much better than the previous occasion, and we were soon writhing naked on the floor of my hallway, rolling into my spare shoes and knocking the coats off of the hook. It was actually surprisingly good and not even lying on top of my smelly trainers put us off the sound of each other's ejaculation.

When it was over, and we lay next to each other red faced and panting. I realised how tired I actually was, so I picked her up, threw her into the bed and immediately fell straight asleep. Little did I know where this would all lead.

September 14th 2007

I worked in the Sales department in the Chelsea office of *Fisher & Irving.* My job involved:

A. Convincing people to put their own house on the market with us.

B. Convincing people to buy their property through us.

C. Convincing people that our own mortgage broker would give the best advice and interest rates in comparison to anybody else.

People often asked me why I ever wanted to become one of those *scum of the earth* estate agents. This, more often than not, was met with one of my sales pitches...

"Well, the fact that estate agents are scum is a common misconception....."

...followed by a reasoned explanation that we always did what our clients told us to do, and it was our clients' differing needs that caused people to get so frustrated with us. I would conveniently omit the fact that clients were easily manipulated into choosing a course of action that made me the most money.

Clearly this rhetoric was just a sham to misdirect so I didn't have to explain that my life as I knew it rested almost completely upon the shoulders of fate. I made no conscious choice to become a salesman. Nobody ever dreams of growing up to be an estate agent, just as I can imagine nobody ever dreams of growing up to be a banker, a management consultant or an accountant. However, I didn't get too depressed about this, as I spent most of my childhood wanting to be a JCB driver. Thankfully, I had grown out of this phase by the time I began my GCSE's and was old enough for it to matter.

My careers guidance as a schoolboy was fairly minimal. My kind-hearted careers officer based our meetings largely on a concept that I was working, or striving towards some kind of goal. Unfortunately there was no goal, there has never been a goal, and until my fated meeting with Elisha Cicero, I was certain that I would be perfectly content bumbling through my life, always hoping that exceeding at the things that I was good at would take me somewhere satisfactory.

It was only after I finished university and it was becoming too embarrassing living off of my parents' good graces that I decided I most certainly needed a well-paid job. Almost penniless and with a single suit, I set out to try to find a career in London. My first role was in a call centre selling double glazing, but I was only there for a few weeks before *Fisher & Irving Estate Agency* offered me a position. I did find it quite ironic that after 20 years of education, the only factor that seemed to get me the job was the 4 weeks work experience in that awful call centre. Estate agency turned out to be a career that I was exceptionally good at, and it wasn't long before I was billing a shit load of money.

My job mainly involved talking, but more importantly, it involved listening. On any average day, I held the following telephone conversation at least 40 times:

Me: "Good morning (or afternoon) *Fisher and Irving*, Chelsea, how can I help?"

Ms Anybody: "Oh hello, I've been looking at your website. There's a two bedroom flat in Flood Street, the one for £150,000? I'd like to view it tomorrow."

This is a bad start for any sales man; she has immediately taken control of the conversation. She has told me exactly what she wants, so I know that she will immediately lose interest when I tell her one of the following things:

A. Although she thinks that she can afford this luxurious two bedroomed spacious apartment, complete with roof terrace and a communal garden, advertised at the bargain price of only £150,000, she most certainly will not be able to afford it.

B. The Property is already under offer, and has been for nearly a year now.

C. The Property is an absolute shit hole.

I would need to take hold of the conversation and put her back in her place. After all, she was only an ignorant consumer who was extremely misguided in her belief that any half-decent two bedroomed property would ever be sold for less than £400,000 in Chelsea. Obviously, I wouldn't want to let her know that I knew this, so would bring her down slowly, then build her up again until she was eating out of the palm of my hand.

Me: "Certainly, let me just take down your name and number, and I'll take a look at my diary and see what I can do."

Ms. Anybody: "Oh! Of course, my name is Ms. Anybody, and my phone number is 0208 (blah blah blah blah)"

Me: "Thank you, now let me just find that property on my system so I can give you a few details. Ah yes! Here we are, Flood St….. Oh dear, I'm afraid that property is actually under offer, and is due to exchange any time soon"

Ms. Anybody: "Oh dear, that property looked perfect for me and my fiancé, it was so much cheaper than anywhere else. I'd be willing to go over the asking price if that helps."

Me: "I'm afraid there was only a 6 year lease on that property so it wasn't such a good investment anyway."

Ms. Anybody: "Oh that wouldn't matter, we would only have wanted to live there for four or five years then move on."

Even the worst estate agent in England would realise this is an incredibly stupid thing to say: this woman knows absolutely nothing about buying a property in London. Thus, she will be easily manipulated into doing exactly what I want. I would now take on an advisory role – catch her off guard with how nice and helpful I could be. I would gain her trust and then, like all good salesmen exploit it completely.

Me: "The real problem with a six year lease is that in five years' time, it will be worth absolutely nothing. In the sixth year, the property will legally belong to the freeholder; you will have lost all rights to it altogether."

Ms. Anybody: "Really?"

Me: "Yes, the only way to keep hold of the property would be to extend the lease, which we estimate would cost something in the region of £300,000. And because it's such a bad investment, it would also be impossible to get a mortgage for this flat, so the £150,000 would have to be paid in cash."

Ms. Anybody: "Oh"

Now to gather all the information I can from her. She has realised she is out of her depth, and all the long hours of scrawling across different websites, trying to find the perfect property amount to nothing. She is begging to be told what to do.

Me: "If you could give me a description of your ideal home, then perhaps if we have anything on the books we could talk to you about some other options.

Ms. Anybody: "Thank you, yes. I would like a two bedroom flat in Chelsea."

What a fucking shit description, I can see she'll need further probing.

Me: "Do you have any preferences in regards to outside space?"

Ms. Anybody: "Not as long as we're close to a park, but with our budget I don't think that we've got much choice."

She has brought up the issue of money. A bad sales person would jump at the chance to sell the mortgage. I, however, would go for a more subtle approach; make her think that I could help her and give her some hope after her recent failure on the property in Flood Street.

Me: "Would you consider an unmodernised property as long as it's reflected in the price?"

Ms. Anybody: "Yes, that would be a preference. We'd like to get as much space as we can for the budget we've got."

She's more than happy that I suggested it; now to make the big plunge and sell our mortgage man.

Me: "So what's your budget?"

Ms. Anybody: "Absolutely maximum £170,000"

With that piddly amount of money she might just be able to afford a cupboard-sized studio flat in Chelsea, nothing bigger. I wouldn't be able to help her with what she wants. Even if I could help, I wouldn't bother with small change like that. I would typically fob off anyone looking below £250,000 onto one of the juniors in the office. Clearly I wouldn't tell the applicant this – it would ruin my mortgage pitch. I would also refrain from telling them that I got paid £50 every time I referred someone to *Woolsten Marks*.

Me: "How far have you come with organising your finances?"

Ms. Anybody: "I have a mortgage in place with my bank."

Me: "Good, at *Fisher and Irving* we deal very closely with a company called *Woolsten Marks* one of London's leading mortgage brokers. Although you've already got your finances in place, it's definitely worth your while talking to them and getting some free advice to see if you can get a second opinion. I'll just take a few more details then pass you over to my contact in that company"

My mortgage pitch never made me feel guilty (Back in the good old days it was more than likely that a broker would get them a better deal than their own bank.) In order to avoid them noticing they had been sold something, I would distract them with my admin requirements:

Me: "Let me just double check your contact details."

I would systematically collect their home phone, mobile, work phone, email address, and finally:

Me: "Could I also have your postal address so I can pop one of our magazines in the post."

(She gives it to me)

Me: "Do you currently own that property or do you rent there?"

I always threw that question in quickly, as if it is almost meaningless, however, in reality it was the most important question of the whole conversation.

Ms. Anybody: "I'm renting there."

Damn it, it would have been easy to persuade her to sell that property through us. I suppose it was bleeding obvious that she was a first time buyer. Still, I could track down her landlord, so that when she finally buys, the landlord could let his newly vacant property through us.

Me: "I think I now have all the details I need, bear with me and I'll just pop you through to my contact in that mortgage company I told you about."

Easy as pie.

Of course, it would be impossible to find her the property she wanted for the price she wanted. I would email her lots of two bedroomed properties entirely out of her price range, and register her with a few other offices, in which she might be able to actually afford the kind of place she wants. It sounds a callous way to deal with her, but while I could have been honest, and told her the truth, she would only have become annoyed with me. It was much easier for everyone to give her a little hope.

My life had continued as such in the days preceding that unexpectedly pleasant meeting with Polly. In contrast, Polly's life had taken somewhat of an unfortunate turn. She had arrived home in Dover, still unsure whether she had got the job or not. Her boyfriend Terry had welcomed her back with a night out in their favourite Italian restaurant. Although not an especially jealous person, he had been a little paranoid about Polly's visit because of my history with her. As their night progressed, he began to make subtle hints to Polly that he was worried that she had cheated on him. Polly should have said nothing. She should have kept it a secret, but in the end she broke down in tears and told him that she slept with me. From what I can gather, Terry didn't take this too well. He threw his plate at the wall and stormed out of the restaurant without looking back. After a lonely taxi ride home she found a rejection letter from her interview pinned to the door alongside a small note from Terry informing her that he had moved out. Although all of his belongings were still in the house, Polly had not seen him since. She couldn't afford the rent on her own and had eventually been forced to move back to Staines with her parents (I assume that she took his belongings along with her). For a short while, a three and a half hour commute each way from Staines to Dover Priory awaited her. Polly had struggled to focus on her work over this period. She had ended up in pretty severe fight with one of her managing partners and had been given her P45 the following day.

She had apparently come up to see me largely to lay the blame at my feet and bite me in the jugular. She had unfortunately arrived at around 6:00 pm, and been forced to wait a good few hours before I came home. This time had allowed her a period of introspection, and she realised that it wasn't necessarily all my fault after all. Thus, when I arrived home, she had been so over burdened with guilt, and misery, she had allowed me to take advantage.

I awoke to a shocking electric buzz at the front door. My alarm clock had not gone off yet, but I was in a particularly good mood. Polly was still asleep; her dark hair splayed out over the pillow. I pulled on a pair of shorts and a t-shirt, and wandered over to the telecom.

"Who is it?" I said, and waited for an answer, but nobody said anything. I frowned in frustration, wondering who had awoken me.

"Who is it?" I said again more loudly.

"It's Terry" crackled the voice.

Shit.

"Terry who?"

"Just let me in."

Shit, shit, shit!

And for some unknown reason, I actually pressed the buzzer. I let him into the hall. What on earth did he want? What was he going to do to us? Had he followed Polly here? But what if he didn't know Polly was in my bed? I ran to my room, and shook her awake.

"Polly, you'd better hide, Terry's here."

Her eyes opened wide as if she couldn't quite comprehend what I was saying.

"What do you mean?"

"Just hide, he's on his way up. Now!"

"Jesus Christ! Where can I hide?"

I looked around, unsure where she could possibly go.

"Under the bed" I said, and without a word, she squeezed under the bed. It was almost comical seeing her naked bottom sticking in the air then disappearing under the mattress. I threw her clothes in after her, so that in the off-chance she was discovered, it wouldn't look half as bad. I heard someone knocking and knew Polly's boyfriend was ready to meet me.

Terry began hammering on my door, this time louder and harder. It crossed my mind that this wasn't going to be a pleasant experience. It also crossed my mind that the person on the other side of the door could be a lot bigger than me, and I could potentially be in for a beating. On the other hand, when a girl cheats on her boyfriend for me, I can't help but think that he's probably going to be a little bit pathetic. I know it's not true, but I can't help but assume that I must be that little bit more masculine, hence being able to woo the girl in question. But then again, what if he was out there with a weapon? What if he had a baseball bat poised and ready to kill me?

I pondered for a while whether I should get my own weapon in case he did attack. I eventually decided against it – my awful streak of British pride worked itself into a frenzy as I decided that it would be much too embarrassing to open the door brandishing a weapon if all Terry wanted to do was talk. So, before Terry had a chance to stew on my affair with his girlfriend, and get really angry, I decided that it might be prudent to open the door.

To my surprise I was not greeted with angry shouts, and hurling fists, but with a blubbering and pitiful creature who fell down to his knees wailing and weeping in huge and unashamed sobs.

I stood still, not entirely sure what to do, weighing up my options.

1. Should I invite him in?

2. Should I stand in the doorway and wait for him to speak?

3. Should I actually make physical contact and usher him into my home before any of the neighbours come out to see?

For a moment I was tempted to close the door, it was almost too pathetic to be believable. I also considered going to get Polly from under my bed, but decided it really wouldn't have helped the situation.

I eventually settled on the highly inadequate phrase: "Urm, would you like a cup of tea?"

I regretted saying it as soon as the words left my mouth – I knew that a brew wasn't going to resolve any of Terry's problems. In fact, I knew that nothing I could say or do could change the fact that his girlfriend was currently lying naked under my bed.

Why didn't he hit me?

Why didn't he stand up?

Why didn't he say something? Say *anything?*

He remained in my hallway, sobbing into my carpet while I stood and watched him. I twitched my fingers nervously, in silence, waiting for him to do something. Surely Polly could hear him crying? Why didn't she come and help?

"Terry" I murmured gently, "come inside and sit down where we can talk properly."

Terry looked up at the sound of his name and stared at me with a glazed expression. I wasn't sure whether he could even see me. A strong whiff of whiskey passed over me and I couldn't help but grimace. He was drunk.

"Terry, what do you want?" I said when Terry didn't move. I looked around the corridor, and began to wonder whether something was seriously wrong. Terry was turning pale, and his eyes seemed to forcing themselves shut.

"I sht'love a, yoknow." I didn't know what he was saying, "ya faulllltscunt"

Each word was slurring into the other, and his head was beginning to sag. Slowly but surely, all of the colour drained out of the human being before me, until he was little more than a ghost. His head hit the carpet with a thud, and his breaths began to stifle.

"Oh my God! What's wrong with him?" Polly, that fucking coward, had finally emerged from her hiding place now that her beloved had lost consciousness.

"I don't know, do you think he's just drunk?"

"I hope so!" replied Polly, now openly weeping.

I knelt down to look at Terry properly, and the world seemed to recoil, as I spotted, clasped in the palm of Terry's limp hand, an empty bottle of pills.

"Polly, I'm going to call an ambulance, sit down and make sure he's okay."

Polly, who still had not seen the empty bottle, looked as if I had slapped her in the face.

"Just do what I say and he'll be alright, ok?" I didn't wait for her reply – instead I ran into my living room and dialled 999.

The ambulance seemed to take forever, but when it did arrive, the paramedics knew exactly what to do. They shook him, and spoke to him and checked his pulse. I couldn't help but feel like a spare leg, realising that I knew absolutely nothing about first aid. In other people's eyes, an estate agent isn't really a profession that commands a great deal of respect. I hushed the thought, and in an attempt to console myself, I reminded myself how much more money I made than them. Still, in this fairly unusual situation, money and career success had no impact whatsoever, and I was reduced to sitting around feeling incompetent. Polly was fulfilling her role as the worried and grief stricken girlfriend, weeping and demanding comfort from the paramedics. I don't think any of the ambulance guys could really work out where I fitted in. With a flurry of blankets, Terry was quickly inside the ambulance and on his way to hospital. Polly got in with them, naturally, I opted to stay behind. I didn't think he would have appreciated seeing me upon his return to consciousness....if he returned to consciousness (I tried not think of what would happen if that turned out to be the case).

On my sombre and introspective return up the stairs to my flat, I found a suicide note that must have dropped out of his pocket:

'Polly

I don't see anybody dear to me anymore, I can't feel what they are feeling, and I long for a friendly comfy face, someone with whom I WISH I can reminisce! Dance with me dance, with me please. Who are these people who claim to be my friends? Why do I claim their companionship? Perhaps I am evil? Perhaps I no longer deserve the kinship of others? Perhaps I am just so drunk that my fingers have gone numb? This night must progress. This night must look beyond my own blurring eyesight. This is why I must say goodbye.

I hate you and I always will

Terry'

It meant nothing to me. It was meaningless drivel. After reading it once, I tore it up and never mentioned it to Polly.

September 15th 2007

The following evening I had a telephone call from Terry. I had gone to work with the events of the previous night already beginning to recede into something that felt like a surreal dream. I arrived home absolutely exhausted after an extremely long day. My aching feet kept me standing just long enough for me to be able to shove some pasta on the boil. When the phone began to ring, I groaned inwardly and was faced with the usual soul destroying choice of either picking up the receiver so as to avoid missing out on something important, or leaving it to ring on and on and keep my life as simple as possible, living in wonderful, peaceful, hermit-like bliss.

The moment I answered it, I realised I had made a mistake

"Hi Shaun, it's Terry"

With those words, the horrible reality of the previous night raised its ugly head, and with stinking breath, bit me in the face. What did he want now? I was too tired to deal with this idiot. I felt like telling him this, but couldn't help worrying that probably wouldn't be a great opener to someone with suicidal tendencies. Instead I settled on a polite, if forced, formality.

"Oh! Hi Terry, are you feeling better today?"

"Yes, thank you."

Was he going to kill himself on the other end of the phone? How did he keep getting my personal details? I was going to make a point of going ex-directory from now on.

Well, at least he wasn't slurring and acting crazy, but I couldn't work out why he was calling me.

"I suppose that you're wondering why I'm calling you, but I just wanted to thank you for saving my life last night. If it wasn't for you, I wouldn't be here today."

An awkward silence followed. I hadn't done anything but call an ambulance, and the only reason he'd tried to top himself in the first place was because I was fucking his girlfriend. WHY was he calling me?

"I want you to come and see me in hospital today."

Oh Jesus tap-dancing Christ, anything but that! Anything but sit on a sick bed for an hour and sympathise with the useless twat.

"I suppose I owe you at least that." What was I saying?? I sometimes thought that there must be something wrong with me. Why couldn't I be rude to weak people?

"Don't say that Shaun, no matter what you think, it's not your fault..."

God I felt awkward, what the hell was he talking about? Just because you've tried to kill yourself, it doesn't mean that you can just talk like a twit to total strangers whenever you feel like it.

"...Ever since the *incident* last night, I've had some time to think, and it was really selfish of me to do that to you. Thank you for calling an ambulance, and thank you for calling Polly and telling her what happened..."

This caught me off-guard and I gasped involuntarily. Polly hadn't told him that she'd slept with me again. This was almost too uncomfortable to allow.

"...you saved my life last night, and that's a really special thing to do...."

It even crossed my mind that he could be gay.

"I am forever in your debt."

He must have been rehearsing for hours. I don't know when it clicked, but in time I came to realise that this speech hadn't come from his heart, but more from his need to add dramatic effect to the most menial of feelings.

September 16th 2007

I knew before I left my flat that actually meeting him in the hospital was a terrible idea. I knew as I walked into the stale air of the Underground that this would be a harrowing journey I would always regret. But when I got there, and both Terry's mother and father who had been weeping in the hallway, stopped mid-sob to glare at me in stony silence as if they knew who I was and what I had done with Polly, I knew this would be one of the most uncomfortable experiences in my entire life.

Terry was propped up by two fluffy pillows and munching on some toast. I looked about my wholly practical surroundings, designed for the sole purpose of maintaining the sick.

"How are you Terry?" I said holding out my hand for him to shake. He shook my hand weakly in return, and smiled condescendingly.

"I'm feeling much better thanks Shaun. Should be out of here in a week"

"A week! Why so long?"

"I think they want to watch me and make sure I don't do it again."

I didn't know what to say to this, so chose to ignore it and talk about something else.

"Was that your mum and dad out there?"

"Yes."

Once again I struggled for direction in the conversation. Nothing interesting would come of this line of questioning. After all, where could it go? His parents had been sobbing uncontrollably, and although I had no idea how they knew who I was, they had stared at me venomously.

What should I have said next? I thought of talking of Polly, but feared that it may make things even worse. In the end, I settled on the mundane.

"Have you called in sick at work?"

"Yes. My mum called them yesterday morning."

"Do you need me to do anything for you? Pick up some papers?"

"No, it's alright; I think they'll be able to manage without me for a few days."

"What do you do anyway?"

"I'm a producer for *Oops! TV.*"

Before I fired out the next benign question, I did a double take. Something in what he said made my subconscious reel with excitement.

"*Oops! TV*? THE *Oops! TV*?"

"Yeah, why?"

I could see that Terry was enjoying that I was impressed. *Oops! TV*, among many other programmes, made *Soma Holiday.*

"Know anyone famous?" I knew I sounded like a wanker, but, fuck it.

"It sort of goes with the job." said Terry smugly.

He then began an utterly dull narrative that involved him meeting a plethora of C-list celebrities and doing something which was supposed to be both witty and charming, but in fact was neither. I refrained from rolling my eyes, and indulged him for two reasons:

1. I had inadvertently caused him to make an attempt on his own life just 48 hours previously.

2. Although I was loathe to admit it, I was incredibly impressed.

So I sat, listening to his ridiculous stories for two whole hours. By the end of it, I was almost ready to strangle him, but still made arrangements to meet him the following day, and the next, and every day until he was well enough to be released. After his release, it didn't stop; he commuted to London for three days a week as part of his job and usually made an effort to track me down. I can't say I enjoyed his company, and at the time I wasn't sure he really liked me either. I thought he was lonely and wanted a life like mine, and perhaps believed a bit of my charisma might rub off.

In all honesty, I had initially hoped that once Terry was back on his feet, he could make his own way through life without my help. I really didn't want him hanging around too much, especially because my relationship with Polly had moved onwards and upwards. Although I knew it was never going to become a full blown relationship with Polly, I didn't think Terry would have reacted well to the truth. Exposing him to more of my life than was absolutely necessary was something I wanted to avoid. As such, when he invited me to a party celebrating his renewed health, I politely declined.

Polly and Terry were now completely finished, and she was steadily growing bitter about the man who she had royally fucked over. It's funny how a few short weeks can change a person's perspective. Originally I had to sit and listen to hours of her weeping, saying things like:

"I don't know what I'll do with myself now?"

Or

"It's all my fault, it's completely my fault, oh God, why am I such a bitch?"

Initially she seemed happy that I was going over to meet him, and liked me to recount everything he said or did. Then one day, out of nowhere, I was recounting a particularly nauseous recital of an encounter Terry had with a photographer, when she slapped her forehead with the palm of her hand and cringed.

"He's such a wanker! Oh God he's such a twat. Why do you bother spending so much time with him?" Perhaps some of my cynicism at Terry's ridiculousness had rubbed off on Polly.

After this initial outbreak of Anti-Terry-ism, it began to grow, and grow, until she was saying truly horrible things about the man she had once loved. Phrases like: "He wasn't really trying to kill himself, he only wanted everyone to look at him; why else would he have knocked on your door?" were never far from the tip of her tongue. Polly began to get irked by my nights spent with Terry, and she knew very well that I didn't like him one bit. When I told her that I had been invited to his party, she couldn't help but vomit out huge tirade of poisonous remarks.

"I hate those bloody parties. I hate them, and those idiots he invites. None of them really care whether he's well not. They just hang around him hoping that one of the famous people he invites will actually come."

I learnt 2 things from her bile:

1. I had created a monster.
2. I was attending the party.

Saturday 4th November 2007

To survive in a high pressure sales environment like estate agency, you have to make sacrifices. To reach your goals, you always need to be thinking about work. Everybody you speak to is a potential client.

It's a very simple equation: People x Contact with Me = £

As such, you have to make the absolute most out of every single day, look the best you can, and charm as many people as possible for as many hours as possible. You need to get into the office as early as possible, lay out your diary correctly, and make sure that your manager knows that you're first in and last to leave. I won't lie, it's not always pleasant. Not everyone would be able to do it. You really need to have focus and to know what you want.

I personally had a routine to set me up for the day:

5:30 AM: The alarm shuddered against my soul.

I snoozed, and buried my face in the pillow.

5:35 AM: The alarm shuddered against my soul once more.

I snoozed again with the covers over my face.

5:40 AM: The Alarm pained me for the penultimate time – the dreadful moment before I pushed myself out of bed.

I lay still for five minutes, thinking about the day ahead of me, what I needed to do, and how I was going to go about doing it.

5:45 AM: Rise

I stumbled across the shag-pile of my bedroom.

I approached the heated marble floors of my kitchen.

Boiling water + Mug + Coffee + Two Sugars + Milk.

I flicked on BBC News, and began:

Press-ups: Three times twenty sets.

Crunches: Forty.

A pint of water with an effervescent Vitamin C tablet thrown in.

Another coffee – this time accompanied by a slice of toast with smooth peanut butter.

Polished my shoes.

Showered.

Shaved.

Ironed my shirt.

Suit Trousers.

Shirt, cuff-links, collar bone.

Then my tie – a Half-Windsor.

06:45 AM: I was out the door.

07:30 AM: I arrived at my office and sorted out my diary.

Every day without fail.

Unless Polly was there ruining it with attempts at intercourse before I was awake. Defiling it with the tepid, bitter coffee she insisted on bringing to me in bed. Destroying it with her insistence on watching some bullshit morning show with Charlie Ekells presenting. And she switched off the alarm. She wouldn't snooze. She switched it off so that it blared once at 05:30, and then not again. I would arrive at work stressed, dishevelled and with a creased shirt.

My clients and my applicants all crept around me. My workmates may not have known what was disturbing my equilibrium, but, they knew I was off my game, and that there was a reason. They watched and waited like a pack of wolves hoping that I'd crack, and licking their fat lips at the thought of inheriting my pipeline of applicants.

Polly and I were destined to be enemies – I came to accept that fact early on. I needed her out of my life and I needed my routine back. At the beginning of our renewed relationship I pretended to care for her, hoping that she would change back to the person she used to be. This small kindness came back to bite me – she effectively moved in with me, staying over five nights in any given week. I didn't invite her to stay – she just turned up one day and remained. Occasionally she'd go home to her parents (her *actual* home), but for the most part, she was just leeching off me like a parasite. I was stuck with her. With no job and no home she had nowhere better to go. To make the nights more bearable, our conversations would often wander onto the good old days, to the time when I actually liked her as a person.

The first time I met Polly, back in 1998 we held hands while sleeping next to each other at a house party. It was a betrayal, my first and worst. At the time, a girl called Susan was my life. Susan, to whom I had lost my virginity under an apple-tree in her father's Orchard. Susan had been in Dundee at University, far away, and although I missed her, and although I thought I loved her – it didn't matter, Polly's hand was warm and close. I broke up with Susan the following day over the phone and ran straight to Polly's bed. Susan is married now and has a son. On Facebook I've seen pictures of the whole family playing around the apple tree in the orchard. I've seen them eating a picnic there and squinting at the sun. Possibly she cares or remembers me fondly, but she probably still hates me.

My remaining relationships at university could be described as somewhat frivolous. Strings of short-lived courtships, and a mutual understanding with Polly, that no matter who else we were seeing, we could rely on each other, day or night, to satisfy each other's needs. Fuck Buddy. That´s all she was to me. No more than that.

Perhaps this was why, years later, I could never take her seriously as a girlfriend. She had somehow lost some of the confidence that made her so attractive when she was young. Approaching thirty now, she worried that her legs weren't firm, and about grey hairs and varicose veins. She worried that her career was leading nowhere and that half of the girls she knew were getting married or having children. She told me she was falling in love with me again and cried when I couldn't say anything heartfelt back. Perhaps she also remembered those university years where she would arrive in my room five minutes after another girl had left, with the smell of the stranger's perfume still on my sheets. Back then, she didn't care. We would talk or fuck and laugh at how much fun we were having. Clearly, she'd make me have a shower before we fucked – that would have been disgusting, even to her.

Regardless of our past friendship, in 2007 she was a drain on my time and resources. Although it would have happened anyway, everything soured between myself and Polly as a direct consequence of Terry's Party. Nowadays I scorn the idea of hanging about with a bunch of minor C-Listers, but back then, although I knew there was something slightly pathetic about it, this was as good a place to start as any. If I could describe my mental processes during this period of my life, I think I would have to describe them as slightly unbalanced. I was confident and I was a salesman, I thought I could charm my way in and out of any situation. I NEEDED to go to this party. The way Terry made his life sound – it seemed that he was close friends with almost every film and TV star in circulation, the toast of London high society. Of course, most words out of Terry's mouth were utter bullshit, but still, I convinced myself that as he was a producer at *Oops! TV*, some celebs would surely be there. My first set of difficulties arose when I realised that on the day of Terry's party, as usual, Polly was going to hang around my flat like a bad smell, sitting on my sofa, watching movies, and generally getting in my way. I eventually had to admit to her that I was going to the party. The exchange of words didn't go too well, and on my departure I had to slam the door to my own apartment, leaving Polly sobbing and alone inside.

Once again it was raining, and my walk to the tube station did nothing to help me ease into the evening with grace. For some reason, a large majority of roads in London suffer from huge drainage problems, and colossal puddles form at the side of the bus lanes. Bus drivers, not being the most sympathetic, patient or understanding of people rarely slow down as they plough through the fords of murky water, in fact I would bet anything that on most occasions they actually speed up, which obviously results in a larger than average tsunami washing up on the pavement. Although I would never admit it to anyone, I like to call them Busnamis. This evening, cursing myself for being honest with Polly for a change, and cursing Polly for being such a whiney twat, I was knocked off my feet by a particularly feral Busnami and drenched from head to foot.

I would have gone back home, but I'd left her inside, with the slam of the door still ringing in my ears. I couldn't face going back and having another embittered conversation about my slowly blooming (and somewhat one-sided) relationship with Terry. So I ushered myself on, knowing that a solution would present itself. On the tube, amongst the hum-drum hordes, I began to wonder if I could actually get away with it: t'was only a stain after all. I made my way, along Camden high road, and no one batted an eye lid. Perhaps I could actually pull it off? Perhaps I would arrive at the night club and tell a witty story about the puddles and the buses, and something that I called a *(scoff)* "BUSNAMI!!!" I passed many a store where I could have bought a half decent replacement shirt, but felt no need. I wasn't a mess, I was rugged. I held myself together with my natural charm and dignity.

Yet when I walked into the club, and handed in my ticket, I caught sight of myself in a mirror, and God damn it, I was a bloody mess. It wasn't just my clothes, the shit stains on my pink shirt would never wash out (even with biological washing powder), my hair had matted into something that appeared very similar to the masses of grit that surround a river-dwelling shopping trolley, my lips were black, and the left hand of my face had a single brown stain streaming from my nostril to my earlobe. In all honesty, I'm surprised they even let me in. It really was too late to leave and change, so I walked straight into the bathroom and washed my face, clawing the worst bits out of my hair. Stoically, I got a piece of tissue and rubbed vigorously at the mess until it was little more than a small brown blemish on a gloriously crimson canvas. I chose not to panic, I chose to carry on, and I'm thankful I did. It was at this point, that I discovered my next step along on my journey to Elisha Cicero.

The bar was the first port of call. It wasn't the right type of social function for Guinness, so I grabbed a Bucks-Fizz, and guzzled it down to ease my nerves. Scanning around for Terry, I caught sight of a busty blond in a tight green floral dress, and had trouble keeping my eyes off of her. She had a delightfully long neck, which swooped and curved downwards into a picture perfect pair of breasts. I raked her up and down with my eyes, and before it became too glaringly obvious that I was infatuated, I turned around and walked in the opposite direction; after all, I wasn't here to pick up girls. Terry was amongst a throng of fake, overtly dramatic friends, and he was mopping up every single ounce of their tiresome attention-seeking sympathy. I gritted my teeth, and entered the circle of vanity looking at the ground, refusing to meet any of them in the eye. Terry welcomed me with a sickly sweet hug.

"This is the man who got me through it all, he was my rock. I would have never left that hospital alive if it wasn't for his friendship." said Terry.

It took every ounce of my strength not to roll my eyes and groan. They knew that he hadn't really tried to kill himself, and so did he, yet they all pretended as if he'd had one of those life altering experiences. Terry hadn't experienced anything of the sort, in fact Terry's only problem was an addiction to amateur dramatics. I would bet money, that almost every single person in that group had almost but not quite made an attempt on their own life. I thought once again about going back home, but the image of Polly waiting for me made me shudder, and without a word to Terry's clan, I walked back towards the bar. When first informed that some celebrities might be there, I had imagined myself amongst a list of talented and beautiful people, who would naturally be attracted to my charm and charisma. Unfortunately, I couldn't discern anyone I recognised, and my eyes were drawn again, and again, back to the girl in the green dress. I didn't approach her. The bar was calling, and my thirst needed to be slaked. Terry unlatched himself from his obnoxious gang, and followed me.

"Hi! Thanks for coming tonight, it wouldn't have been the same without you." He sounded confident and in his element, no doubt scanning the room for someone else he barely knew, with whom he could make meaningless self-gratifying comments.

In the absence of anyone catching his eye, he followed me to the bar and insisted on buying us several shots of tequila. He made whooping noises after every single glass. After a while, our fuzzy minds were sucked of all coherent logic. I moved my face closer to his:

"I thought'd be some of your workmates here?" I belched into his ear.

"There are! They're all around."

I glanced around at the distinctly unglamorous group of nobodies. I refrained from saying: "Where are the famous people?" as I knew I would look like an idiot. In fact, regardless of celebrities, I hadn't even managed to find anyone else that worked at *Oops! TV*. There were people who had worked with Terry at one point in their career, but had since moved on. None of the guests appeared to have any strong connections to Elisha's world whatsoever. Terry was clearly a lonely man, and I guessed that his current employees and colleagues didn't want to degrade themselves by coming to this awful person's party. I had long decided that I was wasting my time, and resolved to get off my trolley on more shots, and try my luck with the blond in the green dress. Terry must have been speaking to me about something or other – we were sitting next to each other at the bar for some time. A Mojito had come and gone, as well as several large glasses of Old-Fashioned. I'm not sure if I actually told Terry that I was going to leave him by himself, or whether I just walked away without a word. I am almost certain that it was the latter. I smiled at the girl in the green dress and she approached me.

"Hi, I'm Shaun." I said shaking her hand and pulling her close.

"I'm Scarlett." she replied kissing me on the cheek.

"How do you know Terry?" she asked me.

"I'm fucking his girlfriend" was on the tip of my tongue, but I bit it back.

"I was the one that found him when he....." I left it hanging there, as nobody really wants to be reminded of the morbid realities of life while flirting. I looked directly in her eyes, and my heart skipped a beat when I thought I saw her pupils widen. Had I caused that, or a change in light? I wouldn't have been any kind of man at all if I hadn't silently convinced myself into believing it was the former.

"HOW ABOUT YOU?" I screamed over the drum 'n' bass music that was blasting out of the speaker.

"I used to work with him."

I raised my eyebrows – was she my ticket into the social circles of the A-list celebrities?

"What do you do?"

She placed her hands on my bottom, stroking it gently and I couldn't help getting a semi. I thought she might get bored of my arse at some point, but she just carried on, smiling while she did so. She didn't answer my question, but in all honesty, I had forgotten my question in the first place. The most reoccurring thought in my mind was to strip her naked then and there, and have her right on the floor of the night club. My eyes roamed the room for the nearest exit, so if needs be, there would be no delays on our way out. Sounds arrogant, but in fact it's just primal instinct. In the back of my mind, I knew that it wasn't going to be that swift. I would have to do some groundwork first. I smiled and moved closer to her.

"What are you doing with my bottom?"

She grinned at me, and her teeth gleamed.

"I couldn't help it."

Not the witty retort that I had been hoping for: maybe banter wasn't this woman's forte. Still, I hadn't dreamt that somebody this beautiful could be so forward. She continued to tickle my bottom so that I began to feel a little hot under the collar. I moved my face towards hers, hoping for a kiss, but she moved away from me, and stopped groping my bottom.

"Drink?" I slurred, miming the action while doing so.

"Yes, please."

"What would you like?"

She had a sweet white wine, and I enjoyed the rest of the evening thoroughly, especially after I managed to get Scarlett out of that green dress.

Sunday 5th November 2007

Under normal circumstances I wouldn't have thought twice about ending the relationship with Polly there and then. However, the previous night had transformed me. My success with Scarlett Smith, a successful producer at the BBC, had hardened my resolve. It was proof that I had the wherewithal to achieve my goal of Elisha Cicero. The plan, as it had formed in my mind was this:

1. I needed to approach Elisha as an equal.

2. The only way to do this was through a close friend on the same standing as her.

3. I had no friends who were on the same social level as her, so therefore must actively seek one.

My days spent with Polly and Terry had allowed me time to consider this plan in great detail. All I had to do was work my way up the social ladder, and I would be able to approach Elisha. I had no doubt that she would find me interesting and charming. She simply had to meet me.

While making my way home from Scarlett's on the morning following Terry's party, I decided to keep my encounter with Scarlett a secret for the time being. Ending my relationship with Polly in my usual brutal manner had the potential to jeopardise my friendship with Terry, especially if Polly felt the need to go blabbing to him. Once Terry knew the truth, he might have decided to cast me aside, which in turn would have some impact on whatever it was that I had going with Scarlett. This would block my most promising route to Elisha, and my plan would come crashing down like dominoes.

By all accounts it was a rather half-hearted attempt – our relationship was over in a blaze of fire within twenty four hours. In my defence, Polly is a rather irritating person.

Sunday afternoons bore me at the best of times. Sunday was a day without work or play, and without these two factors, I was incapable of finding anything which can hold my attention. Back then, more often than not I sat around watching God-awful television with a laptop on my knee mindlessly surfing the internet. YouTube served as a constant source of entertainment, as did many of the gossip columns that let me know all that Elisha was up to. When I was with Polly, Sunday afternoons were doubly bad. She always seemed to want me to do something energetic. I wouldn't have minded if it had been something that was stimulating and interesting, like going on a walk or run, or going to the cinema, but she sat around telling me to clean the kitchen, to cook her something healthy, or sort out some stupid problem with the vacuum cleaner. It was as if she was under the mistaken impression that she owned me and my house, and had the right to boss me around. She seemed to forget that I wasn't Terry, or some other sap who gave a fuck about what she thought.

On the morning after the party, I was hung-over, perfectly content to while away my afternoon watching the Hollyoaks Omnibus on television when she walked through my front door. My own front door! Without knocking, with a key she had somehow purloined without my permission. She walked over to me like a robot and kissed me on the cheek, barely even noticing that I was there. She took off her shoes and walked into my bathroom. My bathroom! While I was still marvelling over what had just happened; she stormed out of it shouting at me and gurning with an over-exaggerated air of disgust.

"How do you live like this?" she moaned like a petulant child, "Your bathroom's disgusting!"

I wanted to point out to her that it was my bathroom, and I should be allowed to keep my bathroom however I like it, and that if she didn't like it, I wouldn't have been overtly offended if she fucked off back home. I wanted to tell her how happy I had been without her at the party. I longed to tell her that Scarlett Smith was as beautiful in the morning light as she had been the previous evening. I longed to inform Polly that just two hours previously, Scarlett's soft warm naked body had lain gently upon my chest. The problem was that I had the King of fucking hangovers and Polly wouldn't let her stupid little bathroom rant alone. Prissy in makeup, high heels and an unflattering miniskirt she stood, blocking the television and demanded an answer from me.

"Well....?" her shrill voice gave me a headache. I tried to ignore her, but she wouldn't go away. Silence was all she would get from me; I couldn't bring myself to bend to her whims. The cleaner would be coming on Wednesday anyway!

Eventually she made some kind of gurgling sound in the back of her throat and clenched her hands into fists. I'm not sure what she was trying to achieve with that noise, there was nothing in it that was especially nasty, or malicious. Probably a cry of frustration more than anything else, but it broke my resolve.

"Fuck off!" I screamed, and suddenly through the cracks that had appeared around my soul, a whole flood of vile truths, and half-truths came bursting from my lips. Needless to say, the revelation of where I had spent the previous evening did not sit well with her. In fact, to my deep regret, rather than fight back, she withdrew from me and crumpled. Her arrogant strut had gone; her eyes pierced me with the pain of a wounded animal. I had lost her trust and her friendship, but I did not care. As to my plan, she was no longer playing an important role, so could be discarded. Of course, a certain amount of damage limitation should have been implemented, but I had little idea of how vindictive a woman scorned could be. She said nothing, still recoiling from my evil words and actions, and faded away out of the door.

I continued watching Hollyoaks in silence.

Step 2: Terry Taylor

<u>Late November 2007</u>

I didn't want to appear too keen so I didn't call Scarlett immediately. I wanted to leave it for long enough so that she would panic, leave her to stew in her own paranoia and self-doubt. If this had been Polly, or any other half-human being, it would have worked perfectly. Unfortunately Scarlett was one of those people whose self-assurance was only outstripped by her beauty. She came from a very wealthy upbringing. She was one of those strange breed of London women who rides horses regularly, who owns several horses which are looked after by her inbred family in some huge country manor, and if truth be told, looks a little like a horse. She wore heels come hell or high water, and regularly ate in restaurants with a plethora of admirers who she only courted in order to ignore. Fortune had fallen on me on the evening I met her. Some poor sap she had met at a party in Wales had travelled all the way down from Sheffield to see her at Terry's party. The only reason I had ended up in her bed, was to torture this plaything of hers. That evening, with nowhere else to go, this northern dolt had been forced to stay in the spare room of her two bedroomed flat in Shoreditch, totally emasculated by the over-exaggerated tempest of pleasure bouncing through the paper thin walls.

Needless to say, she had not worried over my lack of contact, and if anything, had been bored by my phone call when it eventually came. I invited her out for a drink; she told me immediately that she was busy, but to maybe call again in a few weeks. When the phone disconnected I bit my fist in frustration. I hadn't known she was one of THOSE women or I would have played the situation entirely differently. Shit, I shouldn't have slept with her on that first night. Now that she had had me, she could chew me up and spit me out. She knew how good she was, and she knew how to play men. As such, I was forced to fall back on Terry Taylor for the time being, until I had successfully inaugurated myself into Scarlett's network of friends.

As the weeks passed, she deigned to let me see her. I longed in vain for a repeat of that first evening together. A night with Scarlett was like a pornographic film in action. She could anticipate and execute the perfect move, the necessary groan, the most intimate facial expressions for the most ideal and euphoric orgasm. The night of Terry's party, there were moments while I was pounding her that I began to wonder whether it was dream or reality. She was a bloody siren, a real life fucking siren, upon which myths and legends were made. Driving men to their doom with her beauty, luring them to the jagged rocks of peril, and laughing as they drowned.

Daytime with Scarlett was hell on earth – she had a way of simultaneously ignoring me and watching me perform. I turned into a monkey, a spectre of my normal self; into a wraith whose only purpose was to please; pretending to be unaffected while she flirted with any Tom, Dick or Harry. It was only on a rare occasion that she let her gentleman suitors into her boudoir. Those lucky souls were not lucky for long. They were soon enslaved by the night, and it was on an even rarer occasion that they got to experience her gentle moaning frame again. Most of her suitors remained ensnared until their grave, but some learnt about the folly of their love the hard way, when Scarlett tortured them with a public display of affection with another man. The term 'man eater' had never been more apt.

I took her to as many fancy restaurants as my fairly generous budget would allow, but she yawned at them all while quaffing the numerous bottles of bloody expensive Champagne that I placed in front of her. In a final wild and desperate attempt while at the end of my tether, I even took her to one of those weird, yet strangely 'in vogue' hippy/vegetarian restaurants where you can't book a table because the owners have the organisational skills of Wurzel Gummage. We couldn't get in because it was 'BYO' night, and was filled wall to wall with loud-mouthed drama students and struggling actors looking for a cheap night out.

I hate drama students. They all pretend to be so quirky and confident. It's always the drama students marching around and campaigning, dancing stupidly, making meaningless noise and drawing attention to themselves. They somehow seem to uniformly develop the same crazy notion that just because they spend their afternoon lessons pretending to be a tree they are superior to the rest of the world. In some ways the credit crunch wasn't all bad; at least the drama students started becoming unemployed once they'd finished their pointless degrees. The thought of all those loud-mouthed deviants all standing in line for their dole together never fails to bring a satisfied smile to my lips. They should have done a proper degree and pretended to be a tree in their spare time.

Those few months of my life were excruciating. Keeping Terry's garish ego at bay took up the vast majority of my free time, while chasing the dream that was Scarlett kept me awake at night in dissatisfaction. Thankfully work was going well, or I might have imploded in misery. At this point in my life, I was blissfully unaware of the money-flow problems I was going to face in the very near future. In any sales job when things are good, the maintenance of your winning streak tends to suck up a disproportionately large amount of one's life. Of course, this is also true when things are going badly, but in a more soul destroying way. You can see a salesman is doing well by the smug and cocky look in his bloodshot eyes. You can tell a salesman is performing poorly by the nervous tension they radiate, like an elastic band pulled so taught it is just about to snap. Oh the highs! And the awful, miserable, terrifying lows of a life in sales.

Little did I know that 2007 would be the last of my happy days as an Estate Agent, it was all going to pot at the end of that year. Bloody mortgages, Bloody Northern Rock, bloody credit crunch. Back then, if I mentioned credit crunch to people they would have thought that it was some kind of ludicrously tasty breakfast cereal. I really don't think I could have put up with Terry if I had to endure him through the worst of the recession. He would walk into my office and wait for me. He would sit in the chairs where our applicants were supposed to sit, and read a book. It wasn't even as if it was just for ten minutes before the end of the day. He knew that I rarely finished before 20:00, but still, twice a week he would arrive in his ripped jeans and wait for me from 17:00! Don't get me wrong, I don't really have anything against ripped jeans, but Terry's ripped jeans were always ripped in such a deliberately 'fashionable' way, that it couldn't help but vex me. There were always the usual, not-so-hilarious office *gay* jokes thrown about by my work colleagues. I couldn't help but think that being friends with Terry damaged my image.

Over the months that I knew him, I grew to realise that Terry was a very unbalanced and contradictory character. As he grew confident in our friendship, he relied on me more and more as an emotional crutch. One day he would be buzzing with excitement, and then on another he would weep dramatically about how nobody loved him, and I would have to comfort him, feed him lines about there being plenty of fish in the sea etc...

We never spoke about Polly, although her spectre loomed constantly over our fabricated relationship. He was like a child and equally demanding of attention. He would come up with some stupid idea like going on a walk across London to the zoo; or on a day trip to Thorpe Park. If I didn't want to do it, he would grow petulant and sulky. He would hang up the phone on me, and refuse to speak to me for several days, or worse, he would throw a tantrum at me in the middle of a public area. I'm sure that we were often confused as two men having a lover's spat. Still, he would invite me to parties with lots of people in show business, who all made a good show of seeming to like him, and as a bi-product, they also seemed to like me. Scarlett was sometimes there, flirting with someone or other; of course, she barely spoke to me. I would look across the room, trying to catch her eye, only succeeding in making her smile all the harder at the man in her arms.

Behind her back, Terry pretended to hate Scarlett. He called her an 'emotional laxative'. I was never entirely sure what this meant, but all his friends would snigger appreciatively whenever he said this phrase. They would all look at me and pat me on the shoulder, and wish me luck with mock sympathy. This was another problem with being friends with Terry. He would present me to the group as some kind of heartbroken, hopeless romantic, fallen for the wrong girl.

Oh God.

The Bile in my throat was so hard to keep down around him.

He told them that he was compelled to comfort me through this difficult time in my life, as he owed me so much. He would bring up *the incident* and recount his suicide attempt, revelling in the polite gasps from people, as if it were the first time that they had heard it.

I often felt physically ill when he spoke.

I sometimes wondered over what people must think of me hanging around such an obvious attention seeker. Thankfully, most of the people we met were useless plebeians at the bottom of the food-chain of showbiz, so I didn't lose any sleep over it.

December 2007

Christmas approached and slowly the housing market began to shut down. No one wants to move at Christmas time. December the 1st in my mind is the date when people's usual business-like minds turn towards sleigh-bells and wrapping paper and other such mush. The telephones stop ringing; so as a salesman it is your duty to pick up the phone and beat the festive cheer out of everybody you speak to. Force them to put their business heads on.

Here is an example of the standard of conversation you get as an estate agent at Christmas:

Mr. Festive Bloody Arsehole: "Merry Christmas?" (Oh no! not the C word, and in the form of a question instead of hello)

Me: "Hello is that Mr Head?"

Mr. Festive Bloody Arsehole: "Yes, who's this?"

Me: "It's Shaun from Fisher and Irving, how are you?" (Please note that I am not wishing them 'happy new year' or any of that nonsense – it's Mr Business Head and not this Festive Bloody Arsehole that I want to speak to.)

Mr. Festive Bloody Arsehole: "I'm not too bad Shaun, not too bad. Looking forwards to getting the kids round for Christmas."

Me: "Yes, I can imagine. Maybe we'll have you a bigger place by then, so they can all have their own room. How's the search coming along?" (Of course, even if he does get an offer accepted, no doubt his God-forsaken solicitor will be on holiday for the next two weeks, along with my client's solicitor. Solicitors are the worst people at Christmas; they're all so bloody rich they can afford to take the piss when it comes to holidays. God, I hate Christmas)

Mr. Festive Bloody Arsehole: "To tell you the truth Shaun, I've put everything on hold until the new year." (What For? His ex-wife has the Kids! He never has any social life to speak of, in fact I bet he has two friends in his life, and one of them is his mum. What's so chuffing special about Christmas?)

Me: "Ah hah! And can I ask when you plan to start looking again?"

Mr. Festive Bloody Head: "I don't know. Probably when the market picks up again." (Applicants are all so predictable – this is the go to response when they haven't got a clue.)

Me: "Right, OK, I can see where you're coming from there. I imagine you're thinking mid-to late January here?

Mr. Festive Head: "Yes"

Me: "Hmm... the problem with that is that everyone else is thinking the same thing. They're all going to wait until the New Year to move, and although this means there are more properties on the market, there's a hell of a lot of competition. If you find somewhere before Christmas and get an early offer in, because nobody else is looking, it's an easy win"

Mr. Festive Head: "But surely nobody is accepting offers?"

Me: "You'd be surprised! Lots of people are desperate to get out of their house before the New Year and are frustrated with everyone else dragging their feet. Why else would their houses be on the market? They're desperate to move!"

Mr. Business Head:"Alright, you make a good point, when could you spare to see me?"

I'd say that only one in ten people are turned, but that's the difference between a piece of coal in your stocking or a bottle of Dom Perignon.

Although it it my job to ensure people don't put Christmas in front of their house purchase, I'm not a complete Grinch. There are several aspects of Christmas that I actually quite like:

1. The bars packed with happy people.

2. The Christmas songs blaring on the radio (I have a soft spot for the golden oldies)

3. Secret Santa.

I bloody love Secret Santa. I love the mugs I get, the tacky, fat, Christmas themed mugs. I love it when someone tries to be funny, and buys someone something a little 'risqué' like a dildo, or a pornographic magazine. We generally have a £5 budget, and I always enjoy the challenge of buying a present at this price. Invariably I go over the limit and end up buying something for around £7.50. This particular year, I had bought a Shower Radio shaped like The Beatles yellow submarine. Guy, who had been the recipient of this present, seemed mildly pleased that it was something that he might actually use, which, in turn, made me a little warm inside – a rare feeling that made it all the more rewarding.

I received a Christmas card through the post from Polly. It read like this:

Shaun, I'm sorry I pushed you away.
Merry Christmas and a Happy New Year!
All My Love
Polly xx

I threw it in the bin with the rest of the junk mail, irritated. Nothing seemed to be going my way. Over December things died a terrible death between Scarlett and me. I had called a cease-fire on my text messages. I was outright refusing to send her a text unless she sent one first. Every time I heard that familiar 'Bippidy bip bip, bippidy bip bip' sound I prayed that it was Scarlett asking me for a drink. Unfortunately it was never her.

I tried to ignore my frustration; an activity which largely took the form of over-excess. December is an easy month for such things. I don't know how or exactly when it happened, but being young and single at Christmas in modern day England means one thing: booze. Family and giving have been reduced to formal obligations that play a minor role to the P-A-R-T-Y! By December 23rd me and my liver were longing for a break from it all. I realised that I actually wanted to go back to see my family, even if just to have someone wait on me while I rebalanced my equilibrium. Two or three days is all I can handle of them though, after that I become twitchy and restless. I long for my own home, and I need to get back to the buzz of city life.

My sisters spend alternate years with their husbands' family and my parents. As such, the years that my sisters don't come home, my parents travel abroad. This invariably means that I spend every other Christmas alone. Xmas 2007 was one of those years I spent with the family.

I'm not very close to my sisters. This may largely come down to our inherent differences. They are both married, having, from my memory, only ever been with a single boyfriend, and are both utterly dependent upon the attention bestowed upon them from my parents. From what I gather, both sisters phone them every single night of the week. My parents are lucky to hear from me once a month. It just isn't something I can quite get my head around: My sisters for all intents and purposes seem to have their whole 'grown up' lives sorted. If this is the case, then why do they still have this infantile need to maintain their umbilical cords intact? Still, despite their shortcomings, it was always nice to see them.

As is the case with most Londoners, I wasn't raised in the city. I was actually born in Swansea, but my place of birth is of no consequence to me whatsoever. My parents were both from Sussex. They moved to Swansea during their first year of marriage so that my father could finish his PhD. I was born the same year that my father graduated and got a job as a lecturer in Oxford Brookes.

As far as sport goes, I support England first, and Wales second.

I spent very little time with my family as a child. From an early age I was sent to Christ's Cathedral Boarding School in Exeter. It was an all-male environment, and has been given by many a disgruntled girlfriend over the years as the root of my emotional detachment to females. Devon was a fine place to grow up, but, much like Wales, there's nothing much within its borders to attract a man of my tastes. As is the case with most entrepreneurial young people, I had eventually come to settle in London. My parents on the other hand, had ended up in Cambridge. After my father retired, my mother demanded that they move there so they could be close to her sister and her family. It's also a short journey to Cambridge from London where the rest of us live.

I was the last to arrive, rocking up late and fairly dishevelled on the 23rd December. My Mother hugged me with her bangle adorned arms as I walked through the door, kissing me on the forehead.

"Oooh, it's *so* good to see you sweetie, how have you been?"

"Good, thanks mum. Where's everyone?"

"Oh they're all in the kitchen eating dinner. I've made lasagne."

My mum hobbled slowly into the kitchen following the sound of familiar voices, mingled laughter and the tinkle of cutlery. As I walked through the doorway, everyone rushed over to cuddle me. Only George and Harvey, my sisters' husbands stood back; they greeted me with a firm handshake instead. My family's perception of me is that I am the 'outlandish rebellious one'. So, as usual, I was hounded with questions about my life, and begged to recite any amusing or shocking events that had happened when I'd been out 'partying'. It is a continual source of frustration to me that no matter what I say, they always find my exploits, no matter how mundane, outlandishly funny. I could recount the most boring story and they'd still consider it 'wacky'. For example, I once told them a story that began with me walking to the post office to post a letter. The story was leading to an argument I'd had with the lady at the counter, but as it turned out, I didn't need to get to that point to amuse them. Elizabeth, my older sister, snorted garishly and piped up with:

"What did you do that for, why didn't you just send an email?"

Everyone started laughing.

"Well, she didn't have an email address." I replied, more than a little confused at their mirth.

"No email address? How old was she?! You should stick to women your own age!" bellowed my father. From here, there ensued a barrage of jokes about older women, and how I only fancied women if they were going through the menopause. I knew they only did this to try and keep me involved but it was a little irksome at times.

I sat down, and ate, and played up to my reputation. All in all it was a nice and normal evening with my family. My mother, like all mothers, I'm sure, seems to be able to make food much more flavoursome and tasty than anyone else on the planet. I was happy to discover that the lasagne lived up to my expectations. My sisters spoke about work and their 'crazy' friends who went out clubbing to all hours of the morning. I do love my sisters; they are wonderful, funny, intelligent human beings, but it baffles me how they've managed to let themselves become middle-aged in their late 20's. As I finished my third portion of lasagne, my father gave a contented sigh and told us that he was retiring to the living room for "a small drop of whiskey". As we all stood up to follow, the mobile phone in my pocket started vibrating violently. I rolled my eyes when I saw the caller ID and switched it off without answering. As I shoved it back in my pocket, I glanced around the room, and my family were staring back in silence. There was no point explaining why I didn't pick up the phone and I could see they were not going to ask. I followed them into the living room without a word.

My parents have a huge ornate liquor cabinet that they still keep under lock and key, a habit they have retained since my early teens. This was, as you might expect, not down to me, but rather my sister Elizabeth. I guess before she turned into one of the most boring people alive, she had once known how to enjoy herself. The security precautions had been implemented after my parents discovered that the vast majority of a litre bottle of Jack Daniel's had evaporated, and replaced with water, rendering the rest of the bottle undrinkable. I was too young to have been to blame, though I'm sure, even then, they thought of me first. Nobody had ever owned up to the crime, until Elizabeth's Hen Party, when finally the truth was revealed to my mother. Apparently everyone rolled about laughing. It's a little pathetic when you think about it, for something as insignificant as that to be mentioned at a hen party; it must mean that she has done nothing else adventurous, or slightly unexpected since.

In the meantime, my father trudged upstairs to get the key for the cabinet, and the house phone rang in the kitchen. My mother stumbled over and answered. As usual, I heard her reel off the home phone number by way of greeting. My mother always answers the phone by doing this. It was just another thing that made me feel at home, like a child again.

"Yes?" She said, sounding genuinely confused.

"Sorry, who is this?"

"Oh, yes, yes, we've heard so much about you"

"What did you say your name was again?"

"Terry?" A cold shiver ran down my back, surely he wouldn't call me at my parents' house?

Damn! But of course it was him.

Damn, damn, DAMN!

He was still mid-soliloquy when mum, clearly bored of his voice, passed the telephone receiver over to me.

"Shaun! Your mother sounds like a wonderful woman, she was just telling me what a nice Christmas you were all having….."

I refused to respond to his lies. My mother had said no such thing, I had just witnessed her answer the phone and listen to his drivel with a glazed expression. So I waited for him to get to the point:

"….You are so lucky…." Still waiting for that elusive point…

"….So very very lucky…" I was tapping my foot on the floor agitated.

"….Christmas has always been a difficult time for me. And now, after *the incident*, it's even worse."

"So, enjoying your Christmas so far then?" I said flatly, struggling to keep the sarcasm out of my voice.

"Oh Shaun, I'm with my family, but it feels so, so meaningless. They weren't there at *the incident*. They don't know what happened between us! It's like there's a void between them and me. Are you in London?"

"No." I refrained from pointing out that as he had dialled my parents' home-phone number, including the area code, he knew full well I wasn't in bloody London.

My mum passed me a glass of sherry, my whole family was staring at me.

"When will you be back?" – he had me in a corner.

"Boxing Day."

"Yes, boxing day, I thought so…" I really didn't know what he was doing, or why he was doing it, but I wanted to end this painful interchange and get back to my family. Reluctantly, I decided to just give him what he wanted so we could end the conversation.

"How about we catch up then?" I said.

"Shaun, you don't know how much that would mean to me!"

"No problem. Look, I've got to catch up with my sisters now but I'll call you when I'm on my way."

"Have a merry Christmas, Shaun."

"Okay, Terry"

I hung up. Merry fucking Christmas, moron.

Christmas continued as planned: Drink and food and the polite conversation about house-prices with family friends, cousins, siblings and in-laws. Aside from my escapades, that's all anyone ever wanted to talk to me about. I didn't mind, I always felt that it was a good way to practice my New Year Market Chat:

"Well, January is always the busiest time of year, what we find is that over Christmas, very few people will actually seriously consider moving – they're more concerned about buying their turkey – but in the new year, new years' resolutions kick in, and you see hundreds of applicants flooding the market. Yes – my advice would be to get on the market now before the Spring Market really kicks in and you're priced out."

I never gave them my card. They wouldn't have been able to afford the houses that I sold.

On Boxing-day, I said my goodbyes and drove back home, the monstrous image of Terry looming in the back of my mind. I met him in a Starbucks in the trendy part of Camden. With a tear in his eye and an insufferable smile on his face, he plopped down two airline tickets on to the table.

"Merry Xmas!" (Xmas, not Christmas. Who actually says Xmas?)

I picked them up – two British Airways tickets to Cape Town.

"What's this?"

"I thought we could celebrate the New Year in style!"

"These fly tomorrow?"

"I know."

"They don't bring us back until the fourth?"

Raising his eyebrows and glowing a little red he made an annoying "mmmm?" sound indicating that he was hiding something that he wanted me to ask about.

"I'm back to work on the second."

Gushing now "OMG I cleared it with your office! I told them that it was a surprise, and they were fine about it!"

My blood boiled a little as I imagined my manager Lance agreeing to the holiday with a mocking smile. I was already dreading the banter that would greet me on my return to the office

"How was your honeymoon Shaun?"

"Yeah, did you enjoy your romantic getaway in the Savannah?"

"Did you propose to him on top of Table Mountain? It must have been WONDERFUL!"

On the other hand, at this time of year the tickets mustn't have been cheap, and I could definitely use a little bit of sunshine in mid-winter.

"I don't know what to say. This is, this is really kind of you."

"Let's just say it's my way of saying thank you for helping me survive this year."

I drank the rest of my latté with growing excitement.

Now, I did wonder where Terry had got this money from, but at the time it didn't seem to matter – I was going on HOLIDAY. Sunshine, blissful sunshine. Scorching off the winter cold, burning away the blues. Say what you will about Terry, but the man was generous.

Now – many people reading this will be asking the following three questions:

1. Why would any self respecting individual and normal human being go on holiday with a man like Terry?

2. Why would Shaun agree to such a stupid idea?

3. Just why?

My answer is this:

I have ambition.

The most fundamental thing that separates me from your average Joe (apart from the hundreds of pages that show me posing in celeb magazines) is my ability to set myself a goal, and ruthlessly pursue it until it has been reached.   It's basic sales: set yourself a target and achieve it – no matter what that target may be, or who you have to stab in the back to get there.

An idiot salesman, at the beginning of the week pledges realistically; he promises low figures, maybe less than what he hit last week.   It invariably results in accusations that he has taken his foot off the pedal, that he's a man with no confidence. This in turn, leads him into a hate fuelled spiral where he fails and fails and fails again. Gradually losing the respect of all around him and sinking into despair as his meagre figures are continually outshone by all the big players.

To illustrate this phenomenon in terms of women: a poor salesman will pledge for Polly. If he ever achieves her, (and we all know that it's not all that difficult), he'll have to contend with the irritating way she moves, breathes, speaks, eats and cleans her teeth. Despite the meagre reward, he'll pretend that he's happy, may even think that he's happy. I on the other hand, will never be content with less than perfection. Polly will eventually get bored with that poor sap and move on to something bigger and better. Chances are that the confidence of this poor simpleton will be knocked so hard as a result, that he won't ever get anyone half as good again. He'll eventually settle for an old pig.

If you, like me, want to succeed, think of a realistic figure, think of the highest amount your average Joe could possibly sell in a week, and then triple it.   Lie through your teeth; tell everyone that you have enough in the pipeline to hit it. Make a bet with your boss.

At *Fisher and Irving*, when I made a pledge, I knew that there was not a snowball's chance in hell that I was going to hit it. My colleagues knew that I wasn't going to hit it. Even my manager knew in some small corner of his greedy little brain that I was bull-shitting him; but still, he took these figures to the board of Directors and explained that these targets, these pieces of fiction, would be achieved. He then promised that the figures will be doubled in three months' time. It then became 'official' and all our reputations were on the line – we were building an empire on ego and dreams. Amazingly, and seemingly by some massive stroke of luck, I would get a £3 million asking price offer on a maisonette in SW3. Out of nowhere, I would hit my target while the plebeians gawped in amazement. Jealous and stupid people thought that there was no skill involved – being in the right place, at the right time. While they wailed inwardly in desperation, I was off quaffing Champagne, celebrating like the amazing salesman I was supposed to be. Most people seemed to forget that it wasn't just luck; I used to hit my unreachable target more often than I failed. After my reputation was on the line, the only option available was to force myself to hit it. Once I hit my target, I'd triple it again, and work, and call, and show, and drive, and pester, and poach, and sell, until I reached the next target. It was hard work getting to No.1.

So I pledged Elisha and I was going in with guns blazing, Damn it! With Scarlett written off as a failure, Terry was my only tie to 'show-biz', my only client, if you will. If I was ever to reach my goal, I needed to schmooze him until a better offer came along.

The following morning I found myself sitting on the Heathrow express at 5:00AM with the most annoying man alive. Terry didn't even need to actually do anything to get on my nerves, just smile, and exist. Sitting opposite him in the warm stuffy carriage, a few unpleasant thoughts twittered their way around my mind, shitting on any kind of excitement I usually get when going on holiday:

I slept with his Girlfriend, why would he want to take me on holiday?
Is he some sort of pervert?
Will he try and murder me?
Might he rape me?

Clearly these weren't thoughts designed to settle my soul, and I grew silent. No normal person would choose to go on holiday with the man who fucked their girlfriend. In an attempt to find solace, I spent some time devising a theory that didn't end up with my anus being sexually violated. Perhaps he wanted to be like me? Latching on to me realising I was stronger and more charismatic. That was the best I could come up with. Even that didn't make complete sense – as a successful producer he must have been skilled, and confident, and known what he was talking about. He probably had hundreds of people looking up to him. However, try as I might, I couldn't imagine Terry in any roles of responsibility. To me, he would always be that quivering wreck weeping at my doorstep and vying for people's attention. Ultimately, I decided that it wasn't wholly impossible to comprehend: a successful businessman who was also a complete idiot. There are enough successful City brokers that fit that description, specifically those plebeians responsible for my ruined income.

Thankfully he took my silent contemplation as a signal to bring out his book. He began to read, allowing me a few moments to rest my head against the window and feign sleep while attempting to allay my paranoia.

By and by, we arrived at Heathrow. We were relatively early for check-in, and slipped through security with ease. As you might expect, like a child, Terry followed me. He didn't bother looking at the notice boards to find our flight details. I could have been walking the entire way to South Africa and he would have stepped in file. In the departures lounge, I sauntered over to Boots and purchased sun-cream. Terry got some too. Between us, we also purchased: two disposable cameras, two matching pairs of flip flops, two packets of cards, two vest tops, four pints of Guinness, and two full English breakfasts. It irritated the hell out of me. I had also intended to buy myself a new pair of shorts, but couldn't bear the thought of us both having exactly the same wardrobe for the entire holiday. I'm not sure what he thought he was doing, but it did nothing to dispel my fear that he could be unhinged.

There is something rather unsettling about leaving home midwinter and arriving bang in the middle of an African summer. Alighting from the plane with a head full of cold, looking slightly anaemic, and stepping out onto parched, quivering runway, the heat beats down upon your head, and your skin immediately begins to feel scorched. It's such a dramatic change from Britain's miserable climate that I imagine that it's not unlike the shock a vampire would feel when they are burnt to cinders by the sun. There's a rugged feeling to the country, and everything feels so alien, even the dirt in Africa feels alive and breathing.

Cape Town, possibly the tamest, and certainly one of the most Westernised areas of Africa, is still utterly different to anything an Englishman is used to. From the moment we arrived at the airport we were bombarded with unfamiliar experiences – the native Africans carrying our bags out to the taxi over their heads, dressed in smart – but dirty clothes; sitting in the taxi and watching people cross the motorway on foot, not even vaguely wary of cars; the neat white Dutch-style architecture contrasted against the squalor of the Townships. Eclipsing it all – Table Mountain loomed over the city with God-like supremacy. Cape Town was truly scenic and looking out of the taxi window, my mood picked up; the holiday was once again lain out in front of me: sun shining, people smiling, and mountain booming. For a while, during our journey between the airport and the harbour where our hotel awaited, my annoyance at my unlikely companion momentarily abated – at one point I even forced myself to turn and flash a cheery smile at him.

Sadly, this Zen-like serenity didn't last long. Terry's Maestro card wasn't accepted in the hotel we were staying in and, with embarrassed apologies from Terry, I was forced to use the details from my own Visa Card in order to secure the room. To exacerbate the issue, he had reserved us a double room. Thankfully we didn't have to share beds, but it meant that I had to spend every waking minute of every single day with him. The first and last thing I would see for the next few days was his stupid face. With a sigh, I handed over my card to the receptionist. By the end of our first evening together, in spite of the exotic location, I knew that I had made a horrendous mistake agreeing to accompany him on the trip.

Here are some of the many things that bothered me about the holiday:

1. The Weather.

Although I do like it to be sunny, I don't like it to be *that* sunny, especially as I burnt my skin to a crisp on the very first day. Terry thought it was hilarious. He kept saying "I tried to warn you!" In fairness, he had tried to apply some sun lotion to my back. Unfortunately, I was still worried that he may have some kind of crush on me, so I pushed him off and took myself for a long walk along the harbour, forgetting my shirt. The sea breeze fooled me so that I didn't realise how much sun I had caught. When I returned, I had the aura of a Lobster Bisque about me, and for the rest of the holiday I was in agony.

2. The disappearance of Scarlett

I had completely lost at her game.   Over Christmas I had eventually gotten fed up with her silence, and desperately sent her a flurry of text messages. I received nothing in return. She had abandoned me.   Terry explained that he had heard a rumour that she was seeing someone else. This riled me, and I didn't have any proof to the contrary. Terry looked at me pityingly every time I checked my phone; no contact for weeks, and I couldn't think what I had done wrong. She had simply vanished off the face of the earth. I tried to quiz Terry on how much he knew about this new man, but he didn't know anything. Unsurprising really, there's not a chance in hell Scarlett would ever divulge anything personal about her life to Terry: He was one of those people who built up a vast number of acquaintances and contacts, few of which he interacted with in any meaningful sense. Typically he was incredibly vindictive behind their backs. It was unsurprising that none of his colleagues actually liked him very much. They would come to his parties if he invited them, but they would rarely extend an invitation back to him.

3. The People

Cape Town seemed to be made up of two types of people: the arrogant rich, and the filthy poor.   The Townships spilling out meant that you couldn't walk ten metres without someone clinging to you and begging for something. Then, right next to these wretched slums, there are fortresses built high with spiked fences, security systems and dogs barking to keep out the undesirable neighbours. It was so different to what I'm used to in London, it didn't feel right. More than this, the white South African Men seem to be reared on protein, standing a foot taller than me and twice as wide; and what's more, they knew it. On more than one occasion, I nearly ended up in a fight in a bar with one of these meat-heads who made some sarcastic comment about rugby, or the English, and expected me to back down. When I argued back, they quickly ran out of 'clever' things to say, and ultimately started cracking their knuckles. Night after night, I went out hoping for something sophisticated. I wanted to find something similar to the London Club scene where I could brush shoulders with the rich and famous. I found none of this in Cape Town, possibly because without any inside knowledge, we typically hung around the tourist traps and yokel bars. Only on New Year's Eve did I have a good night out, and that was because I copped off with a beautiful petite French girl called Sylvie so I was able to avoid Terry for the entire night.

4. Terry's endless need for Tourism

I worked damned hard in my job, and when I did take time off, I liked to relax. Apart from skiing, I don't tend to go on active holidays that involve exercise, or walks, or sightseeing of any kind. Unfortunately, Cape Town seems to have an endless number of things to see – Nelson Mandela's Prison on Robben Island, Cape Point, penguins, safaris, vineyards, slums, 'scenic' walks, and on and on. It led to several awkward and embarrassing arguments between us, and in the end, we grew miserably tired of each other's moaning. Every now and then, he would flush red with anger as I barged him out the way and made my way back to the hotel on my own, refusing to have any part in the horrendous itinerary he had planned. Throughout the holiday, our differing wishes and requirements became a torment to each of us – not a breakfast went by without us butting heads. Terry became bolder in expressing his frustration at me, which never ceased to shock me. Ultimately, it was Terry's need to "experience" everything that led to the end of our friendship.

On the penultimate day, his alarm clock sounded at 07:00 AM, so, no lie-in as usual.

"Time for breakfast!" he said.

Terry had a habit of stating the obvious. I rolled over and buried my head in my pillow while he rumbled around the room, showering, using the hair dryer, singing to himself, switching on the television, whistling, and generally being a nuisance. I eventually gave up trying to get back to sleep, and forced myself out of bed at 07:30. We wandered down to the dining room together, but I don't think I spoke a single word to him until I'd finished my third cup of coffee. I do love the cooked breakfasts one gets at hotels. The smell of bacon in the air, the cool jugs of orange juice lined up in a row and the conveyer belt toasters; there is something altogether satisfying about it. Typically, I'm still full from the large meal the night before, and despite the slightly sick, over-stuffed feeling that eventually overwhelms me, I will always make room for a cooked breakfast on holiday.

"Looks like a great day to climb Table Mountain!" said Terry.

I stared back in disbelief, climb Table Mountain? CLIMB it?

"I'd rather get the cable car if that's okay; I think it's a bit too hot for all that exercise." I replied.

Terry looked a little crest-fallen, and then flushed red. I knew it was time for the daily argument.

"This is my one favour I'm asking of you. Walk up with me"

I had considered all of his excursions my 'favour' to him. Other than the day out in the catamaran, they had all been tedious. I knew this walk up a mountain in the blinding heat would turn out to be more trouble than it was worth. My favours to Terry were all but used up.

"Look, my sunburn hurts and I fancy a rest. We can go up the cable-car, and the view will be just as good."

"No, that's not good enough. I want to climb up. A-J from work said he climbed it, and it was one of the best experiences of his life." His cheeks were puffed like a five year old on the brink of having a tantrum.

"Terry, I said I don't want to."

"Why not?"

"I just fancy a rest."

"Look, if you don't fucking come with me, I'll make you pay for your half of the holiday."

This was a whole new level of petulance and I ground my teeth in frustration.

"What the fuck Terry? You can't do that!" I had an urge to mash in his teeth with my coffee mug.

"It's your credit card details sitting behind the front desk. I can just walk out of here right now, and you'd have to pick up the bill for the whole week".

Blackmail seemed to be his forte. Perhaps this was how he became a business man after all? I had to hold myself back from hurling my plate of food at his face.

Eventually the desire to cause him harm with my eating apparatus became irresistible. It would have gone badly for Terry but for the fact that my neanderthalic urges were tempered by my common sense and dignity. My inner struggle manifested itself in the rather pathetic course of action I took: I picked up a glass of water which was very nearly empty. Only two millimetres of luke-warm liquid remained. With a wild and flamboyant hand gesture I hurled the water at him.

"Fucking cool off, why don't you?" I said, with as much venom as I could muster.

Terry was unmoved by my actions, and but for a small wet-patch on his chin, he was otherwise completely dry. I dare say he might have even found it refreshing.

I took a deep breath, and considered my options. I didn't believe he'd actually make me pay, but I was certain that he wouldn't shut up unless I agreed to go.

"Terry mate, I'm sorry. I'll come with you then if it's that important." I was feeling a bit foolish about the water. My embarrassment was enough to mollify me into an apology. Terry stood up and indicated that I should follow him. We left the table in silence. The other guests' eyes followed us as we walked to the exit and my ears burned red in shame. Terry had got his own way again, so we headed back to our room and began to make preparations for the trip.

Terry decided that he wanted to travel up the back of the mountain starting in some Botanical gardens, following a route called 'Skeleton Gorge'. Hearing the name of our route didn't make me any more inclined to climb. Once at the summit, we would continue along the top to the highest point (apparently this was the same route 'A-J' from work had taken). From there we would walk towards the cable car to take in the waterfront views. For some stupid reason, instead of taking the easy route down the cable-cars, the intention was then to turn back on ourselves and climb down the way we came.

Before catching a taxi to the Botanical Gardens, we stopped off in a supermarket to buy some snacks for lunch. We grabbed a loaf of bread, cold meats, and some Samosas. Terry insisted on buying several large bottles of water. Although I too was concerned about the risk of dehydration in the blinding heat, I felt that 8 litres of water was excessive. I said as much, but this almost brought out another temper tantrum from Terry. After I lost the argument about the water, it turned out that Terry's backpack wasn't big enough to hold more than two litres, so I ended up carrying 6 litres of water while Terry carried only two litres, and our lunch. Needless to say, 30 Degree heat coupled with a heavy back-pack did not make for ideal mountain climbing conditions.

Initially the walk through Kirstenbosch Botanical gardens was fairly flat; still, the sun beat down on my head and within 10 minutes I was drenched in sweat. I looked at the mountain ahead, and considered the feat before us. It seemed impossibly high. I've long since Googled Table Mountain, and it's actually only 1086 Metres above Sea level. When I tell people that I've scaled Table Mountain, I think they probably imagine me using a pick, and climbing up a vertical face. I don't usually tell people that it's only 1086 Metres, and could probably be accomplished wearing sandals. If they specifically ask how high it is, I usually tell them that it's 3563 feet above sea level which sounds a lot higher. We followed signs that directed us towards Skeleton Gorge as the incline grew steeper and steeper. After a little while, the path led us into a forest. I had been hoping that once we got into the shade the walk would be more bearable, unfortunately I had been wrong. The dense foliage around us sapped the cool sea breeze, so we were trapped in a green sauna. Slowly, the sound of the busy gardens petered out, and I was alone with Terry. It would have been completely without noise, if it were not for Terry's insufferable panting. Although I was a reluctant climber, I was in much better shape than Terry and found the exercise a lot easier. Within half an hour he was complaining of shin-splints. I'm not entirely sure what he had been expecting when he demanded that we climb the mountain; a walk in the park, it was not – mind you, technically, we never actually left the botanical gardens – so technically, a walk in the park is exactly what it was. A set of steps had been etched into the dirt track using wood and rope. It was steep and fairly heavy going.

My back grew impossibly hot and uncomfortably damp, my heavy bag pressed against my shoulders, trapping in unwanted heat. Although I had been forced into this trek, I've always enjoyed exercise, and although I didn't want to be exercising on my holiday, that day was no different. Frustratingly, even this small pleasure was ruined by Terry. I would get my groove on, get into a strong rhythm and begin to cover good ground, but every ten minutes I would find myself alone. So I was forced to stop over and over again, waiting for Terry to catch up. He would turn up eventually; purple faced and wheezing uncontrollably. The closeness of the air prevented us both from ever properly catching our breath. The mud steps grew uneven and steeper. The forest was so close that the trees were creeping down our necks and it was difficult to say how far up we had come, we only got the occasional fleeting glimpse of the world beyond the canopy. The mud steps turned into stone where some poor soul in the distant past must have had to chip away at the rock with a pick axe. When Terry caught up with me, I would try and get on as quickly as possible, but Terry would hold me back by hanging on to my arm. The irony of our breakfast argument was not lost on me; I took no small amount of pleasure at seeing the trembling mess that Terry had become.

"I've always had trouble with shin-splints" he kept on repeating.

I don't even know what shin-splints are, but it seems to be a common problem amongst people who are crap at sport. Terry would stop, and bend, and stretch his hamstrings to try and ease his pain – I'm not sure how that could have made any kind of difference to his shin-splints, but he seemed to feel it helped. He looked weak and I was embarrassed for him. Over the next hour he grew slower and ever more pitiful. Unfortunately the smug satisfaction that I had been feeling quickly wore off and I grew more frustrated with our pace. We had our first reprieve from the monotonous 'stepping motion' when the path met what looked like a dry river bed. For a few moments I wondered whether we had taken a wrong turn somewhere, but quickly realised that we were expected to scale the huge boulders blocking our route. Surprisingly, Terry accomplished this with little or no moaning (thank God). Apart from a few other almost identical river beds, and a set of rather rickety looking ladders the route was quite simple: Step and step and step again. Just when I thought it would never end, I burst out of the canopy directly under the midday sun. The view was stunning and the city suburbs spanned into the distance. I even managed to pick out few landmarks, Newlands International Rugby stadium being but one of them. Straddling a small boulder, I removed my bag. The wind cooled my sweat-sodden back and I took a long hard drink of the water I'd been carrying. I removed my top despite my burnt and peeling shoulders and donned a pair of Oakley's. I crouched, basking in the heat until Terry finally caught up. By and by we reached the end of the eternal steps and the path took us up over a plateau at the crown of the mountain. From the harbour looking up, the mountain looks perfectly flat, but in fact it is surprisingly hilly and uneven. There is little vegetation, and the path is hard and rocky. It would be quite easy to trip and turn your ankle. A huge stone gorge surrounding us emanated heat from all sides, and the sun beat down upon the back of our necks. Although physically easier, the hot dry air sapped away our strength and Terry began to complain again. I was forced to stop and wait again, and again, and again.

When we emerged from the chasm, according to our map we were still a few hours walk from the highest point, but Terry wanted to stop for lunch. Although I would have preferred to wait, I could see how much pain he was in, so sat down beside him and unzipped the bags. I bit my tongue when I saw that we had not yet touched three of the four bottles of water I was carrying. We sat with our backs against a huge sandstone precipice looking out at the City. Although the climb should have built up quite an appetite, it was too hot to eat too much, especially after our large breakfast. We were the only people around, and apart from the rustle of the wind in our ears, it was deathly silent. Terry was unusually untalkative; I couldn't work out whether it was because he was tired, or if something was troubling him. He opened his mouth as if to say something but seemed to think better of it and took another bite of his make-shift sandwich. I regarded everything around me, I hate to admit it, but for a few minutes I almost began to enjoy myself. It was galling that I had to share this experience with Terry, but just to experience it at all was enough. I finished up the last few crumbs of my bread and stood up to clear up the remainder of the picnic. The heat overwhelmed me and I stumbled a little, my hand snapped out onto Terry's shoulder. We remained in this position until the dizziness had passed.

"Let's stay here a bit longer." said Terry "I don't think I have enough energy to reach Maclear's Beacon anyway" (Maclear's Beacon is the highest point of the mountain)

I regarded my companion with displeasure, he was so weak.

"I think we should be able to make it." I responded, well aware at how our roles from the morning's exchange had reversed. I'm not sure why I wanted to push on to the top. It was partly due to something sick inside me that takes pleasure in other peoples' pain. That, and the fact that I'd now set the peak as a target that I needed to hit. Reaching the peak was one of the few things that had made this pointless waste of my time more bearable.

"I don't think I can."

I clenched my fists in frustration.

"Why don't you give it a try? We can't be far."

Terry rolled his eyes, took a deep breath then shrugged in defeat.

"Okay, I'll give it a try…." As he stood up he let out a huge lady-like squeal and dropped to the floor.

"….OMG I've got Cramp! Oh, it hurts." He writhed around on the floor, tears streaming from his eyes. It was pitiful. I took his foot and stretched it to the sky while Terry breathed in through his nose and out of his mouth.

"Let's go back! Let's go back! I can't go on."

"For fuck's sake, maybe you wait here while I go up on my own."

"No! Don't leave me on my own up here. I can't even walk! What if something comes after me?"

The only wildlife I'd seen so far were small birds and several small brown Guinea Pig type creatures that looked about as harmless as, well... an oversized Guinea Pig.

"I don't think anything will come here"

"Are you kidding? We're in Africa! There could be anything out here. Please don't leave me. OMG, please don't leave me."

"I won't be long."

"NO! NO! NO!"

This time it was my turn to shrug in defeat. The peak was now lost to me, and I thought longingly about the hotel swimming pool where I could have lounged all afternoon under an umbrella sipping cocktails. It had been such a waste of time, to get so close to the top, and still turn back because of a little bit of cramp.

"Okay, we'll wait here for another 15 minutes then go down."

We remained in silence with the world in miniature laid beneath our feet, but now that I wanted to get moving, I became well aware of how uncomfortable it was in the sun. All the irritations I had previously been ignoring became glaringly obvious. It was all that I could think about. Three blue bottle flies landed on my skin, tickling and crawling on my arms. My head pounded under the unyielding sun. One of the flies flew upwards towards me face. Terry rubbed his legs snivelling and breathing deeply, giving the impression of Mummy's brave little soldier battling on against the odds. I flapped my hand at the fly in my face, and the two others jumped into the air. My stomach churned in the heat. The flies flew to my lips, to my eye, to my ear, to my neck and to my lips again. My sunburnt back was rubbed red raw by the stupidly heavy bag I was carrying. A fly landed on my ear, and one of the stupid Guinea Pig things that Terry was so afraid of hobbled past us. My irritation mounted and the heat clouded my senses. Terry looked up at me.

"Polly emailed me the other day" he said. Two more flies joined the original three and landed on my back, drinking up my sweat. What was he drivelling on about now?

"She wants to meet me when we get back." He continued.

"What do you mean?" I stifled an angry shout. The flies continued at my face, and I glared at him.

"I don't want to meet her unless I know what happened between you two though."

"You know what happened." The cluster of flies got in my eyes.

"No, I don't think I do."

"Yes you do, she told you, and then you tried to kill yourself."

"Look, let's leave *the incident* out of this. Did you see her again after that night?"

"No." I tried to slap the flies off my skin, but they jumped out the way, and landed on the hand I'd used to slap them.

"You're lying to me."

"No, I'm not."

"Why do you keep on lying to me? I know you've seen her since! I know she was there the night of *the incident*."

"No she wasn't! I thought you said not to mention *the incident*?"

"Shaun, just tell me the truth for once in your life. You owe me that much."

"Look I don't fucking owe you anything. I'll pay for the hotel, Okay? Let's just get off this God-forsaken mountain and talk properly over a drink."

Without a word, Terry slowly stood up and began tracking back the way we came. I took one last look in the direction of Maclear's Beacon and stepped in line behind him. The infuriating insects took their own place behind me and in a misguided attempt at outrunning them, I picked up my pace. Within minutes I was ahead of Terry, but this time decided that I would wait for him only after long distances, that way I didn't have to spend any time with him. Half an hour of solitude later, my stomach really began to ache, and without warning I was forced to empty my bowels behind a rock at the side of a path – it seemed that the Samosas had been a bad choice. It is a little known fact about shitting behind a rock at the top of a mountain in Africa, that the only thing you can wipe your arse with, is your pants. This is exactly what I did. I expect my pants are still up there behind that rock, covered in the last vestiges of my shit.

When I came out from my hiding place, there was no sign of Terry. I couldn't be sure, but I doubted that he would have kept in pace with me. I stumbled round the corner and checked for any signs of him down the mountain as far as I could see. I couldn't see anything, so I waited, and all the time my stomach pained me. I couldn't leave the path again for fear of missing him. I began to get frustrated again, and the Bluebottles straight from the fifth circle of hell tormented me enough to give up the wait and walk back on myself to find him. He wasn't there; I retraced my steps all the way back. I hadn't realised how far I'd come until I noticed our lunch-spot to the left of me. I couldn't work out whether I was angry or concerned. Surely he hadn't passed me when I rushed off the path? Had he gone on to the summit? Had he taken ill and hidden in the bushes? Had he collapsed somewhere? I was so angry and unwell I took a shit right on the spot where he'd been sitting. I briefly considered using a sock to wipe my arse, but decided that I would have to go without and take the consequences.

I would like to point out that shitting in public is not something I tend to do, but I was on my own in the middle of nowhere, and I had very little choice. It dawned on me very quickly that he was most probably down at the bottom of the mountain; after all that whining, he was actually able to keep up with me until I fell ill.

At the back of my mind I still had some concerns that he had gotten lost or done something stupid. I tried calling his mobile for the second time – still no answer. One of the stupid fat Guinea Pig things started sniffing around the crap on the floor. The flies flew down to it, and then flew back at me. I kicked out at the creature on the floor, and it bit my ankle with some exceptionally large teeth. It made several high pitched noises then shuffled off into a little hole. My leg was bleeding and the flies flew straight at it. I grunted in frustration; swatted the flies away and began running down the path towards the bottom of the mountain. Within minutes, the sweat was getting in my eyes, and my lungs were panting against the harsh dry air in the gorge, but I continued until I tripped and fell hard on the ground. The bluebottles landed on a gash on my knee and I felt like crying. I tried to keep my calm and stood up. I brushed myself off and stolidly made my way back, trying to ignore the bruises on my legs and the grit in the graze. My knee throbbed in dull mechanical discomfort. The skin had also come off the palm of my hands, but I could ignore that as my knee and the Bluebottles took up all of my attention.

The journey back down the mountain is not something that I would want to repeat ever again. It took three hours and every footstep was a struggle. By the time I reached the botanical gardens at the bottom, I was at the end of my tether. Terry was sitting in the shade in a café drinking a cool ice tea reading a book. When I saw him, he calmly looked up at me over the top of his book.

"I was wondering when you'd show up" he said in a maddening tone. "Have you finally built up the courage to speak to me about Polly?"

Like a switch, I was Shaun Valfierno no longer. I become a ball of rage. My eyes filled with scowling patterns of menace, reminders of every little annoyance Terry had ever perpetrated. I ran at him and pushed him off his chair. The table fell over and the ice tea smashed on the floor. Ploughing down into the desert of my soul I began shouting, cursing, and everything came out. Amongst many other things I told him about my relationship with Polly, I told him my true feelings regarding our friendship, and I told him I was only using him to rub shoulders with the rich and famous. Like Polly before him, Terry crumbled.

"I only wanted to know if you still had feelings for her, you fucking dick!" he screamed back.

My anger quickly subsided along with our friendship. I didn't apologise, I walked into the car-park where a taxi was waiting. I took the first taxi back to the hotel, showered, changed my clothes, and checked out. At some considerable cost, I moved my flight forwards to the first available out of that God forsaken country. I didn't speak to Terry again for quite some time.

Step 3: Scarlett Smith

5th January 2008

If I had been more medically aware I would have gone straight to hospital to test if I'd contracted Rabies from that stupid Guinea Pig. Instead, I returned to work trying not to think of the look of despair on Terry's face. Thank God I didn't get Rabies. God had something else in store for me on my return. Something only marginally better than Rabies: the credit crunch had arrived. When I first entered the office it wasn't immediately apparent what curse had befallen my profession over the Christmas period. I do, however, remember noting how bizarrely full the office was for January. When I say 'full', I mean that all of my co-workers were sitting at their desks making phone-calls. This was bizarre in the fact that they shouldn't have been at their desks, they should be out on viewings, making sales. Initially I thought that the Christmas lag had somehow spilled over into the New Year. It was only when I began to call my existing applicants that I began to get worried.

"The market's going to crash."

"I've decided to wait."

"My parents told me to wait."

"I can't get my deposit together."

"Have you seen the news? They say property prices are going to plummet."

"I've been made redundant."

"The bank won't give me a mortgage."

"I've decided to rent for another two years, I've already signed the contract."

"I'm moving to Australia, there aren't any jobs here at the moment."

"I'll see what happens with the economy, perhaps buy next year with a bigger deposit."

"There's no chance I'm moving in this market."

"I'm going to wait for a while and get a repossession cheap."

"It's not financially viable to get a buy-to-let in this market."

"The markets going to crash"

"The markets going to crash"

"The markets going to crash"

"The markets going to crash"

Nobody thought that it would last as long as it did, after all people *need* to live somewhere; London is overpopulated, and there is nowhere near enough property for everyone.

Time proved us wrong.

The weather was cold, the days were short, and nobody wanted to buy a house from me. It got worse, and worse, until it was all over the newspapers every day. The damn press: I was certain that if they would give us a break, we could make just a little bit of money. It was like being kicked in the face over and over again. Estate Agents sell confidence, but the press took away any chance of us doing that. Each and every news story felt as if it were specifically designed to ruin us: stories of banks failing, mortgage companies balking under the pressure, first-time buyers completely disappearing from the market, redundancies growing and pensions diminishing. You name it; it was there in horrifyingly final black and white. All of a sudden, the job became a little too difficult for my liking. Life as a salesman became a living nightmare, battling against a relentless tide, trenching through a well of shit with no end in sight. I didn't have time to rebuild my burnt bridges with Terry, and for that month, my quest for Elisha was completely put on hold.

No matter what we told people:

"Now that prices are beginning to drop, it's time to upsize! Sell before they drop anymore. Buy six months down the line moving into something twice as big....."

"It's simple supply and demand. The London property market cannot crash...."

"Well, yes, the first-time buyers are no longer able to afford a mortgage, but Chelsea doesn't get first time buyers anyway, it's all too expensive around here. Chelsea won't be affected....."

None of it worked: nobody would budge. For the first time in my life, I became a failure. Deal after deal fell through. Property after property left waiting. Houses to sell that no one wanted to buy, and lists of applicants who didn't want anything to do with us. The atmosphere in the office became oppressive. We were stuck together, working every waking hour, united only in our frustration and disappointment.

29th January 2008

Early in the morning, 02:00 AM, I received a text message. I was half asleep and worrying about my future, my career, and my mortgage payments. I didn't bother looking at my phone. Instead, I blasphemed at whoever thought it would be okay to send me a message at that time of day, rolled over, stuffed my head under the pillow, and remained in that position until my alarm-clock pierced my restless sleep. After showering, shaving, and ironing my shirt, I eventually took stock of the text message. This is what it said:

"Hey sexy – come over, I'm in need of ur services xx"

It was from Scarlett.

More to the point, it was a bloody booty call from Scarlett, and I'd bloody missed it. Initially close to slitting my wrists, I soon talked myself out of my slump like a true champ. After all, she'd now shown she still thought about me, and still wanted me, and oh God! I definitely wanted her back. I considered playing games, but decided to favour the 'guns blazing' approach instead.

"Hey sweetheart, I'm sorry I missed you last night (I was getting my beauty sleep). Any chance of a morning quickie?"

And what's more it worked. I waited barely five minutes before the following response beeped away on my phone:

"Come over right now Big Boy, you can pound the hangover out of me."

I called work immediately, explaining away my lateness with an 'early morning' viewing, and battled the rush-hour traffic down to Shoreditch, where she lived.

The front door into her building was mysteriously left ajar. She had also left the door to her flat unlocked, so that I entered it completely unannounced.

I climbed the stairs, slowly, and silently, hoping to surprise her. A pointless attempt, as she had hoped I would get the hint, and come up the stairs. It was she, who surprised me – she lay completely naked, legs apart, masturbating. Her soft brown skin glistened with moisture; I jumped on her, and breathed in her scent. I would like to say that on that day, I was a champion in bed. Alas, it had been a month since the girl in Cape-Town, and I was ridiculously turned on by her efforts. Don't get me wrong – I wasn't premature or anything. I fought bravely, trying my hardest not to ejaculate. When I got close, I tried to slow down, change my angle so that it was slightly less vigorous on my Chap, giving me some time to recuperate. Unfortunately she writhed back and forth, over and over again telling me not to stop. Her actions were too much for me, and caused the opposite effect to what her words had pleaded. All the stress from work, my fight with Terry, my frustrations at my drop in income, all bubbled out of me into her warm vagina. I made a half-hearted attempt at finishing her off with my hands, but she brushed it away impatiently. Instead, she lit a post-coital cigarette, and said:

"You should probably leave."

My heart dropped a little, but I picked up my suit from its crumpled heap on the floor, and with the smell of her still all over me, I went to work. For the first time since my fight with Terry, I was in a fantastic mood.

I sent her an email while eating my lunch that same day:

From: Shaun.Valfierno
Sent: 29 January 2008 15:41
To: Scary.Smithy

Hey there Scarlett, it was great seeing you again. We should deffo do it again sometime. Perhaps next time we should precede it with some dinner? Let me know when you're free xx

Then I waited. Again.

Waiting for Scarlett to respond to anything is an excruciating experience. It's like clock watching, waiting for something awful to end, but it never does. I wish I could say that I was un-phased by her silence. I wish I could say that I always had my eye on the ultimate goal of Elisha, but I didn't. For a second time, I had been ensnared by this horrendously aloof woman. And God, I wanted to have sex with her too. She was so confident, so exciting, so easy-going. But she didn't really want me. I could see it in her eyes. She needed me because she had wanted sex. Nothing more.

Clearly I wasn't the only person that could give this to her. She was a sexy, beautiful, business woman, and dynamite in bed. I, on the other hand, had completely failed to live up to expected standards.

It took her a week to respond to me, and once again, almost exactly the same thing happened. She had her way with me, and then disappeared off the face of the planet. She was a mystery. I tried, and tried to get her hooked on me. Going forwards, I always ensured that I would not ejaculate until she had screamed out my name in fits of passion. Still, she could take me, or leave me. She made no attempt to keep me if I pretended to have somewhere else to be, and had no intention of entering into any kind of normal relationship.

I don't think that she even liked me as a person. If I told her a joke, she wouldn't laugh. If I went to kiss her, she would turn away her face. We didn't walk down the street, hand in hand. We never went on dates. I wouldn't bring her flowers, and she wouldn't beg me to come over. It was sex, and that is all: cold, soulless, brilliant, sex. If I had retained any ability to 'keep her', I would probably have given up my childish quest for Elisha, remained with Scarlett – such was her power over me. As it stood, I was frustrated and unfulfilled. Without Terry in the picture she was my closest tie to the world of show-biz. Eventually I would need to use her in order to seek out Elisha, but for now Scarlett remained a mystery, and it was as annoying as hell. For weeks it continued in that way – frustration and frustration. I could not think of any way that I could force my way into Scarlett's life: she wouldn't introduce me to anyone, or be seen with me in a public space. She was a brick wall, and completely impenetrable (apart from in the obvious sense).

Valentine's Day came and went, and although I had reserved a seat in The Ivy, Scarlett avoided me for the days surrounding it. I called her mobile on the Day in one last attempt at contact; it had a foreign ring tone and went straight to voicemail. I decided against leaving a message. For a moment, I almost called Terry. In some ways I actually missed his company. He had been like a little puppy snapping at my toes, jumping around in excitement to have a friend. My diary was a lot more open since Terry had ceased contact, and my precarious situation with Scarlett seemed to take up a lot of my time, without actually filling up any of my evenings. In the end I cancelled my reservation and sat at home with a glass of wine and a curry. I knew that Scarlett wasn't abroad because of business; she was on a romantic getaway with some other beau. This wasn't a very happy thought, and before I got to sleep I found that I had finished off the whole bottle of wine, as well as half a bottle of *Jura*. To say the least, it was a lonely Valentine's Day.

Then, one evening in February, after a brief but happy mid-afternoon session of all-enveloping Darkness, lying in each others' arms, listening to the rain patter against the window, Scarlett's doorbell rang. I jumped up, alarmed, and began putting my clothes on. I don't know why, but I was panicked, it felt like I shouldn't have been there. Perhaps it was one of her other lovers arriving unexpectedly? Perhaps **shudder** it was one of her lovers coming to attempt to commit suicide (please no, it can't happen twice!) Scarlett had been dozing, half asleep. It was only hearing my idiotic flapping around the room that roused her.

"What are you doing?" she said.

She received silence as a response, I was too busy unbuttoning my shirt (in my panic, I had pulled it over my head inside out). I think some of my nonsense terror rubbed off on her – she sat bolt upright on the bed.

"WHAT are you DOING, Shaun?" her voice was stern, almost hateful. Still not thinking, I blurted out:

"The doorbell!"

I was running around the room now, desperately trying to find my trousers – where the flying shit did I put them? All her clothes were strewn across the floor, and for some reason, each and every garment of clothing was the exact same colour as my suit trousers. I crouched down, hands shaking, fumbling through the mess – they must be here somewhere, quick, quick, quick. Until

Scarlett's anger knocked me for six. It appeared as if from nowhere and caught me off guard:

"DON'T YOU FUCKING DARE ANSWER THAT DOOR!"

She had mistaken my intention: she thought that I was planning to go and greet her guest as opposed to jumping out the second floor window and running away. Too shocked to explain, I sat back down on the bed in silence and gestured towards the door – *you answer it, no problem.* As I did this, the doorbell rang a third time and Scarlett jumped out of bed. She put on her fluffy pink dressing gown and sauntered through the bedroom doorway, hips swaying.

I remained on the bed until my senses returned. Then curiosity got the better of me. I crept over to the banister, and took a look down the stairs towards the front door hoping for a sneak peak of whoever it was. Shock horror! I actually recognised her: she was one of my applicants. She had come into my office enquiring after a £200k purchase price studio flat in Chelsea Villas – an ex local-authority skank-hole populated primarily with wannabe *nouveau riche* and mid to high level prostitutes. I couldn't put my finger on her name, but I remembered that her father had been filthy rich and a bit of an arrogant prick. Whatever the reason for her knocking on Scarlett's door, their exchange didn't last long. Scarlett didn't come upstairs immediately – first of all she made a phone call. When the conversation was over, she called up to me:

"I've got to get ready for a party tonight, so I'm going to jump into the shower, could you show yourself out, please?" No explanation as to why she had been angry, no apology, just the standard emotional slap in the face.

I drove straight to work. I use the word '*drive*' in the loosest possible sense, seeing as one doesn't drive through London – but rather, one curses their way through the labyrinthine nonsensical layout, weeps amongst the standstill of traffic, and rages at every living creature within a ten metre radius of the steering wheel. It's almost an art-form, and on that day, despite being in a company car, I must admit I was on particularly good form. I strolled into the office and was almost bowled over by the sense of frustration in the room: nobody was making any money. Arty, the mortgage broker, the only one in the office to get his own desk, hadn't even bothered returning after lunch. I sat at my laptop, and scrolled my way back through my Microsoft Outlook diary, trying to remember who the girl in Scarlett's flat was.

In my social life, I am not all that great with names. On most occasions when I am introduced to someone, no matter how charming, or friendly, or outrageous they may be, I can't remember their name. No matter what I do to wrack my brain, it vanishes into thin air.

On the other hand, when it comes to clients, applicants, potential business associates, or basically anyone who can make me some money, my memory is infallible, it becomes God-Like. For that very reason, I could remember the father's name – Edward – but could not recollect the name of his spoilt little prig of a daughter. As luck would have it, Edward had taken a particular dislike to me, so I remembered him very well.

When dealing with people of Edward's ilk (pompous know-it-alls) there are various routes a salesman can take:

1. Kiss his feet and grovel, bend over and let him fuck every last drop of dignity out of you.

2. Back off and apologise – give up on the hard sell, and pray that in a few days he'll have a change of heart.

3. Blast them with your knowledge of the intricate details of the market that only someone working in the industry day in, day out could know. Unsettle them to such an extent that, despite the fact that they earn ten times your salary, they feel completely out of depth. Try

to embarrass them with how little they know compared to you. Begrudgingly, they sometimes actually give you their respect.

Now, there isn't really one route here that works a lot better than others. Some individuals like to have people grovelling at their feet, some need to feel that they are in control and aren't being sold to, and others need to know that they are dealing with an expert. In my time, I have used all three tactics, depending on how I thought the person would react. It will hardly surprise you that my favoured tactic is number 3, mainly because I like to feel in control. With Edward, I used tactic number 3, and it blew up in my face. He was buying a property for his daughter, and was convinced I was trying to rip them off. I'd gone on about the London property market doubling in value every decade since World War Two, I'd discussed the strength of the economy (this was before September 13th 2007), I'd spoken about off-shore developers until I was blue in the face, and I pretty much laughed off his nonsensical view that property prices would soon begin to fall. He stood up, flushed red and said to me:

"Nobody talks to me like that, and I can see that you're just a cowboy."

He stormed out of the office, and his peroxide bimbo of a daughter ran out after him, her orange skin shimmering in the sunlight, her back-combed hair bobbling in the wind.

As a result of this little interchange, I had turned the note next to their names in my diary bright red, explaining what had happened, and to remind myself to grovel the next time that I got to speak to him. Regardless, he hadn't returned any of my calls, and I'd eventually given up on him.

Still, I found the red note in my diary easily enough, and thankfully, I had been wise enough to retain both the father and the daughter's mobile numbers. I played to my strengths and called the daughter.

February 20th 2008

She walked into my office in a tight brown dress that clashed with her orange skin. Her oversize fake breasts were bursting over the top of a bra two sizes too small. Her teeth gleamed, and her hair was so light, it was almost white. I knew I *shouldn't* want someone like that, but I wanted her all the same.

"Abigail! Great to see you." (I'd rediscovered her name on the phone the previous day) "Is Edward coming?" I took her hand to shake it and pretended to look around for her father.

"No, he's in Dubai."

I breathed a sigh of relief and ushered her out of the door towards my *Fisher & Irving* branded BMW.

The Rule of Three was always the way to conduct viewings in our office:

> *First stop*: show them a scummy property that in no way matched their 'ideal' home, but was within their price range.
>
> *Second stop*: show them a half decent home, just slightly higher than their budget – say between £10k and £20k too high, so that if they were be able to pull a few strings and get more cash from somewhere, they may very well be able to afford it.
>
> *Third stop*: Show them their perfect home, which was at least £50k above their budget.

The philosophy was that it shows the buyer what they actually need to pay for that 'extra' bedroom they've been holding out for, and to see how much of a difference an extra £10-50k will actually make. Your average buyer will pull a few strings (typically the heart strings at the bank of mum and dad), and settle on that second stop property.

That day, however, my mission was a little different. I didn't actually want to sell Abigail (Abz with a 'Z' to her friends) anything; I wanted to glean some information about Scarlett. In fact, with the market the way it was, I didn't actually have anything on the books that would appeal to her. Luckily, she was too damned stupid to cotton on to this. Instead, I took her to a place way beyond her budget, a mansion worth £25-30 Million, and decided to show her a good time.

"This, Place, Is, Amazing!" she screamed when she entered the main lobby and looked up at the chandeliers hanging from the ceiling. She swaggered onwards, and my heart jumped into my throat when I noticed her stilettos making small dents in the pristinely polished wooden floor. I'd get an ear-ache from the vendor in the morning – a rather eccentric 70 year old millionaire hypochondriac.

"How much does it cost? I'm not sure Daddy would let me have it." Tragic really, she 'wasn't sure' that her father would increase the budget from £200,000 to £30,000000; clearly this girl had no concept of money.

"Actually, you'll be pleased to hear that this place is already under offer to a developer..." I lied, "...their intention is to keep this traditional style décor, but break it down into a set of smaller and more compact apartments. Ultimately they'll be going at around £200k if you buy it off-plan."

"Off-plan?"

"Buy it before it's been built."

"Oh."

I knew that this still hadn't really helped her understand what I meant.

"Basically, you can buy it cheap before it's been built; when it finally gets built you get to live in it. It will be worth a lot more once it's been finished." While I said these words, I began to feel rather apathetic about the whole thing. This supposed 'developer' was a figment of my imagination. It was really an excuse so I could get her to spill the beans about Scarlett.

"It's still a long way from going through, and I wouldn't usually bother showing it to you, but I saw you pass by my car in Shoreditch the other day, and I couldn't help but get quite excited because I knew it would be perfect for you."

"Shoreditch?"

"Yeah, you were walking down Hoxton Street with another blond woman."

I saw the cogs slowly turn trying to work out why she would have been anywhere as far east as that. I expect that she rarely ventured further east than Russell Square.

"Oh you must mean Scarlett?"

I tried to pretend I didn't jolt at the sound of her name. I hadn't expected it to be that easy, in fact, after the painful conversation about the make-believe developer, I'd expected it to be a long and drawn out conversation that didn't lead anywhere.

"Trust me, if I had any choice, I wouldn't hang out anywhere near that woman."

I raised my eyebrows and smiled, inviting her to continue.

"She's going to be my step-mother, and I can't stand her."

Abz began to cry. She wiped her eyes with a tissue turning it orange. The fake tan had come off around her tears, panda eyes.

"Mummy's inconsolable. He must have been seeing Scarlett for years. Just before Christmas he finally decided to split up with mummy. The divorce isn't even through yet and daddy's already making me go looking for wedding dresses with that bitch."

I don't know what I'd been expecting, but this hadn't been it. Scarlett was engaged?! It stung a little, but I wasn't distraught. The first thing that crossed my mind was that it was going to be incredibly difficult to convince her to introduce me to all her high profile friends, not the fact that I had been cheated. Still, at least I knew what I was up against. Scarlett really was one royally screwed up woman. Now that I had the info I needed from her, I tried to shake off Abz as soon as I possibly could, but in the car on the way back to the office she put her hand on my knee and looked into my eyes.

"You know, I know daddy didn't like you very much, but actually you're really just a darling. Thanks for being so sweet to me today, sorry for freaking out a bit…"

I made an embarrassed coughing noise in my throat.

"…Do you fancy going for a drink sometime?" she finished.

I briefly considered it; she had a sickly sweet sexuality about her, but ultimately I felt that it would be too risky. She sat with her hand rubbing my thigh, and she moved her mouth closer to my ear.

"Go on," she whispered "I know you want to try me."

I had an erection the size of the Eiffel Tower, but I couldn't, I had to stop shitting so close to my doorstep. The traffic lights flashed red, I stopped the car and I turned my face towards her. She pouted and moved her lips until they were millimetres from mine.

"Abz, I'd love to…" my voice had gone all husky with excitement "…but I've got a girlfriend," I lied.

"Don't let a little thing like that stop you…" said Abz looking distinctly unperturbed "…I like it when my men are a little bit naughty."

She rubbed her hand further up my thigh and I felt myself leaning towards her, my heart beat in my eardrums. Luckily the lights turned green and the arsehole behind started beeping his horn. I was forced to withdraw before our faces met.

"I can't" I repeated stoically.

Her bottom lip came out, and she removed her hand from my leg.

"Fine." Her face turned to the window. She seemed to have completely lost interest in me now.

When I pulled up outside my office she got out of the car, slammed the door and walked away without saying goodbye. Spoilt little brat, I was glad I'd knocked her down a few pegs. Twenty minutes later I received an SMS from Scarlett, she wanted me to see her again. I cleared any thoughts of Abz from my mind and made my way across to Hoxton Street to meet the bride to be. For the first time since meeting Scarlett, I felt that the power struggle had shifted in my favour.

<u>February 25th 2008</u>

I thought that I was well shot of Terry and Polly. My separate angry outbursts had forced them away from my life. Sadly, like two unflushable turds, the pair of them just wouldn't go away. It was on a wet and windy day that I received a call from Polly. I hadn't even realised who it was until I put the receiver to my ear. She didn't bother to introduce herself.

"You absolute twat!" was the first thing she said, and I hung up, well aware of my mistake.

The phone rang again, and in the pit of my stomach, I knew that I shouldn't answer it. Despite my brain's clear instructions to remain still, my retarded hand moved forward. Something deep-routed within me wanted to make sure Polly wasn't in any kind of serious trouble. Regardless of our problems, we had once been very close friends. If it weren't for the passage of time and different rolls on the dice of fate, we probably still would be. Don't get me wrong, I couldn't stand the woman. But fond memories of her still haunted me at night.

"Don't fucking hang up on me you prick!" was the next thing she said to me. When it became evident that I was neither hanging up or in the mood to exchange pleasantries, Polly quickly got to the point. She wanted my help sorting Terry out (again).

According to Polly, this was Terry's story: Following the rage-fuelled quarrel at the bottom of Table Mountain, Terry sat weeping for several hours. The effort placed into our friendship had amounted to nothing and he had spent huge sums of money on an airline flight for someone who hated him. Dejected, he returned to the hotel to find that he had nowhere to stay. His Maestro still wouldn't work so he was unable to book another room. He was forced to spend his last night in Cape Town at the airport. He slept in the departures lounge on a single, incredibly hard and uncomfortable seat. 24 hours later, he boarded his plane. He looked around to see if he could find me, I was not there, and the seat beside him remained empty for the duration of the flight. He searched the entire plane, eventually coming to the conclusion that I wasn't on the flight. It upset him that I did not feel the need to resolve things. Following his return home, he must have called Polly and let her know what had happened as she seemed fully aware of the confrontation at the foot of the mountain.

Upon his return to the UK, *Oops! TV* fell into a crisis. In wake of the credit crunch, the vast majority of their advertising agencies had tightened their budgets for the first quarter. *Oops! TV* had lost hundreds of sponsors, and made several high profile and a few more low profile redundancies. Terry found himself without a job. Most people with his qualifications and experience would have been fine. Most people would have landed on their feet and found a job within weeks – after all, at this early stage of the credit crunch, a lot of companies were still doing well. Alas, the world of television is a small and inbred community, and Terry is such a horrendously annoying individual that the job offers did not come through as expected. Polly tried to call him. He refused her. He refused a total of 70 calls over the following weeks. In fact, after four weeks of unemployment, he refused everybody's calls. Terry slowly but surely went completely off the rails.

Polly made her way to his new home in Dover and refused to leave until he came out to see her. She rang the doorbell and knocked and screamed to try and see where he was. He did not respond. Eventually she gave up and went home. Two days later she had a call from Terry's mother screaming that Terry had disappeared. Terry's mother had eventually called the police to try and track him down. Terry was nowhere to be found, the world had crushed him, and now he had disappeared. I must admit on hearing this news I felt a little guilty. I hadn't ever intended to seriously hurt anybody.

I could entirely understand Terry's refusal to let Polly back in his life again. He must have hated her. After a string of text messages and emails from her pleading him for a second chance, I had revealed the truth to him, and it had broken his heart, again. Polly's life also seemed to have gone from bad to worse. She had been unable to find another job, and had been forced to work as a waitress in the restaurant she had worked in as a teenager. It was like her life had been pushed back ten years.

She had begun to look back fondly on her life with Terry. The glamorous parties, the house with a garden, the long weekends away. So although just a few months previously she had hated him with every ounce of her being, she rather selfishly convinced herself that she missed him. Poor Terry had no idea how shallow and materialistic her motives were. It was probably a good thing that I broke the news to him.

I am still convinced that on the day of her interview she had come up to London specifically to assassinate her relationship. She knew what I was after when I invited her to stay, but she came anyway. She could have travelled to her job interview without needing to even see me. Before I dumped her for Scarlett, she had told me she loved me; there was no thought of going to back Terry then. I hadn't taken her declaration of love seriously – this was the seventh time she'd said she loved me throughout the years we'd known each other.

Maybe in her own obscure and gullible way, she did in fact love me. I could never love someone like her, even when she was young and attractive, before her bum grew to the size of the Isle of Wight. She was just so easy, too willing and desperate to please. Worst of all, she had made nothing of her life. She had never been given a high-paying job, always flitting between different professions. She never remained long enough to gain experience in any one thing or climb the ladder beyond a couple of rungs. At least Terry had known people of consequence. He had stayed in the same company since university, gained a certain amount of notoriety and had collected a lot of high profile contacts on the way. Polly had used Terry like a leach, to bolster her own lack of self-esteem. Maybe she had thought to take one last stab at me before accepting that a life with Terry was going to be her existence. No wonder she had tried to go back to him when I gave her the boot. This reminded me that she was equally to blame for all of this. It was her, and not me, that had cheated on him. I told her that I would let her know if he called me.

"Is that it?" she screamed.

"What do you mean?" I replied.

"Are you really that unconcerned? Don't you want to help?"

"Look, I told you that I'd let you know if he got in touch. I'm working thirteen hours a day at the moment and the market's only getting worse. What do you expect me to do? Go running around the streets, calling his name? He's just looking for everyone's attention again, he'll turn up!"

She hung up.

With further press reports that house prices were in free fall, it wasn't an easy day. I even spoke to Lance about being allowed to take applicants out on viewings for rentals. Typically the sales and lettings team didn't get on in my office. With rentals, you have to prance around the landlord and pretend to care about the tenant so that they give you their business again in six to twelve months. It's not the type of sales that I am ideally suited for, my job is a little more smash and grab – you typically deal with someone once every four or five years, possibly once and then never again. I have a tendency to burn bridges, and cut off ties once the deal is done. I'm not one of those Estate Agents that accepts invites to 'House Warmings' and the like. It's a waste of time.

In my opinion, the lettings team were a bunch of drama queens; most of them probably studied drama at university. They were always pawning at their applicants, and often became 'good friends' with their big landlords with 'in-jokes' about tenants.

The commission for lettings was also less than for sales – rather than a solid margin, you take a percentage of the cost of the annual contract. It was more a case of 'little and often'. At that point though, I didn't care: Sales wasn't bringing in any money. Good news came rarely, and even if it was good news, the papers surrounded it in a shit sandwich so that nothing ever sounded truly good. Take Northern Rock, for example. The morning paper explained that the government had bailed out Northern Rock. They had made a firm promise that they wouldn't let any of the banks fail. This was good news. No one needed to worry that the banks were going to go bankrupt. Still, the paper surrounded the story with doom and gloom – house prices falling, the injustice of our taxes being spent on greedy irresponsible fat cat bankers, unemployment levels rising, blah blah blah blah blah. If they'd just left out the other faff, then some of my old applicants may have come back to the market. I swear, the credit crunch was a self-fulfilling prophecy.

People got scared to spend money because the banks were going to pot, and as a direct consequence of this, everything else went to pot. Confidence! Why couldn't the papers sell some confidence? Then we would have been OK.

Unfortunately, Lance, my manager, had no choice but to refuse me. The office was split into two separate departments and he had no power over the lettings department. He looked back at me, his eyes blood-shot and stressed, and apologised. It was galling to see the lettings team doing so well, while the Sales team broke their backs against a brick wall. It was such a difference between the glory days when I had first started. This was only the tip of the mother fucking iceberg – the worst was yet to come. By February, the housing market was only slowing down. In February I still made the occasional sale; but by the end of 2008, it didn't even feel like sales anymore, I felt like an undertaker working in a morgue.

I didn't really feel that sorry for Terry being made redundant. In redundancy you get benefits, you have a reason for losing your job. If you're smart, you would have even insured yourself against it and you would have the right to claim an income. In sales, and especially in estate agency, people do not get made redundant: they disappear.

I think the only lucky buggers to be made redundant in *Fisher & Irving* were our recruitment team. The company's strategy was simple – stop hiring new people, and weed out the weak. Once recruitment stopped churning in new recruits, it quickly became obvious how big the turnover was. I hadn't considered it before, but we had been bringing in new recruits every single week. New starters always seemed so naïve. They had all been promised astronomical amounts in commission, and a 'live hard play hard' glamorous way of life. It only took a few weeks for the reality of life on the sales floor to truly settle, and by then, we all knew who was going to sink or swim. I could tell when someone was going to cut the mustard: they had something about them, a certain charisma that radiated confidence and trust. Those ones were always the first to wise up to the tricks of the trade; they were the ones who realised that charming the secretary on the front desk meant that she was more likely to assign the best applicants to their diary as soon as they set foot into the office; they were the ones that built up a network of friends in the Fulham and Mayfair offices so that when applicants looking in Chelsea mistakenly phoned up there, they were transferred directly to them; they were the ones that bought morning treats for the mortgage broker ensuring that he'd chase their applicants' mortgage offers as a priority. More importantly, they were the ones who prized money above everything else, the ones that worked 14 hour shifts and weekends without days off in lieu, without a complaint.

Now that the commission had disappeared, most of the team were living off a basic salary of £12K. Without the new recruits rolling in, the evaporation of team members who were slightly slower on the uptake became glaringly obvious. Within four months the population of the office had halved without a single redundancy. Some quit in a blaze of fire. Others were beckoned from the sales floor, led calmly and quietly to a room where nobody could see them, and unceremoniously shown the back door. Most of them probably thought they were just going into the room for a private chat with Lance. Meanwhile, the secretary had their belongings packed up and sent to greet them after they had been given their exit interview. We never saw these people again. Lance could have been shooting them in the head for all I knew. We could always tell when someone was close to cracking, close to breaking point. *Dead men walking*, that's what we all called them, and for good reason. Their figures decreased, and it was the management's responsibility to watch every single tiny thing that they did and to always criticise. To always find something lacking and never praise. We lingered around these retched individuals like vultures ready to pick at the carcass. There were always one or two good applicants that could be stolen from the pipeline of dead-meat if you knew where to find them.

Needless to say, I couldn't bring myself to feel sorry for Terry. He was overreacting to a situation that could have been much worse. I knew he would turn up, and I was right. Polly called me the following day to tell me he had been found, and although it had slipped my mind that he had even gone missing, something inside me breathed a sigh of relief. He had been found swimming in the Thames shouting abuse at passers-by, and was consequently institutionalised as a manic depressive, or bi-polar, or whatever it's called. Polly made it quite clear who she felt was responsible for the cause of Terry's downfall. There may have been a grain of truth in her words, some of it could have been my fault, but ultimately I consoled myself with the knowledge that being depressed is a chemical imbalance in the brain: I couldn't be held accountable for that. Her admonishments and curses fell on deaf ears, and I made a promise to myself that I wouldn't bother answering the phone when next she called.

March 2008

In appearances, my relationship with Scarlett, our illicit sexual tryst, remained unchanged. Her impending marriage to Edward went unmentioned, and I never brought it up. I was her dirty secret, living in the shadows. As far as I could gather, Edward had been on the scene from the very beginning. It was only recently that her relationship with him had moved on from the 'mistress' phenomenon into 'fiancé' territory.

Scarlett didn't love Edward; or me, or anyone for that matter. I think that concepts such as love were beyond her. She wanted wealth and notoriety. Her own career had already given her a certain amount of that but there was always more to be had. I don't know why she risked it all to be with me. I could tell that she didn't really know herself. Maybe she saw in me a kindred spirit. She could tell I wanted something materialistic from her, and knew I wouldn't hang around if I felt I couldn't get it. I think she enjoyed the excitement of it, knowing we were both playing the same game. We never spoke about such things, but there was a subconscious connection, a mutual understanding, a certain presence between us, like static electricity – don't get too close or you'll get a shock. More than this though, the sex was fantastic. It was animalistic and spontaneous. Arriving at her flat, she would jump on me as soon as I walked in the door, unable to keep her hands off me. We would meet during the day in my car, on a public street; she would raise her dress and slide on top of me; passers-by probably guessed what we were up to, but we didn't care. We would hire a hotel room over lunch and copulate passionately on the floor, on the clean sheets, in the bathroom, in the shower. On one occasion, she started to cup me as I tried to take the keys from my pocket to get into our room, and we made love in the hallway, her peachy bottom turned towards me, her hands pressed against the unopened door.

All the while, I was trying to work my way into her life. Secure some connections from her. It seemed impossible – I couldn't gain any vantage point. I couldn't blackmail her – that would have broken the terms of the game. Following her engagement, other than our risqué sexual encounters, she point-blank refused to be seen in public with me.

One crisp sunny afternoon, she left the sheets of our hotel room to go to the bathroom. I turned my head towards the window, and had my solution. Her Blackberry had been left on the side-table, just calling me to examine it. I picked it up, but it was locked with a password. It was a failed attempt, but I had my answer. If I couldn't break into her life by force, I would do it by stealth. Her Blackberry held all the answers.

Over the following weeks I would watch her in the corner of my eye trying to work out what keys she pressed. The buttons on a Blackberry are tiny, and her fingers moved so quickly when she entered the password that it was incredibly difficult to tell what she was typing. She was naturally secretive and knew I was untrustworthy, so typically turned the phone away from my inquisitive eyes.

She wasn't all that careful though, and within two weeks I knew that it began with an 'A', ended with a 'Y' and that it consisted of a total of six characters. She would occasionally be forced to answer work emails, and text messages while lying in bed with me; it only took another week to get the rest of the letters bar one. From the sequence of letters I guessed that the final piece of code (positioned between an L and the final letter) must have been another vowel. One afternoon, as she took a shower, I input the letters into her phone; I added an 'e' and got it on my first try. Sheer excitement overwhelmed me as I scanned the emails between her and her fiancé. All these fake iterations of *I love you* plastered across the page. It was laughable.

Although Edward clearly had money, and charisma, from looking at the emails he sent her, he lacked any kind of care or charm. I was surprised at how caring Scarlett's words were, she sounded like she actually loved him. Here is one example of an email conversation they had in February:

Scarlett: *"Hi Honey. I've had a great day with Abz looking at wedding dresses. I don't know, maybe she's finally coming round ☺ I wanted to tell you that I've managed to find something that's absolutely perfect (the only thing is that it's £38k). Even Abz said it was beautiful! Have I told you recently how much I love you! I can't wait for the big day when I can finally tell the world that I'm your wife!*

Xx"

This was Edward's reply:

"Put the dress on your own credit card, I'm not paying for something that expensive."

This wasn't just a one off either. Her inbox was littered with similar conversations. I almost felt sorry for her. He was always so cold. I guessed he did care for her, but for some reason he was completely incapable of expressing himself. It was so strange that the language they used was at polar opposites to the loyalty they actually showed each other. I scanned each email until something interesting caught my eye:

Scarlett: *"Baby, now that the divorce has finally come through between you and Georgina, I thought it would be a good idea to have a proper engagement party! It would be a great way of showing the world how serious we are about each other. I want to let everyone see how much I care about you and that I'm here to stay. I know not everyone is happy about your divorce, but if we show them how happy we are together it's bound to change some of their opinions!"*

Edward: *"Who did you have in mind?"*

Scarlett: *"I've got a list of people I think would be great to get through the door, what do you think about the following?*

Peggy Thrace

Charlie

Damien (Smith)

Damien (Woland)

Abz

Jimmy Baldrick

Sam

Billy Pirou

Katelyn Robinson

Ali

Mum

Gabby and Lisa

Gav

Tim Sisters

A-J Bright

Mindy Ocelot

Edward: *"Abz won't come. Where & when?"*
Scarlett: *"5th April at mine? I'll cook dinner xxx"*

Gold! I had struck Gold! I knew that I would be a fool to miss that party if Damien Woland would be there. Damien Woland was the co-star of *A Better Class of Enemy* alongside the one and only Elisha Cicero.

Unfortunately, attending the party would mean single-handedly assassinating all semblance of friendship between myself and Scarlett, but she had left me with little choice. It looked like Edward had some powerful connections. I pondered on how Edward would receive me. I knew Scarlett would have to remain silent – she knew that I could destroy her relationship with Edward *et al* if I wanted to. I absolutely had to crash that party.

Over the next few weeks I ignored several calls from Polly, each voicemail she left more irritable than the last. She wanted me to visit Terry and set things straight. He refused to see her, and was currently on a hunger strike, being force-fed through a tube. It sounded like he was in a pretty dire situation. His parents had been forced to bail him out of mounting debts – those run up on a credit-card in order to buy plane tickets for our holiday, and many other expensive things that Polly felt were also my fault.

Meanwhile the sun began to shine, and spring came to London. The bitterly chilling winds that swept the grey dust along the grey streets became a little more bearable; flocks of the various birds that had left England for warmer climes came back to join the army of grotty London pigeons that are a permanent feature. This all passed me by; I was focused on my job and obsessing about crashing Scarlett's engagement party. I had considered my options and at one point even deliberated upon convincing Abz to take me as her date. Ultimately, I felt that this plan would be too risky and decided to turn up alone, brandishing a bottle of wine and pretending to be a legitimate guest.

Scarlett invited me over to her place on the Friday night before the party – although she still tried to hide it from me, now that I knew to look out for it, there were signs of her impending marriage to Edward everywhere. A spare and rather masculine looking toothbrush next to the sink, a pair of black brogue's under the shelf next to the door-way, bridal magazines on her desk, and the smell of someone else on her bed sheets. I had no idea what their plans were once they were married, but I couldn't imagine Edward living in Shoreditch. The sex that night was disappointing; my head wasn't in the game. I couldn't help but think about how she would most likely hate me the following day. It would be the end of our glamorous secret. If it didn't work out, I would have nobody.

I wondered how she would react, and at one point even found myself working out the odds on the likelihood of Scarlett ending up in the nut-house being fed through a hose-pipe. I considered all my actions over the past seven months, and whether I really should take some responsibility for Terry's ill-health. In fact, I was thinking all of this while I was inside her. The thoughts were so pathetic, and the guilt so awesome I couldn't even climax. In the end, I gave up. She must have sensed that for some reason I was upset and even tried to kiss me good-bye; it was almost human, almost heartfelt. Perhaps she even suspected that I knew something about Edward and was feeling her own brand of guilt. On my journey home, I picked up a fresh bottle of Jura, plonked myself on the sofa, and slowly drank myself into a stupor.

I have always been a great believer in the healing power of whiskey; the furious scent entering the lungs on inhalation; the warm bursts of tranquillity as it gently and warmly slithers down your throat; the dizzy cool inebriation it brings to the soul. Needless to say, I woke up with a light hangover, but felt at peace with the world. I was ready to storm into Scarlett's life and blow her own tranquillity to smithereens.

Saturday 5th April 2008

My day passed slowly, I wasn't on duty to work that Saturday shift, but popped into the office anyway, as I had some high profile viewings with the CEO of a multinational publishing firm and was feeling vaguely hopeful about it. I took him to three large houses, all of which he rejected for various reasons. Price wasn't a concern for him; it was all about location and style. This was unfortunately something that the majority of our stock was lacking at this point in time.

The viewings were over by lunch. I didn't eat. I couldn't eat. Instead I attempted to relax and watch a film. I kept checking my watch and the clocks to see the time. Needless to say, the afternoon dragged.

I spent a few hours thumbing through *A-List* and on the internet, researching anyone of note who would be attending the party. My hope was that I might find some scrap of knowledge that could help me gain their favour. I also looked up Edward. There was no real tactical advantage to it, but while I was in the swing of things, the mood took me there. He didn't have much of an online presence, other than a small summary about him on the Lexicus Subran website.

Edward Subran

Founder and CEO of <u>Lexicus Subran</u>

Edward Subran *was born in Southwark in 1955. He studied Mathematics at St. John's College, Oxford. Before founding Lexicus Subran he embarked on a successful tenure as Managing Director at STNC Finance. Edward's vision of transparency and client-centric management has been the driving influence of the Lexicus Subran culture.*

After my exertions online, I began to feel drowsy. The spring sunshine beat through my windows and the warmth in my flat became stifling. I closed my curtains, but the dark in my living room combined with the drink from the night before and the soft cushions on my sofa, were enough to make my eyelids sag. To stop myself from dropping off, I stood up, opened the window and pushed out twenty press-ups. I put on a jacket and wandered down to the nearest Café Nero to get myself a double espresso. The fresh, crisp, spring air, coupled with the caffeine boost worked its magic, and my drowsiness was conquered. By the time I returned to the flat it was approaching 18:00, time to get ready.

I showered again; I had already shaved that morning before work, so moisturised, deodorised, plucked my eyebrows, and shaped my hair. It didn't sound like it would be a formal dinner – just at Scarlett's house, so I donned a chequered shirt and a pair of chinos for a smart casual look. I had also purchased a bottle of Veuve-Clicquot to bring along for the 'happy' couple. Although my income had been steadily declining, I still couldn't accept that it would stay that way for long, so I refrained from getting public transport and opted for a taxi. It pulled up outside my front door at 19:00. I finished the glass of port that I had been sipping to calm my nerves, and stepped on to the pavement ready to declare war on Scarlett Smith.

The taxi engaged in a battle of wits against the evening traffic and took a rather unusual route to Shoreditch. When we arrived, I hastily paid the driver, and walked up to Scarlett's front door. Scarlett lived on the third floor of a block of modern, purpose-built flats. It was impossible to enter the building without buzzing the intercom and being granted access by the occupants. I didn't especially want to announce my arrival: if Scarlett heard me over the intercom, she would refuse me entry – probably tell me that she was unwell and to call another time. I had hoped to arrive alongside a group of other guests so I could discreetly let myself in behind them. Unfortunately I was alone. I waited a while, out of sight of the front door, watching for other guests, but nobody turned up. I began to panic that I was the last guest, so I readjusted my plan to suit my needs: I rang her next-door neighbours' door number – but nobody answered, so I rang another. This time, a childish voice answered:

"Hello?" said the voice

"Hi, I'm looking for Scarlett Smith." I replied

"That's next door!" said the voice. Whoever it was pressed the buzzer to let me in, and I entered feeling rather smug. I walked towards the staircase passing a strange menagerie of bikes and prams in the hallway, and quietly made my way to her apartment. With butterflies in my stomach, I launched my kamikaze attack and gravely knocked three times on the door.

Thankfully Scarlett wasn't the person who came to the doorway, it was some chap called Tim who shook my hand heartily. He was already slightly inebriated, so welcomed me into the flat with a huge bear hug.

"Welcome to the Nut-House!" he laughed and led me through into the kitchen.

"Scarlett!" boomed Tim, "Shaun's here!"

If looks could kill Scarlett's would have torn me to shreds. She was silent for a few seconds, then walked up to me and kissed me coldly on the cheek."

With gritted teeth she whispered in my ear: "What in living Christ are *you* doing here?"

I didn't respond, instead, smiling I replied: "Congratulations on your engagement." I handed her the bottle of bubbly, and sidestepped her into the throng of other guests. Nervously, I scanned the room for Edward or Abz, but I couldn't see them, nor could I see Damien Woland. Scarlett walked up behind me grabbing my arm.

"Shaun, please just fuck off." she hissed.

The poor girl was clearly petrified that I was going to ruin her life, but I had no such intentions. Once again I ignored her; I brushed her off and strolled over to the fridge to examine the drinks. It was quite a homely little gathering – I had been expecting a crystal service. All the food was home-made, or brought by other guests. It was little more than a family gathering, with a few friends scattered about for good measure. Scarlett wasn't even wearing any shoes! I'd never seen her in anything less than six inch stilettos in public. Admittedly, the wine was all fantastic – expensive vintage and varied in taste. To begin with, I felt a little awkward and had to keep reminding myself that nobody other than Scarlett knew that I was not invited. I kept looking over my shoulder to see if Edward was about, but luckily he wasn't anywhere to be seen. I assumed that he had popped out on a beer run, or to collect someone from the station, so I didn't worry too much about it all.

After pouring myself a large glass of *Meursault Les Narvaux*, I made my way to the living room, hoping to catch site of Damien. Unfortunately, he was not present at Scarlett's soiree, but his sister Charlie was sitting alone on the sofa, weeping silently into a tissue. Charlie was a well-known television presenter. It was she, who had gotten her younger brother a role in his first film: a gritty Brit-flick in which he played a troubled teenager on the run from the police for killing a catholic priest who had molested his best friend. Due to the controversy, and the rugged good looks of the young protagonist, Damien very quickly became a hit sensation in Hollywood.

The fame and cult following of Damien Woland somehow jarred with the homely image of an inhibited woman of plain tastes that surrounded his sister. Based on what I had seen of her on television, there would be little or no common ground with this woman. I was reluctant to even make an attempt at charming her – so close was she to Elisha's inner circle – if I played my hand wrong and added a disgruntled sister into the equation, I would be creating another barrier between myself and my ultimate goal. I eventually decided that it could do no harm to try and make her feel a little better. It might be useful to have someone to back my corner if Damien did turn up. Slowly, I walked up behind her, my heart beating in my chest. The knowledge that my very future depended upon the outcome of this meeting was ever-present in my mind. I considered the *A-List* articles I had read on her that afternoon, one from June 2005 sprang to my mind:

*"...After two years working on BBC's **The Sunday Sermon**, children's TV presenter, come religious zeitgeist **Charlie Ekells** will be joining **Oops! TV** to helm their flagship breakfast show **Charlie's Brekkie Time**. Ekells, who is often seen accompanying her hunky younger brother **Damien Woland** to his film premieres is said to be looking forwards to showing off her lighter side.*

*The move to **Oops! TV** may prove controversial to fans of the **Sunday Sermon**. Ekells, whose alcoholic father was convicted of killing her mother in 1988, is renowned for her outspoken views on teetotalism. She was once quoted as saying "I choose not to drink. On the odd occasion that I've slipped off the bandwagon, it has been out of sheer curiosity. Each instance has solidified my resolve that it's a waste of money, and a waste of life."*

Oops! TV *whose programming to date includes the booze fuelled reality shows* '*Soma Holiday*', '*Lads on Tour*', *and* '*Sex, Sun and Brits Abroad*' *are said to be pleased to have her on the team.* *Oops! TV* *are hoping to broaden their audience with the new show..."*

Before approaching, I tried to consider my angle – what could I use to my advantage against such a person? Her fame to date had relied heavily upon her being young, beautiful, but most problematically – completely chaste. Nothing I had read gave any indication that she had any personality beneath her Christianity. My last vestige of hope relied upon the hypothesis that if she had *slipped off the band wagon* before, she could do so again. On that note, I suddenly knew what my primary objective for the evening would be: namely to take a match and burn her wagon to smouldering cinders.

"Sorry to intrude…" I said in a soft voice that didn't sound anything like my own. "…is there anything I can do?"

Charlie looked up from her reverie straight into my eyes. She looked older in person – the blemishes ironed out in the make-up room and with the bright lights of the television studio were all on show for me to see. Despite this, she was still gorgeous. She looked me up and down then touched me gently on my wrist.

"What a sweetie! Thank you but I'll be ok,"

"I can see you're empty, how about a drink?" I replied.

"No thanks, I don't drink," She said, still smiling.

"Are you sure? It looks like you need one." I said, still in that silk smooth fake voice. She shook her head.

"In normal circumstances, I don't drink either…" I lied, "…but when I saw those £300 bottles of wine flowing, I thought it would be a shame to miss out on the experience. I'm usually offered revolting bottles of cheap plonk." She smiled at that, and I could tell she was sizing me up.

"One glass, you've convinced me to try one glass."

"Your wish is my command, madam." I bowed and trotted out of the living room towards the kitchen. Scarlett was waiting for me in the hallway ready to strike.

"Shaun, I don't know what the fuck you're trying to do. I'm engaged to someone else, deal with it."

I laughed out loud.

"Do you actually think I give a damn about you and Edward? I'm not going to do anything to mess up your sham of a marriage with that idiot."

"Oh yeah? Then why are you here?"

"Relax honey, I'm just here to network."

I could tell that she was completely baffled by my responses. I think that she'd been expecting some sort of fight, a spectacle in front of her family and friends, but on hearing my calm responses to her interrogation, her eyes narrowed, then she visibly relaxed. Once again, she must have seen herself in me and realised that I wasn't here to ruin her life, there would be no tactical advantage to that.

"Please can you leave?" she repeated, but I could tell that her heart wasn't in it this time.

"No" I replied indifferently.

She stood on tip-toes and leant forward as if to whisper in my ear. I could feel her soft breasts pressing against my arm through her silk dress. Finally, she rested her mouth against my ear and spoke in a clear and firm voice, it was so loud that it rattled my ear-drum.

"Listen here you worthless creep. If you fuck this up, I will do everything I can to destroy your life."

"No problem." I responded, I put my hand to her neck and pushed her against the doorframe. It was supposed to be an aggressive act, but I could tell that to her horror, she had become aroused. I ignored this and turned my back on her, making my way into the kitchen.

I could feel her eyes boring into my back with malice. For the first time since we met, it was I who had wounded Scarlett's pride and I revelled in the feeling. Still, my mind remained on my true purpose, so I poured Charlie an enormous glass of red wine – easily one third of the bottle.

When I gave her the glass, she took it without complaint. She was still whimpering a little, and nobody else had come to check on her. We sat in semi-awkward silence for 30 seconds or so, while she tasted the wine I had given her.

"I'm not convinced that this expensive wine isn't completely wasted on me." She said grimacing as she took a sip. "This is the first drop I've had since the millennium. It all tastes the same to me."

"I'm not quite as strict as you, it's been a little more recent for me since I last partook, but I'm certain that I can tell the difference."

The aura Charlie had about her had a significant impact on me, she seemed so innocent and unworldly that I found myself talking like a character from a bad adaptation of a Jane Austen novel. She didn't find anything unusual about the way I had been speaking, but I noted that she took another large sip of her wine.

"How do you know Scarlett and Edward?" She asked after a few more moments' silence.

"Oh, I'm an old friend of Scarlett's."

"She's never mentioned you? How did you meet?"

"Do you know Terry Taylor?"

"No."

"No, I suppose you wouldn't, well we met at the party he threw for me."

"For you?"

"Yeah, it's a long story."

"Try me."

"It's not a nice story."

"Oh, you MUST tell me now!" she laughed.

I hesitated for a second, and put some real gravitas into my words.

"He tried to kill himself at my house."

"My Gosh! That's horrible."

"Yeah, he overdosed outside my front door."

"What for? Was it a cry for help or something?"

"I don't know; I didn't want to ask him, it's always been a sensitive subject. Anyway, I called the ambulance and managed to keep him alive until the paramedics arrived. When he was better he threw me a party."

"And that's how you met Scarlett?"

"Yeah, me and Scarlett really hit it off that night. We've been great friends ever since." I had quickly decided that I should make the story of my relationship with Scarlett strictly PG13 for Charlie's benefit. I felt this would be easier to swallow than the explicit reality of "we have sex like rabbits behind her fiancés' back". I also embellished the story a little, deciding I came across a lot better in this new version with a 'hero's party' held in my honour.

"That's an amazing story, well done you. Your friend is lucky to have someone like you."

I cleared my throat nervously, and took a sip of my wine – Terry's recent swim down the Thames jumped to the forefront of my mind.

"How about you? How do you know them?" I was eager to get off the topic of Terry as quickly as possible. She took another large gulp of wine and finished her glass.

"Another one?" I said, not really expecting her to accept my offer, but she nodded in affirmation. I went into the kitchen and poured her another, even larger glass; Scarlett had clearly invested in some fairly hefty glasses – these were almost pint sized.

120

As I turned to go back into the living room, the front door opened, and I heard the distinctive voices of Edward and Abz as they entered the apartment. I was in no hurry to speak with either of them, so darted back into the living room. People appeared to be avoiding the living room; this was probably because of the hysterical celebrity on the sofa. Lingering in the doorway for a moment, I considered the fact that she was talking freely to me. I had tried to approach other celebrities on the clubbing scene with Terry, and while they had been friendly in a distant sort of way, they had been entirely unwilling to open up to me. I guessed it was the homely atmosphere that tricked her into deciding I was her friend – Scarlett's lounge had befuddled her mind.

"So, why so miserable?" I said to her, trying to ignore the chatter of Abz in the kitchen – I thought that she had decided not to come.

"I don't want to talk about it tonight." said Charlie.

"Sure?"

"Yeah, thanks though," she wrinkled up her nose and smiled. I had a feeling that the wine was beginning to have an impact on her and that she had convinced herself she was feeling a little better. For the time being, the source of her misery remained a mystery. She stood up and walked in the direction of the kitchen.

"Where you off to, eh?"

"I'm going to tell my brother congrats."

"Damien?"

"No silly, Edward!"

Edward was her brother? A horrid feeling crept over me as if someone had walked on my grave. Being close family, it would be hard to become close to Charlie and Damien if Edward and Scarlett both stood in my way.

He was over twenty years older than her, and he had a different surname – half-brother perhaps? There had been nothing about this on the internet, but for better or worse, I knew I would soon be getting to the bottom of this little conundrum. I stood up and reluctantly followed her into the kitchen. I imagined that when I went into the room, there would be deathly silence, and perhaps a tumbleweed. In the end, only Abz looked up at me in confused silence. I could tell she was trying to work out why I would be there. Scarlett completely ignored me, and Edward didn't recognise me, so long ago had our viewings been. He shook my hand and perhaps a glimmer of recognition crossed his face, but he must have written me off as one of Scarlett's friends.

I looked on at the man who had decided to devote his life (and his bank balance) to Scarlett; it was a devotion that an imbecile could tell was misplaced. He was clearly intelligent, confident and extremely wealthy, but other than that, he had absolutely nothing that would make him attractive to the opposite sex. He was grey, balding, and over-weight. From all I had seen of him, he appeared to be a self-righteous, pompous, boring old fart. Nothing he did or said on that evening led me to change my views. He ignored me, assuming I was unimportant – something which on this occasion, I was very happy for him to do. In fact I tried to steer clear of the three of them (Edward, Abz & Scarlett) as much as possible. At one point, Abz caught my arm and said to me with hatred in her voice:

"Why is Scarlett getting you to spy on me?" I took this as a reference to my interrogation regarding Scarlett. The conceit of that girl astounded me; she really thought it was all about her. I harboured no ill feelings towards either Abz or Scarlett, but this was not a battle I wanted to enter into.

"Look, she only asked me to check up on how you were coping with the engagement."

"Really, what did you say?" she began to look a little concerned. Ultimately, she was a daddy's girl, and no matter how much of a prick he was, she didn't want to upset him – possibly the reason for her last minute change of heart in attending his engagement party.

"I didn't see any point in fucking everything up. I told her you were coming round to the idea."

"Yeah, right." her voice was laced with sarcasm; now that she knew her daddy wouldn't find out her real thoughts, she had resorted back to her usual ugly façade.

I felt pretty pleased with myself – that bullet had officially been dodged. In the meantime Charlie had apparently consumed several more of the large glasses of wine, and looked decidedly worse for wear. Her eyes were blood-shot, and she was having a lot of trouble standing up.

"Eddie," she said, tears rolling from her eyes, "It's my fault, Eddie! Don't marry her."

Edward's eyes widened at this. I'm not sure what he reacted to worse, being called 'Eddie' in public, or the fact that she had insulted his bride to be.

"Charlie, you need to stop drinking and go home," he said.

"No! No! You've got to stop this wedding. You've got to stop it." She stumbled over to Scarlett and tried to push her, the result of which, was that she tottered a little and lost her own balance. After this failure, she stood up and punched Scarlett clumsily in the face. It wasn't well aimed, as such, didn't land particularly hard, but Scarlett let out a dramatic scream and clutched her cheek.

"Someone get her out of here." commanded Edward.

Tim, the bulky man who had let me in the house took Charlie by the arm and showed her to the door. She was screaming and crying, though she did not put up a fight when she was led out of the house.

"You're going to hell! You're going to hell! Go back to Georgie!"

After the door had shut her out and muffled her prophecies of eternal damnation, the atmosphere in the party turned frosty. Clearly, not all of the guests felt that Scarlett was the right match for Edward, though it had only been Charlie that had the balls to say it out loud. Scarlett had turned a little pale, her epic night of family and friends gathering to celebrate her marriage was going down the pan. I found it hard to feel sorry for her: ultimately Charlie and the rest of them were all right about her, and what's more, Scarlett knew it too – I was a shining example of her deceit.

I could tell that Damien would not be coming that day; half of the guests were looking at their watches itching to leave. I decided to make a swift exit to see if I could catch up with Charlie and get her number before she got home. I was surprised that Edward hadn't sent anyone to look after her; he was, after all, supposed to be her brother. Scarlett nodded to me as I left the flat and smirked, she knew exactly where I was going, and could tell I wanted to bag myself a celebrity. As her lips curled, I could see the malicious cunning in her eyes.

"Happy hunting, Shaun. Give me a call sometime" and she blew me a kiss.

She wasn't upset, worried or angry; in fact, it almost looked like she was enjoying herself. I knew she wanted me to do something bad with Charlie to get back at her.

"I'll see what I can do." I winked at her and shut her front door. After walking down the stairs and out into the fresh evening air, I caught sight of Charlie swaying along at the end of the road. I followed her into the night grinning, happy hunting indeed!

Step 4: Charlie Ekells

<u>Sunday 6th April 2008</u>

The following morning, I awoke feeling rancid with acid in the pit of my stomach and a jagged pain threatening to tear my head in two. Charlie plodded out of my room wearing the same clothes from the night before.

"Where am I?" she said.

"Islington." I replied.

She sat down beside me and began to cry again. By this point, I had begun to find her constant blubbing a little irksome. I put my hand on her shoulder in a half-hearted attempt at comforting her, but frankly, I was too concerned with my own poor state. I hadn't even drunk enough to deserve how bad I felt.

Unfortunately the hangover fairy had other plans in mind, and despite my reserved intake of wine, had deemed that Sunday 6th April was the allocated day for Shaun Valfierno to suffer. My only respite was that the pain I felt was nothing compared to the way Charlie looked that day; she had well and truly been cursed.

"I've been an idiot, haven't I?" she said to me.

"Ummm," it was awkward. She had been so wretched the night before I couldn't bring myself to kick her while she was down.

"My Gosh, I tried to punch poor Scarlett! Oh, this is why I shouldn't drink." This wasn't addressed to me, she was mumbling, almost to herself. She looked a mess with her make-up smeared down her cheeks and a deep look of concern on her face. She fixed me with an icy accusing stare.

"Why am I here? Why have you brought me here? I don't even know you."

I could tell that she was worried about the tabloids. A whole host of problems would crop up if something had happened – I could ruin her clean image, and probably her career. Hell, even if nothing happened, if someone got a picture of her doing the walk of shame out of my front door, her career was still as good as dead.

"You've got nothing to worry about." I said, more than a little annoyed. Although my intentions weren't entirely pure, I hadn't made even the most minor of sexual advances on her. She noticed the genuine indignation in my voice and her face furrowed into an apology.

"What happened?"

I explained to her that after she had been thrown out, nobody else checked whether she was going to be alright, so I went after her; then I told her that I had found her vomiting onto the pavement, and how she was unable, or unwilling to tell me how to get her home, so I took her back with me.

Although lesser mortals may have taken advantage of Charlie that evening, somewhat to my surprise, I found myself being a perfect gentleman. I hate it when girls get too drunk; all the grace and composure they spend the rest of their lives attempting to simulate is completely lost. Wretched she looked as she tripped over her own feet and skidded on her knees. I couldn't help myself but pick up the blubbering mess and take her home in a taxi. I hadn't the foggiest idea where she lived, and she was in no fit state to tell me.

When we got home I had made myself a bed on my sofa and gave her my bed to sleep in. Knowing her religious background I had sensed that she would not have appreciated my presence when she woke. Even though I was currently speaking to her still wrapped in a blanket on my sofa, she had still jumped to the worst possible conclusion. She was clearly quite highly strung when it came to sex, and I found myself wondering whether this 30 year old unmarried Christian woman was still a virgin.

"Shaun, you looked after me? Oh sweetie, I'm so sorry." I could tell that with my indignation I had won her trust.

"It's OK" I replied.

I stood up and made us both a cup of coffee. She took it in silence.

"Can I stay here until the evening?" she said to me.

She went on to explain that she was panicked about the paparazzi seeing her in her current state. If she could stay, shower, and recover, she could wait until the evening and make her way home in an evening dress. This was better than perfect. A whole day to charm her, put her in my debt and become true friends.

"Stay as long as you want! Weren't you scared about them yesterday?"

She explained that she had been; which is why she had gotten to Scarlett's so early, but in her state of idiotic drunken idiocy, she had forgotten herself and let her guard down. She confided that she was still worried there was a chance someone would have taken a picture of her in that state, getting a lift home with a tall and handsome stranger. I smiled inwardly at the 'tall and handsome' part; she picked up on this, and blushed a deep red.

"Luckily a small engagement party like that isn't likely to attract their attention. Even then they'd be unlikely to bother – I'm usually a bit of a bore to the sensationalists!" she said this last part like she'd said it a thousand times before. It was well rehearsed and sounded false. I thought I may have read it in at least one interview I'd seen of hers in *A-list*. Did she really think she was boring, or was she just saying that?

"From what I've seen of you so far, I can't imagine anyone would think you were boring." I said smiling.

Charlie laughed at that.

"Perhaps you bring out the worst in me!" she said.

Looking back at the tabloid scandals that surrounded Charlie following the end of our friendship over a year later, I am ashamed to say that this off-hand comment turned out to be the truth. At the time though, I thought it funny and smirked into my coffee cup.

"Chill out, and let me look after you today."

Over the course of the morning, we took it in turns to run to the toilet and vomit, but we were united in our pain, so despite the nausea I actually thoroughly enjoyed myself.

By mid-afternoon I felt well enough to order food; such were our cravings that we had pizza, sushi and ice-cream all delivered to my front door. We ate the lot while watching films; she dressed in some pyjamas my mother had given to me for Christmas, I wore shorts and a dressing gown. I could tell that Charlie was really warming to me and by 18:00, I worked up the courage to ask her directly about her relationship to Edward.

"Is Edward really your brother?"

"Yes, sort of."

"What does that mean?"

"He's my foster brother." The idea that someone could refer to another person who was in no way related to them as their brother seemed odd to me. My upbringing was so far removed from any experience of 'foster care', I had assumed that foster parents raise their children, and when they are old enough, they lose contact – otherwise they'd adopt, wouldn't they? I'm not sure why, but I always considered a 'foster home' as something akin to a half-way house. Let the troubled kids get back on their feet until they were old enough to look after themselves. To consider your foster home as your family hadn't occurred to me as something that would happen.

It transpired that a few years after Edward had flown the nest; his parents had taken Charlie into their Foster home. In spite of some lack-lustre attempts from social services to keep the siblings together, Damien had been adopted by a different family. Edward's father had been a priest, and the source of inspiration for Charlie's turn to religion following her mother's death. Despite her less than happy life history, she had kept up the religion with great fervour. Charlie spoke about religion like very few other people I know. She spoke about it without embarrassment, or discomfort; she believed what she believed, and that was that.

"How did your mother die?" I asked at the end of her story. I already knew what her answer would be, but I wanted all the sordid details.

"My dad killed her" she replied.

I put my hand on her shoulder, and ushered for her to continue.

"He still claims it was an accident, but I know that she didn't fall down those stairs."

I felt a little remorse for bringing the topic up and silence crept in amidst our happy friendship for a moment or two.

"Have you seen him since?"

"No, he was convicted of manslaughter. Me and Damien would never go back. He isn't the easiest person to forgive."

As she said this, a distant memory of my old man trying to cook me breakfast flittered across my mind. He would cook pancakes for breakfast as a treat during the holidays when I was home from school. It glimmered in my mind's eye for a second or two, and then vanished. Upon hearing the misery Charlie's father had caused her, I couldn't help but feel a bit more love for my own dad. I had had a privileged upbringing, even if my folks were absent for most of it.

"Is Edward religious too then?" I said, breaking our reverie by speaking my thought processes out loud.

"Only when it suits him," said Charlie.

"What does that mean?"

"It means that his father would be turning in his grave if he knew what he was doing."

"What?"

"Matthew 19:9."

I looked even more bewildered, but she didn't elaborate on what Matthew19:9 was in relation to. When I got to know Charlie a little better, I realised that it was not uncommon of her to cite random chapters of the bible in the middle of conversation. This bizarre habit generally forced people to finish the conversation in incomprehension – it was not her most endearing habit. I quizzed her about it once and she told me it was her way of adding a little mystery into conversations in the hope that it would force her loved ones into reading "God's message" in order to understand what she was talking about. It hasn't worked on me once – I have a natural aversion to all things religious, and there was nothing she could ever have done to change that. To this day, I don't know what Matthew 19:9 means, though I imagine that it says something like "And behold! God went forth and sayeth that sex with Scarlett Smith is evil." In which case, I suppose that I should begin to accept that if God is real, my soul is doomed to hell for eternity.

After several hours passed in messy bliss together, her eyes smiled at mine and I knew we would stay friends, true friends. Although we talked of many things, she revealed to me why she was feeling miserable:

Scarlett was introduced to Edward via Charlie.

Scarlett had worked with her on *Charlie's Brekkie Time*; in fact, it was the programme that made Scarlett's career. Once she had worked on that, the BBC offered Scarlett a senior position at almost double the salary she had been earning on *Charlie's Brekkie Time*. She and Charlie had remained friends and regularly met to discuss their lives. Over the years, Edward and Scarlett's paths had crossed on several occasions, and at some point, out of sight of Charlie's judgemental gaze, Scarlett had committed the ultimate treachery by hooking up with her foster brother.

On a side note, what the fuck is a producer anyway? I mean, I know they 'produce' stuff but what the flying hell does that mean? Even now, I have no idea. I asked Terry once what his actual job involved on a day to day basis. His response began with an extremely flatulent explanation about 'getting the job done through thick and thin and rape and pillage'. After which, I stopped listening and decided I didn't care. I never bothered asking Scarlett, it would have been the kind of question she would have turned her nose up at. She would have laughed at me and asked "Do you even care?" This, in fairness, is probably the best response to most of the questions I ask.

At first, Charlie had been worried about Scarlett, and had specifically befriended her because she felt that she was someone who needed to be saved, someone full of sin, but who had the potential to be a truly good person. Over the years, however, Charlie had given up trying to save Scarlett. She came to realise Scarlett would never change, but to Charlie's surprise they had remained friends. Scarlett had always made an effort to meet up, especially if Charlie was unhappy for whatever reason. She would cancel her plans, and cook Charlie dinner and listen to her woes, always having something insightful or helpful to say.

Then Scarlett ensnared Edward, Charlie's faith had suffered a huge dent. Charlie couldn't remember when she had introduced the two, but now, despite being completely oblivious to the affair until Edward's double announcement of an impending divorce and engagement, she was racked with guilt. In short, Edward had doomed himself to the room next to mine in the *sex with Scarlett* section of hell, and Charlie thought it was all her fault.

There is little more to say about that first lazy Sunday spent with Charlie. We parted ways at 20:00, and she made it home safely without any photographers taking the least bit of interest in her journey. It was such a fun, and funny day that we tried on many occasions to recreate it. She would turn up on my doorstep wet through in the pouring rain, smiling and holding a pot of pancake mix, or several DVDs for a back to back movie fest, or a bag full of chocolate and cheese. Me, usually hungover, and her, generally exhausted from her weeks waking at 04:00 AM to present her breakfast show. We would lie on my sofa together and tickle each other's feet. Time after time I go back to that year in my life and wonder what it was that Charlie saw in me. She was such a sweet and fun-loving girl; kind and gentle, and always giving. I often wonder whether it was because she was raised by a priest – she was so innocent and unworldly that it was easy to conceal my true and selfish nature from her. Sometimes it didn't even feel like I was pretending, maybe, just as I was able to bring out the worst in her, she was able, for a short time, to bring the best out in me.

Friday 9th May 2008

It is very rare that any transaction in a property goes without a hitch. Something always goes wrong and it's exceedingly frustrating – this problem was exacerbated by the credit crunch one-hundred fold. Even though I had learned this truism through bitter experience, whenever it happened, it always caught me off-guard. With the vendor happy, the purchasers happy, and the offer in place, I would always find myself foolishly hoping that maybe, just maybe, if, as Charlie would say, '*God willed it*', everything might just that once go through smoothly.

Sadly, it never did; whether anti money-laundering regulations called into question the source of the applicants perfectly unsuspicious deposit; or something weird like Japanese Knot-weed turning up in the survey report; or the divorcee vendors falling into an idiotic argument about who should be on the receiving end of the money; or most commonly, the solicitors being lazy pigs and refusing to do their job in a timely manner – something always held up the process.

I even had someone turn down a purchase the day before exchange because they found in the lease that they weren't allowed to have pets. It was even more ridiculous because the vendors had a pet cat, and four of their seven neighbours owned dogs. I tried explaining to them that the freeholder wouldn't care, but they still wouldn't go through with it in case there was a small chance of giving up their pet rat, Mister Snatch. I don't know what the average life-span of a rat is, but I bet the commission I lost on that deal could have bought enough rats to last that woman a thousand rats for a thousand years.

It was at times like this, when the deals fell through, when the frustration threatened to overwhelm me, when the office walls began closing in on me in claustrophobic strangulation; that I truly hated my job. The only method I found to stop myself from screaming and tearing my hair out was to take a deep breath and leave the office. I used to go on a short walk to a small café called *The Victorian Tea Rooms* which was run by a sweet old lady. Despite its central location, there was hardly ever anybody there. Usually, I wouldn't be seen dead in a place like that, I tend to frequent the big brands, like *Starbucks* or *Café Nero*, but it was the quiet calm in the poky little room, the lack of other patrons, and the fascinating way that the old lady (whose name I always forgot) talked to herself and laughed as she made me my coffee that made it my post-trauma haven. I would sit there, amidst a sea of doilies and read *A-List* magazine for an hour until I had reclaimed my demeanour.

Similarly, my journey to Elisha wasn't without its moments of despair and frustration. On Friday the 9th of May 2008 my journey seemed to have petered out completely, just as it had begun to lead somewhere. It was within *A-List*, my usual place of solace that I discovered the humungous shlong fucking the shit out of my best laid plans. It was like any other warm morning in May: the alarm shuddered against my soul, I planned the day ahead, I drank my coffee, I did my exercises, I watched BBC news, I drank my Vitamin C, I polished my shoes, I showered and shaved, I ironed my shirt, I got dressed and I put on my tie, but still, even before I had left my home, my day was completely ruined.

I was thinking about Charlie when it happened – I had decided to check my mail, I hadn't bothered for a few days and was expecting the latest copy of *A-List*. When I opened my letter box, it was hidden amongst a throng of junk-mail and bills. I wondered whether Charlie would ever appear on the cover. For some reason, nobody really hounded Charlie like they did other TV stars. I think it was because, apart from the minor blip at Scarlett's engagement party, she led a completely clean and wholesome life. She often joked that almost every other celebrity in the world would have to disappear in order for a story about her to be considered interesting by the public. She got the occasional paparazzi trying to catch her off guard, and occasionally they caught her without make-up or something, but she didn't care, and the photographers didn't get paid much for them as they were entirely uninteresting photos. The biggest problem as far as I could see it, was an almost endless speculation in the lad-mags and daily tabloids, as to whether she had ever 'popped her cherry'. Even that didn't really upset her – she simply ignored it. When I quizzed her why she didn't get upset, she would never give a real answer, just quoting another meaningless bible chapter.

Unfortunately, it wasn't Charlie whose name was plastered over the front cover; it was Elisha. She had gotten married over the weekend to an American Football star. She had married him in secret, accompanied by just a few close friends, including none other than the enigma that was Damien Woland. It was such an absolutely enormous fuck-up, that not even a trip to *The Victorian Tea Rooms* would have been able to help me. Something inside me snapped. Until that moment, I had been able to convince myself that the goal I had set myself was all in good jest, a happy experiment that was likely to fail, and if it all went wrong I would shrug my shoulders and accept defeat. However, when I read the news of her marriage and the tears ran freely down my face, I realised that I had been mistaken. What I had been doing was a sick game; not quite stalking, but not a million miles off either.

How had I become this person; this obsessive manipulator of minds? The world was threatening to overwhelm me. I couldn't help but look at the picture on the front cover again, and again, and again. She was dressed in white (of course), smiling and grasping her Yank husband with her right hand; her fingers curled into his, interlocking and firm. I looked upwards at the hallway ceiling and laughed manically, loud, and deep. How could I have done this – wasted all this time on a chance in a million? How could I have thought that her life would lie still as I battled my way to her? Still, I couldn't dwell on it for too long. I lived in the real world now, in the chaos of the credit crunch, and I had my career to rescue. I left my house, numb to the spring sunshine, and went to my office, and hid my shame and instability from the world in a sea of dead-end phone calls.

May 10th – May 31st 2008

With my focus gone, over the next few weeks my life meandered along amidst a sea of grey boredom. My work was too agonizing to be able to grip my attention, and the mundane routine of everyday life began to itch at my soul. I was unable to keep focus, and the desire to become the best salesperson in my office began to lose its appeal. I had walked into a life of limbo, no longer satisfied with my previous life but unable to cross the void into the life that I wanted. I kept on imagining what could have happened if I had succeeded with Elisha: the lifestyle, the photo shoots, the respect and the money.

So miserable was I, that I had even begun to contemplate making do with Charlie; at least she was famous. She wasn't a superstar like Elisha, but she was beautiful, she was kind, and she had her own breakfast show. Our friendship really bloomed over those troubled times, and I was able to use my genuine dissatisfaction with my life as a method of drawing her in. She made such an earnest effort as an amateur psychologist that it was heart-breaking for me to have to hide the true reason for my misery. Such an honest and frank person was she that the fact I would deliberately keep back any important or incriminating evidence from her wouldn't have crossed her mind. At first she had been a little stand-offish, but after two months of daily contact, be it on the phone, via email, or face to face, I believe that she considered me as one of her best friends. True, it was a young friendship, and consequently she held a lot of herself and the skeletons in her closet back, but she showed true affection towards me.

Surprisingly we had quite a bit in common, she had quite a dry sense of humour, and although she rarely made any dead-pan jokes, she never failed to laugh heartily whenever I made one. She often impressed me with her political knowledge, things that she had picked up interviewing famous politicians. She was also an absolutely amazing cook, something she attributed to being lucky enough to be close personal friends with a variety of celebrity chefs. The one thing I usually tried to avoid discussing was religion. Charlie was a Jesus fanatic, always talking about God and all that other nonsense. The only experiences I'd had of the Christian world was when forced to attend Church once a month at boarding school. I hated it, all the strange things that the odd-ball religious kids would do in order to prove they were the most religious – like claiming to have talked in tongues and getting Confirmed and other such guff. The religious boys always seemed to have some kind of sight deficiency, were socially awkward, had bad acne, and the worst B.O. It was a curse that blighted the entire Christian population below the age of 18 at our school. I also hated the R.E. teachers, religious freaks hell bent on proving that Christianity was the only true religion to young and impressionable minds. It's really odd thinking about it, my parents were in no way religious and having grown up in the Swinging Sixties, would hate to have thought that they were paying some small-minded 50 year old unmarried man to preach about the sins of sex before marriage to me – it made me uncomfortable then, and thinking about it now, it makes me even more uncomfortable. I couldn't help but think that such apparently restrained people must have been hiding some awful secret, and that they hated themselves for it.

Despite this clear divide in religious views, Charlie and I got on like a house on fire. I developed a theory – partly because she still liked me regardless of whether I liked Jesus or not, but mostly because she was a girl – that surely she was attracted to me... True, I had no cold hard facts to base it on, but I had a hunch, and I tend to rely on these hunches when it comes to girls.

One late evening in my flat, as we sat and ate a meal, a situation arose which was so tempting, that I couldn't help but put my theory to the test. It all began when she complained that she had a bad back, consequently I offered my skills as a masseuse. She seemed a little reluctant at first, but I was so eager and confident in my abilities to cure the back-pain, that I eventually persuaded her to lie down on my floor and to undo her top so that the oils I would be using wouldn't leave grease marks. When her blouse was removed, she blushed deeply and hurried to face down onto the floor. Her bra was still clasped firmly on her back, and with one hand, I undid it. I didn't see her face when I did this, but her whole body shuddered, and I'm certain she was thrilled. I warmed the oils in my hand, and pressed down onto her shoulders, kneading out the knots while she groaned. Basically, she lay there semi-naked on my floor, covered in oil and groaning – something which in my opinion left only one single and overwhelmingly logical course of action – attempting to have sex with her. After ten minutes of rubbing her back, arms, legs, and neck, I moved my hand up her inside thigh from beneath her now-hitched skirt and felt her warm vagina with my fingers. I only felt it for a second, but her knickers were sodden. She had clearly been aroused by my touch, but unfortunately she did not react positively; in fact she leapt up and kicked me off.

"What do you think you're doing?!" She yelled at me. She stood up, clearly intending to storm out of the room but her unclasped bra fell off her pert little breasts so that I got a full frontal. Her chest was burning deep red with arousal and her cheeks were flushed. All at once, she looked down at herself and couldn't cope; she grabbed her clothes and ran into the bathroom. After four or five minutes she came down, fully dressed in shoes and coat.

"You shouldn't have done that." she said

"You seemed to be enjoying yourself," I replied

"It's not right, Shaun; I've made a promise not to."

She seemed less upset with me, more genuinely angry at herself – although admittedly there was some healthy anger at me sprinkled in for good measure. She sighed deeply and put her hand on my shoulder.

"I can't do anything like that with you, not now," she said, and left the flat before I had a chance to respond. I spent Saturday night on my own, fiddling around on the internet and watching television (fiddling being the operative word).

Charlie called me at 07:00AM the following day.

"Are you awake?" she said.

It was Sunday, and before midday, of course I was a sleep.

"I'm coming round."

"Ok."

I hung up and slept for what seemed like 30 seconds but must have been over an hour. In no time at all, Charlie was calling my phone again and telling me that she was outside, and that I needed to come with her. Cursing, I scrabbled my way to the front door and buzzed her in. She refused and told me that I needed to get dressed and come with her straight away. I complained quite a bit about this, but I was feeling a little guilty about my conduct from the night before, so I relented and got into her car. Sitting in the car, unshaven, unwashed and feeling sorry for myself I asked her where we were going.

"To Church!" She smiled at me pulling out of the driveway and heading north.

I felt like clawing my way out of the car. I knew that she was interested in that kind of thing, but I never thought she'd resort to hijacking and forcing me to endure two hours of awkward boredom in order bring us closer together.

It was everything that I remembered it to be as a child. Stuffy, long-winded, and completely nonsensical. Happy hippy morons all sat around feeling self-righteous in their smug satisfaction believing that they knew something that other people didn't. It wasn't even a nice church, apparently this group of people felt that the Church of England had become too secularised and devoid of values, so instead of sitting in the comfort of a nice old fashioned stone church , they decided to meet every Sunday in a run-down hall in a run-down school a couple of hundred yards from the type of tacky, seedy hotels only frequented by drug-addicts, low-class prostitutes and the less discerning football supporter travelling up to see Arsenal playing at home. Just off Seven Sisters Road, it was a stone's throw from Abu-Hamza's favourite fundamentalist hangout in Finsbury Park.

The hymns weren't even any good. They didn't sing any of the old stuff that I knew. Gone are the days of 'Jerusalem' and 'Amazing Grace', instead they sang modern stuff, which to my uncultured and unchristian ears basically sounded like shit pop music (think Take That in the early 90's, but with less talent). I surprised myself at how disappointed I was not to hear the Christian songs I had sung at school; it was like going to a concert for a one hit wonder from the 80's and only getting to hear their crappy new stuff. They all stood around listening to this rancid tripe and lifted their hands in the air and closed their eyes. Surely they knew that it was bad music? Badly thrown together by people who had no idea about modern musical tastes, played by a bunch of talentless nobodies who had only taken up playing the guitar in order to impress the vicar. Surely someone must have realised that bad music is bad, regardless of whether it mentions love for God or sympathy for the Devil? But nobody seemed to realise, and they put their hands to their hearts and screamed, completely oblivious of how stupid they all looked.

It was awkward to watch them, and I cringed every time the priest told everyone that it was time to sing.

I praised the Lord with genuine affection when it was all over. But that spiteful bastard was out to get me, and there was a post-service tea and biscuit thing that Charlie insisted on dragging me to. Everyone wanted to speak to me, including the vicar; I was a guest and therefore a potential candidate for evangelical recruitment. They crowded around asking about my life and my own religious experiences. I am rarely intimidated, but this bunch of middle-aged Christians frightened the fuck out of me. Everything they said put me on edge; I was forced to think outside of my usual comfort zone, and pretend that I actually gave a crap about any of it. Charlie didn't help matters either, when she introduced me to the priest – a happy go lucky skinny man with a goatee beard and a cheap suit – she told him I was an atheist.

"No, I'm an anarchist! Ha ha ha." I tried to joke.

The priest didn't smile, his beardy little eyes scratched at my skin, and I thought he would be angry.

"What experience do you have with religion?" he asked me.

I was uncomfortable, but I told him as politely as I could how much I had hated church when I was a child.

"Ah yes, I know your story well. It's such a shame when childhood experiences put people off."

It sounded like a very reasonable statement, and for a moment I considered his words. He spoke in such a gentle and accommodating manner that I couldn't help but feel relaxed.

"What's stopping you from looking into it yourself?"

I shrugged my shoulders. Charlie was smiling and nodding at me, evidently pleased at how I was responding.

"There's nothing out there stopping you" continued the priest "God's not going to come down and strike you with lightening you know. It's up to you."

It was about this point that the feeling of discomfort came flooding back. I realised that the priest was embarking on a sales pitch. Everything he said had the unmistakable signs of a hardball sales pitch – I had never realised that this is what priests were nowadays. They are no longer the esteemed pillars of our community – their job is now to convince people to come to church. They were all desperately trying to get their attendance numbers up; they had probably even been given a target to do so. In our office, every morning we chalked up our pledge and what we had achieved upon a white board in the centre of the room. While the priest was talking at me, I couldn't but help but conjure up an image of a room full of men in dog-collars chalking up their attendance figures, cat calling at low performers and wolf-whistling and cheering the top salesmen.

Any good salesman knows the structure of sales:

1. Market Chat

All through the conversation every step of the way don't forget to speak in depth about the market you are selling in. Make it clear from the word go that you are an expert in your field. Allow them to feel confident that you know what you're talking about, and that you're only selling it to them because it must be the best thing in the world.

2. Rapport building

Be friendly, find some common ground. Mirror the customer – if they are young and bullish, talk about football (even if you don't like it), speak about amazing nights out in wherever they have been or are planning to go on holiday. If they are old become the perfect example of how the youth acted in 1950's rural England – become a living breathing caricature of Dick from the Famous Five. If it's a girl, assess their type and flirt. I personally have a set list of things to talk about with girls on a viewing, dependent upon their type:

• Goth chicks respond well to talk about tattoos or piercing that I pretend I wish I had.

• Intellectual looking girls just want to talk about work. I used to speak politics with them, but you can't always single out a Tory from a Labour supporter and I was found out on more than one occasion, so I tend to steer clear of political chats nowadays.

- Ladettes essentially love the same chat as their male counterparts – holidays and big nights out.

- Daddy's girls glisten with glee when you refuse to recognise their existence and speak to their daddy instead.

- Most girls love reality TV, so at a pinch, it's something easy to fall back on when all else fails.

3. Qualification/ Information Gathering-

Questions Questions Questions. Get the person to whom you are selling to speak about themselves; their needs and their troubles, what they want, what they don't want, and why. The more information the better. Take a mental note of all their requirements so that you can use it to close them later.

4. The pitch

Go to great lengths to ensure they know to what intimate depth your product matches their needs and desires. Downplay any negatives.

5. Objection Handling

If you've done a good job on the rapport building, this bit should be easy. For every concern they have about your product, be ready with a counter argument that proves that any problem, no matter how seemingly serious is merely a trifle considering that you're about to make all their dreams come true. This bit can be really awkward if you've judged incorrectly when trying to get them to like you, as it essentially becomes an argument.

6. The assumptive close

Basically make it really difficult for them to say no.

Here are some examples of what is meant by an assumptive close.

- "The vendor has categorically stated that they won't accept offers less than £240K, I'll call you tomorrow morning so you can give me your formal offer."

- "To get your phone transferred, all you need is to cancel your existing provider, I'll just pass you through to them right now so that we can get you set up straight away."

- "I look forward to seeing you in Church next week, Shaun."

That's exactly how my visit ended, with a greasy second-hand church salesman closing me into visiting the following week. Charlie was clearly thrilled that I had such an "in-depth" conversation with the priest. As we walked back to her car, she put her head on my shoulder.

"Thanks for doing this Shaun," she said.

I shrugged but couldn't hide my disgust – the last few hours had truly been a waste of life.

"No problem," I lied. "I actually quite enjoyed myself," I lied again. "I'll come again sometime," I lied again, and the cockerel crowed thrice.

Meanwhile, Charlie held my hand and gazed into my eyes.

"You must understand that I didn't run away last night because I don't like you. I have a responsibility to Jesus to save myself for marriage, and I ….."

I forget what she said after that. It was probably something else to do with God. I was occupied with other thoughts – "Jesus Tap Dancing Christ! She is a virgin after all!!!" – was the main and somewhat reoccurring thought that swept through my mind over and over again.

It really wasn't very far from her church to my house, and I realised that each Sunday visit when she had come round to watch films and cook pancakes had been preceded by a visit to this run-down church and the salesman priest. Charlie offered to come home with me to cook me some lunch. I made up an excuse and politely declined. I'd had enough of God for one day.

June 2008

Soma Holiday month!

For those of you who haven't seen the show – it was quite simply the most addictive thing on TV: the show you love to hate. My interest in the show started off as a way to build rapport with my applicants as I drove them to their viewings; that, coupled with the fact that *A-List* is literally filled cover to cover with references about it, meaning I find it impossible not to watch.

By no means do I claim that it was intelligent viewing. Everyone that went on there was an absolute idiot, and talked loud repetitive nonsense. With their screeching, their bored conversations, their cat-fights and their personality clashes all combined, it became utterly compelling to watch.

It was only on for the month of June, and every year I couldn't help but stay in each night and watch it live. I'd tried recording it and watching the following day, but usually someone in the office ruined everything by talking about what happened.

The rules of the show were as follows: 10 celebrities and 10 *'common folk'* would enter the house together; all of their movements would be filmed. The aim of the game, was to last the whole month in the house without being voted out; but it was more complex than that. For the first seven days, the common folk would have to wait hand and foot on the celebrities, cooking, cleaning, ironing and washing. Typically, most of the celebrities would grow arrogant and make their servants perform the most menial of tasks. By week two though, the public could vote house-mates out of the house, as well as being able to vote whether certain celebrities should become servants, or vice-versa. This was when the common folk would be able to get their revenge on the celebrities who had mistreated them for seven days. That's when most of the fun happened.

My friends used to despair at me, even Charlie refused to watch it with me – a strong statement considering she had to do a regular segment on her show, and pretend that she knew or cared what was going on in the *Soma House*. On some occasions, she was forced to relent and sit beside me, but she would watch the bare minimum so that she was able to talk knowledgeably about the inner-workings of the house.

In 2008, Charlie's commentary on Soma Holiday upped a notch – she used to call me at the crack of dawn and get me to give her a blow by blow account of what had happened on Soma the night before. She always pretended to like the house-mates I liked, and towards the end of the month pretended to feign interest when they sat on her sofa for an interview. I would watch lying in bed, unsure what to make of it. In previous months, if I'd seen one of my friends interviewing a *Soma Holiday* contestant I would have been ecstatic. With Charlie though, it was underwhelming. I would plead with her to introduce me to these people, but she outright refused; she called them all "awful awful people". Typically Charlie wasn't a snob, but she well and truly scorned those poor people trying so desperately to become famous on reality TV.

29th June 2008

Following my betrayal and the gate-crashing of her party, my relationship with Scarlett had gone from strength to strength. She had moved in with Edward in South Kensington and put her own flat on the market. She had even asked whether I could sell it for her; I don't work in Shoreditch, so to my regret, I was unable to help. None of these new complexities made any difference to our sex life; it was much the same as ever. Further to this, we now knew each other's secrets, which added previously untapped depths to our relationship. We were able to cut out all of the head-fucking and game playing, and focus solely on the sex. On occasion, Scarlett even agreed to visit me in my own home. She was not the least bit jealous or perturbed when I told her about my blossoming relationship with her adoptive sister in-law. On the contrary, I think she found it amusing. She laughed long and hard when I told her about my misguided attempt at instigating intercourse.

One warm Sunday afternoon, Scarlett told Edward that she was going to the gym. With the intention of returning red in the face from exercise of a slightly more dynamic nature, she came straight to my place.

"Charlie tried to get me to come to Church again today." I smiled as she jumped into my arms. Scarlett laughed.

"What was your excuse this time?" She said as she bit my lip.

"Same as always – the hangover."

Scarlett rolled her eyes, and unbuttoned her trousers. For half an hour or so, Scarlett's scorn of Charlie Ekells was forgotten. It was only later, when we lay together in my sweat-sodden sheets that I remembered Charlie was likely to want to call on me after Church had finished.

"Scarlett," I said, "When is Edward expecting you back?"

"Don't worry about him Shaun, he's playing golf all day. He won't be home until late this evening."

As if on cue, my phone began to vibrate. A flattering photograph of Charlie's elfin features flashed on the screen. I went to answer but Scarlett held my hand.

"It will be easier if she thinks you're asleep," She explained to me as I glanced anxiously at my phone. The sun had found a crack in between my curtains, it shone upon Scarlett's necklace and for a brief second, I was completely blinded by the light.

"Well, Charlie's promised to cook me lunch," I said playfully, "what have you got to offer me?"

Scarlett grinned mischievously.

"I'm sure that I can offer you services that young Miss Ekells may struggle to provide you with."

"Ah!" said I, "but you already provided me those much needed services, less than ten minutes ago."

Scarlett pretended to frown, "Well if *sir* is tired, I'm sure I can take my services elsewhere." She sat on top of me, her blond hair hanging into my face and began to kiss me. Just as it was getting exciting, Charlie called my phone again. Scarlett rolled her eyes.

"She must like you, Shaun. She doesn't usually spend this much effort on mortals."

All of a sudden Scarlett lost interest; she looked at her watch and grimaced.

"I should probably get going anyway. Can I use your shower?" She kissed me on the forehead and walked into my bathroom without waiting for an answer. While she was out of the way, I thought I would take a look at her phone for old-times' sake. I had never told her exactly how I found out about her engagement party, but I assume that after a thorough investigation she believed it all came through Abz. Consequently, her password was the same. As the distinctive hum of the shower met my ears, I picked up the phone and delved into its depths. As before, I was met with the unexpected. Arrogance is perhaps a flaw of mine, and my swollen cranium was forcibly deflated when I came across a rather ominous text conversation with another man:

Mystery Man: *"I'm flying into London tonight. meet me in the bar at the Savoy at eight."*

Scarlett: *"I'm getting wet just thinking about it.*

Mystery Man: *"You better not disappoint me this time bitch, or else"*

Scarlett: *"I'll be there as soon as I can get away"*

Mystery Man: *"Fuck you. Don't bother you ugly cunt"*

Scarlett: *"I'm sorry. I'm on my way"*

Scarlett: *"I'm here, call me."*

Scarlett: *"Call me when you can."*

Scarlett: *"I've bought myself a bottle of bubbly. Come and join me!"*

Scarlett: *"I'll wait around for one more hour, call me"*

Mystery Man: *"Room 142"*

Scarlett: *"Thanks for last night x"*

Frustratingly, neither one of them signed their name, nor had she added the number to her contacts. Who was this arsehole? Why was he able to treat Scarlett so badly and get away with it? Why couldn't I be so demanding and utterly demeaning?

Scarlett abruptly entered the room. So deep was I in thought that I hadn't noticed the sound of the shower being silenced. I fumbled with her phone in a panic, and knocked it to the floor. To me, the guilty party, it was glaringly obvious what I had been doing. Scarlett either didn't notice or didn't care; she busily tied back her hair and donned the baggy clothes that she had been wearing in order to keep up the pretence of going to the gym. My cheeks flushed red; I had somehow assumed that apart from Edward, I was the only man in Scarlett's life. It was galling to think that I had let myself be taken in by her, again. I told myself that there must be something wrong with her, some kind of mental deficiency that meant that she was always hungry for cock. I was happy to discover that this small lie made me feel slightly better about myself, and before she had left my home I was busy concocting a whole plethora of problems with Scarlett's psyche. Ultimately, it was lucky that Scarlett left when she did. Not fifteen minutes after she left, her chaste sister-in-law-to-be called by uninvited to my home. We played cards on my balcony, and drank filtered coffee until the sun set.

Wednesday 2nd July 2008

Despite my sincerest intentions it seemed to be physically impossible to extricate myself from irritating people's lives once they had labelled me as someone of importance. One sunny morning, Polly called and gave me an unnecessary update on her life. After failing miserably to find another job, she had decided to go travelling. I don't know why she always felt the need to update me on what she was doing in order to fulfil her miserable existence, but this wasn't an uncommon occurrence. Whenever she felt that there was something for her to boast about, she would call me, and tell me all the sordid details. Some of the calls over the months included:

1. A new boyfriend (who didn't last two weeks).

2. A sexual conquest with a tall and dark stranger (who never called her back).

3. A holiday in Portugal (with her parents).

4. An invite to a wedding (which she attended, but was unable to find a *plus one*).

5. That she had lost weight (I'm sure it wasn't that much).

6. That she had her teeth whitened (who even cares????).

Now she was going travelling for a year. She hadn't had a job for over 6 months and had decided to rack up a load of debt in the middle of the recession without doing anything that would further her career. I had no clue as to why she felt that this was something to boast about.

She wasn't even going anywhere interesting – a year backpacking around the east coast of Australia and North America. Both countries are basically England except with hotter weather, lower IQs, louder voices, and more racism. I don't know what she hoped to learn about other cultures on this trip, but I had a feeling that she would come back tanned and completely un-enriched. She asked me whether I had called Terry recently, to which I replied that I had not.

"Please call him, Shaun. He's not in a good way. Now that I'm not going to be around to look after him, he has nobody."

I shuffled my feet nervously as she said this. I knew that Terry was now living in Earlsfield in a flat that his parents rented out for him, I knew that he was still taking medication to battle his depression, and that every now and then he would go absolutely mental and do something completely bizarre. I'd heard stories of him chasing down the CEO of *Oops! TV* with rotten fruit, and of him getting thrown out of live television shows by shouting continuously at the top of his voice that he wanted his job back. I even heard that he may have killed his neighbour's dog, although this was yet to be proven. These stories, often related to me by Polly, seemed so far removed from the person that I had grown to know the year before. Terry was irritating, yes, but I couldn't imagine him being capable of such weird and freakish behaviour. Something must have seriously gone wrong with him. I don't know if he killed the dog or not, but the fact that his neighbour suspected him at all was testament to how erratic his behaviour had become. Polly had taken Terry on as a charity case. She had visited him at least once a week, and had on more than one occasion picked him up from the police station after he was arrested. I had no intention of calling him, and Polly unfortunately knew this.

"I've given him your number again in case he wants to call you." She said. This was annoying; I'd rather he didn't know how to get hold of me. I had assumed that he hadn't called me because he didn't want to. His old phone, with my contact details must have been somewhere at the bottom of the Thames.

"Do you think he's likely to call?" I said, more than a little panicked.

"Yes." said Polly, and she hung-up.

Polly. What a Bitch.

Thursday 3rd July 2008

I had been keeping my eyes open for any signs of Elisha's marriage being on the rocks; I wasn't hopeful, as it had only been a few months. Only the 10 pence magazines showed any hint of trouble, but those magazines don't count. Their stories are almost never true and always ridiculous. Nothing else though; not even a picture of them looking fat and miserable. Each day I opened *A-List* with baited breath, scanning the front page for a sign that it had all gone wrong, but to no avail. That morning, before I picked it up from my doormat, I closed my eyes and said a prayer. It was the first prayer I had made since discovering that I didn't believe in God at the age of 13. The prayer went like this: "Please God, let her be divorced. Amen." Admittedly, it wasn't the most altruistic prayer ever made, but it was a prayer nonetheless, I even said 'Amen.' After realising that I had prayed to a God that I didn't think I believed in, I felt a little odd. I was clearly spending too much time with Charlie, something about her was rubbing off on me.

As I stared down at the front page I was confronted with bold yellow letters screaming at me on a pink background: "Elisha's Expecting! Sexy starlet Pregnant!"

Fuck You, God.

I realised that Charlie's mission to turn me into a Christian was futile. I just couldn't bring myself to believe, it was just too stupid a notion to contemplate. Some bloke 2000 years ago performed some magic tricks, and impressed some very naïve idiots. I'm pretty sure that David Copperfield would receive similar treatment had he lived at the time. Not only did I have that bombshell to contend with, but I had two rather unsettling telephone calls.

The first, luckily, I did not answer, as I was on a viewing. Though the voicemail was enough to dampen my spirits:

"Hi Shaun! It's Terry here! Uhhh…..I wanted to get in touch and organise lunch with you. I want to go back to the way it was. I mean we had some perfect times together and I want more. No! I mean….I know you didn't think they were perfect, but I liked being your friend. I wonder why you ever hung around me. Shit it's all gone wrong and I hate the way you ignore me. Don't ignore me. I don't know what I ever did to you and you ignore me. Why? You're still ignoring me. I know you won't call me back. You seemed to like me and I needed a friend and you were my friend but you weren't. At least I don't go around Fucking other people's girlfriends you prick. You fucking prick. I fucking hate you and you've ruined my life. YOU'RE A FUCKING PRICK. Am I evil, AM I EVIL? WHY AM I ANGRY? WHY ARE YOU ALL SO SHIT? IF YOU DON'T CALL ME I 'M GOING TO COME TO YOUR HOUSE AND SLIT YOUR THROAT!"

I listened to it in the office, and I'm pretty sure that Guy, who shared my desk, heard it too. Thankfully Guy pretended he didn't hear, as I would have done had it been him. I loved that about Guy. He didn't want to know me; he just wanted to talk banter, make money, and drink. It was an uncomplicated relationship and I always knew where I stood with him. If I ever wanted to confide in him he would have avoided me like the plague, but if I wanted a night on the lash, he was my first choice every time. When I disconnected the phone, Guy stared down at his feet while I saved the number into my contacts list as 'Terry (Mental Don't Answer).'

The voicemail hadn't been a complete shock – I knew he would try to call me. I hadn't counted on the fact that he was off his fucking rocker though. I continued with my day regardless, trying not to let the morning's events get me down too much.

That evening when Charlie called me, I hope it would cheer me up. As usual, the first fifteen minutes of conversation were all about me – Charlie had quite a cute habit of asking all the right questions, and getting me to speak about everything that had happened to me throughout my day. I told her how glum I was feeling, but refrained from talking about Elisha or Terry. After this, she consoled me, and invited me to dinner at hers in order to cheer me up.

"Yes, I'd love to!" I replied eagerly.

"How does next Tuesday sound?" asked Charlie.

"Perfect – more than perfect."

"Would you mind if I invited Edward and Scarlett along too?" she said.

"Uh, not at all, why?" the smile didn't altogether leave my face. Scarlett and Charlie still hadn't made up since the engagement party, and I couldn't help but hope they wouldn't: it would be too complicated for me.

"I want to see Edward." The words 'and Scarlett' were poignantly absent from the end of her sentence.

"Anything wrong?" I asked, knowing there must be a reason that she was inviting Scarlett as well.

Charlie went silent for a moment, evidently deciding whether to confide in me.

"Can you keep a secret?" she whispered.

"Yes, of course." My interest piqued.

"Edward suspects that Scarlett is cheating on him." This made me smile, and I was glad that Charlie couldn't see my face.

"What? Why?" I asked her, pretending to sound shocked.

"He contracted Gonorrhoea from her"

"What the fuck?" What the FUCK?????? It was all I could think. My head felt hot with embarrassment and I began to feel an itch in my nether regions. Psychosomatic or not, I began to scratch furiously. Perhaps I should have indulged Charlie, asked her why that wouldn't constitute conclusive proof for Edward, or why he would stay with her if she'd given him an STD? But I couldn't think of anything apart from my knob, and what might happen to it. In fact, I needed to end the conversation then and there.

"Look, I've got to go."

"But….." she began and I put down the phone.

So, to sum up my shit day:

1. Elisha was pregnant.
2. Terry had threatened to murder me.
3. Scarlett had given me Gonorrhoea.

Friday 4th July 2008 – Monday 8th July 2008

The following day I went straight to the GUM clinic. I was certain what the result would be, but wanted to know whether I'd caught anything else from that disease-ridden bag of filth. It took three very long working days for the results to come through, so my weekend was completely ruined. I tried to call Scarlett several times to question her, but she refused to answer or return my calls. Luckily I wasn't working, so I stayed in and pissed my day up the wall stalking Elisha on the internet and feeling sorry for myself. On Sunday, I voluntarily accompanied Charlie to church. You'd think that I would learn from my past mistakes, but she seemed so happy that I was there. It was the same pious salesman priest spinning the same tired lines, singing the same stupid songs and attempting to engage me in pointless conversation. This time I refused to play the game and avoided him as much as I possibly could. Charlie could tell that I was miserable about something, and when she asked, I replied:

"Work."

It was the standard response I gave to her. The only good thing to come out of the credit crunch was that it gave me the opportunity to lie about why I was feeling miserable.

"Have you ever thought about trying anything else?" said the priest overhearing our conversation (the smug git.) Charlie smiled and looked at me as if it was the best idea in the world. I looked at her, then at him and sighed.

"Of course I have."

That was the end of the conversation as far as I was concerned, but they both waited for me to continue. There followed a few moments of awkward silence.

"Ecclesiastes 4:8" said Charlie.

The silence was renewed for a little while longer.

"I think I need to go" I said finally, looking at my watch and walking away. Charlie followed me over, she looked nervous.

"I think I know why you're so miserable all the time…"

Now, that was a shock. How much had she figured out? Did she know I'd been sleeping with Scarlett? Did she know about the Gonorrhoea?

"You like me, don't you?" she smiled and my heart tumbled to the floor at how cute and uneasy she looked. She thought I had fallen in love with her. It was such a sweet and pitiful conclusion to come to, that I nearly did fall in love with her then and there. Innocence such as this, I hadn't experienced since my first girlfriend. The moment passed quickly though, and my brain kicked in.

Does she like me?

Maybe I can make some money from this?

Maybe I'll be on the cover of *A-List*?

There she was, radiant and glorious in the house of God, her breasts pressed tightly against her cotton jumper, and me with a belly full of Gonorrhoea, the object of her affection. I almost hated myself for doing it, but I smiled back and looked directly into her eyes. Her cheeks turned pink, and her breasts heaved against that tight little jumper as a red flush crept up her neck.

"This isn't the time to talk about this," I said, teasing her desire. "I want to speak about this properly on Tuesday."

Her face fell a little bit at that, and the arousal I had seen in her only a moment before dissipated in a flash. She was nervous again now – I could see her thinking *'maybe I've got this wrong, maybe he doesn't like me?'*

I smiled at her and kissed her on the cheek.

"I really do have to go."

I waved to the priest, strolled out of the doors and down the grotty street towards a vandalised bus-stop. As I waited for the bus, the sun peeked out from behind the clouds and warmed my face.

Tuesday 8th July 2008

Despite Charlie travelling northbound beyond my house for church every Sunday, it was in fact quite difficult to get to Charlie's home in St John's Wood from mine, so I decided to head straight there from work. I am unsure why she chose that hell-hole of a church in Finsbury Park when she lived nowhere near it, but I imagine it had something to do with 'giving back to a poverty stricken community', or some other bullshit that would never make sense to a normal person.

After the standard long hard slog in the office, I was the last to arrive. There was nothing unusual in this – being the last to leave the office does have certain drawbacks.

Charlie greeted me at the door with a glass of red wine in her hand. This was the first time I had seen Charlie drink since Scarlett and Edward's engagement party. What was it about these two that drove her to drink? I knew that she felt guilty for introducing Scarlett and Edward, but, quite frankly, I found her behaviour bizarre. She had clearly been drinking for some time as her teeth and lips were stained dark red with it. It almost looked like someone had punched her in the mouth – like she had dead teeth.

Charlie lived in a spacious two-bedroomed mezzanine style house. The living room and open plan kitchen spanned the entire length of the building. The dining table was big enough to seat eight people and was placed at the very centre of the room. She had modernised it to her own tastes when moving in, and although I am loathe to say it, the giant oak Crucifix on the wall actually looked rather stylish suspended above the immaculate floor boards below. You could even call it 'religious-chic'; it was homely, modern, and devout.

Scarlett and Edward were sat at the dining table holding hands. Scarlett was completely unphased by my entrance – she must have known I was coming. She stood up to hug and greet me.

"Shaun, it's so good to see you. It seems like an eternity." It had in fact only been one week since I was last inside her – something I now regretted. I couldn't help but wonder whether she had known then that she was afflicted with knob-rot. I hadn't used a condom – we were too caught up in the moment and she hadn't stopped me. Neither Scarlett nor Edward were drinking – which was odd in itself – but I took it to mean that the empty bottle of red on the table had all been consumed by Charlie. This was unheard of – she had to get up at 04:00 AM the following day for work. After extricating myself from Scarlett's embrace, I shook Edward's hand. Shortly after, I picked up a wine glass and poured myself a large one. Charlie was busy in the kitchen stirring pots and pans. I looked at them both and tried to think of something to say.

"How are the wedding plans coming along?" I eventually asked. Scarlett rolled her eyes. She was obviously bored by the inane question that she had answered a thousand times previously.

"Great," said Edward.

He still didn't recognise me as the estate agent that he had hated so much, and I found it unsettling.

"We've found the perfect venue!"

"Oh really, where?"

"Obidos."

"Where?"

"It's in Portugal, there's a beautiful old castle there."

"How is Abz coping with it all?" piped in Charlie, dampening the atmosphere. Scarlett rolled her eyes again; I could tell that she didn't want to be here with the only two people in the world who had a chance of jeopardising her life with Edward. I wondered whether I would get an invite to the wedding. I was apparently invited to the engagement party, would Scarlett keep up the pretence of us being old friends? While we were together, we skirted around the awkward issues in their relationship, though it was blindly obvious that Edward and Charlie wanted to catch up in private when possible. After a delicious three course meal, Charlie was drunk. I knew she wouldn't have wanted to make it obvious, so when she said "Oh, no! I forgot to water my flowers. Edward can you help me?" It was clear that she intended to speak with him about Scarlett. I wasn't sure whether there even were any flowers in the house. There certainly weren't any to be seen in the living room.

They walked up stairs together holding hands. Charlie seemed to really care about this sanctimonious buffoon marrying Scarlett. When they had gone upstairs, I thought Scarlett and I could have our own private chat.

"Why didn't you tell me you had the clap?" I hissed tactlessly at Scarlett. For once, I saw a human side to this marble deity; she blushed and squirmed uncomfortably in her seat.

"What did that little bitch tell you?" she hissed back. Not even an apology. She had responded to my legitimate anger with venom. My blood was boiling.

"Edward knows you're sleeping around." There was no point in being coy – this was the woman who had shamelessly given me an STD.

"Well, if I didn't get it from Edward who do you think I caught it from?" She glared at me. She didn't know that I knew about her other lover, the one who was able to treat her like crap.

"Well, it wasn't me!" I rasped back at her.

"It could only be you, *darling*." The *darling* was laced with sarcasm. This really got on my wick and I stood up, chest bursting out, and eyes glaring. I'd never wanted to punch a woman before, but fucking hell, if someone needed a punch it was Scarlett. I was itching to hit her, I was burning to kick her to the floor, I needed to feel her stupid nose break; but I refrained, took a deep breath and walked upstairs to the bathroom.

I was so angry I had shocked myself. By the time I got to the toilet I was burning with shame. I sat on the toilet seat with my head in my hands. I nearly lost it, I nearly hit her. My hands were shaking. After a few moments of contemplation I stood up, washed my face with cold water and looked at myself in the mirror.

"Get a grip, Shaun, hold it together" I said out loud. My sad eyes stared back at me, and I forced myself to smile. My eyes didn't smile back, but I felt I could carry on.

As I descended the stairs into the dining room, I was happy to see that Charlie and Edward had returned to their seats. Scarlett seemed completely unperturbed by our sparring moments earlier. On the other hand, Edward looked awkward – he was avoiding eye contact with everyone, staring out of the window and refusing to acknowledge my return. It was strangely quiet.

"Scarlett!" slurred Charlie.

It seemed that Scarlett didn't want to respond.

"Scarlett," said Charlie again.

Scarlett sighed.

"Yes. Charlie. What is it?" Poison was evident in the undertones of Scarlett's voice, but outwardly she smiled and seemed polite.

"You're my friend, Scarlett. You've been my friend for over three years now."

"Yes, I have. Oh, I hadn't realised it has been so long." Scarlett didn't want to be having this conversation.

"If you care about me," Charlie paused and smiled. "If you care about me, you know, as one of your best friends," She stopped again; her head was swaying and her eyes looked vacant.

"Yes?" said Scarlett through gritted teeth.

"If you care about me at all, you need to leave Edward alone."

Before Scarlett could reply, Edward stood up.

"Charlie, this is now the second time you've insulted my fiancé in front of me, and I will not let you get away with it again. I don't know what kind of influence that this – this estate agent here has over you, but you've got to control your drinking. If I was you, I'd run as far away from Shaun as you can."

I couldn't believe my ears, was I getting the blame for this?

Charlie stood up and tears began pouring from her eyes.

"You can't talk to me like that in my own house! GET OUT!"

Edward had already taken Scarlett's hand and led her briskly out of the room. They slammed the door without another word, and then they were gone. Charlie was sobbing; she slammed her hands down on the table screaming, and began softly banging her own head against the table over and over again. I pondered my next move for a moment, then walked over to her, scooped her into my arms and kissed her long and hard. As my tongue entered her mouth, I could taste the salt of her tears. Her face was wet, but I kissed her eyes, her forehead, her cheeks. I stroked her arm, and she kissed me back harder and more passionately than before. It was unreal; I had never imagined her being so forward. We continued in this way for some time until all at once she pulled back from me, still holding the tips of my fingers. She was still crying though, red and radiant she stared into my eyes.

"I don't think you're a bad influence, Shaun. I think you're wonderful."

I held her close in my arms, and knew that she wanted me.

"Pardon?" I said "Could you say that again as I'm not sure I heard the end of that sentence?"

"You're wonderful!" she said.

"Louder" I said.

"You're WONDERFUL" she said.

"Once more, please. I want to make sure I'm getting this right."

"YOU'RE WONDERFUL!"

"What me?"

"Yes you, you idiot."

"An idiot now? Perhaps I'm just wonderfully idiotic."

"No, you're just wonderful, plain and simple."

"Well, thank you! What a compliment."

She was smiling now.

"You're good at cheering me up."

"I bet I know how to cheer you up a little bit more." I put my hand between her legs and began to massage. Jesus Christ, she was wet. She was drunk and wet and she wanted me inside her.

"Come on," she said, biting her lip, "let's go upstairs."

My goodness, what was this sweet music coming from Charlie's lips? She wanted me to sleep with her! I tried to ignore the fact that Charlie was blind-drunk. I tried to ignore the red wine stains on her teeth and lips, and thankfully, I was very successful in this endeavour – I led her upstairs without feeling the least bit guilty. It was only when I got to the top of the stairs and saw a framed photo of Edward and his ex-wife that I was reminded of Scarlett and her God-damned Gonorrhoea, and I have to admit, my mood was more than a little bit dampened. Fucking Scarlett, what a scumbag!

If I used a condom, what were the chances that she would catch it from me? I would be her first, she would know it was me, there would be no getting round it.

"Come on, Shaun!" said Charlie as she clumsily removed her top and her bra. I stiffened at the sight of her, and reached for my wallet to find my condom. It would be a calculated risk, and one that I'd be happy to take. Unfortunately matters became a little more complicated when I fingered the section in my wallet reserved especially for condoms, only to discover it was empty. Damn. How could I be such a fool not to stock up? It was Charlie's fault; if she wasn't always so fucking chaste I would have anticipated the need. I knew that Charlie wouldn't have any; her sober self could never imagine herself in this situation. The calculated risk had already become slightly less calculated, and a bit too much risk for my liking. But she was naked, and she was reclining on the bed calling for me, begging me to "make love to her", and it was incredibly difficult to resist. I jumped onto the bed and kissed her. As she reached down to grab my cock, I began worrying about the way she had begged me: Make love? I couldn't do that in my situation, I could fuck her, I could nail her, I could come inside her, I could screw her, I could break her and I could pound the living Christ out of her, but by definition, it's impossible to make love to someone if you're knowingly giving her Gonorrhoea. Would she ever forgive me?

All of a sudden, I came to my senses and broke away from her.

"Charlie," I whispered.

Charlie leaned forwards trying to kiss me again.

"Charlie, we need to stop this."

"What?" she said, looking genuinely offended.

"You'll regret this in the morning," I said.

"I won't."

"You will, and you'll never forgive me."

"Please, Shaun, I really want this."

"No, you don't."

"Please."

"Look, if you still want it in the morning I promise that I will go ahead."

Charlie looked as if she would begin crying again. Although she was drunk, it had taken every ounce of her confidence to ask me into her bed, and now I had turned her down.

"Babe, this doesn't mean I don't want you."

She didn't reply.

"Look, there are many other things I'm more than happy to do for you."

Without warning, she smirked and pulled me towards her.

"Really?"

"Many WONDERFUL things," I repeated, and slowly, kissing her breasts, then her stomach, and then her inner thighs, I put my face between her legs. Charlie moaned, put her hands onto the back of my head, and opened her legs wider.

Wednesday 9th July 2008

The alarm went off God-awful early; Charlie groaned loudly and leant over me to switch it off, her breasts brushed lightly against my cheek. She didn't say anything, but as reality crept up on her she became tense and embarrassed. The pleasure from the night before had been replaced by a stinking hangover and memories she would have preferred to forget.

"You ok?" I said, stifling a yawn.

"Mah," said Charlie, not committing either way. She stood up without looking at me and donned a towel, covering all the bits that she had been so eager to display the night before.

"Uh, d'you want to talk about anything?" I didn't want her freaking out.

Charlie sighed and looked me up and down without smiling. I could tell she wanted to say something, she had an anxious look on her face and was playing with her fingernails. She didn't say anything. I searched my brain for some way to comfort her but came up short. What was she thinking about? How much did she remember? Was she worried that I might have taken her virginity? Was she going to tell me she loved me? Was she going to tell me she hated me?

In the end she didn't have the courage to say anything. Instead, she walked out of her bedroom to wash and get ready for work. I truly *meant* to say something to her but it was 04:00 AM, and while she was in the shower, the gentle hum of her combi-boiler, and the warmth of the sheets sent me straight back to sleep.

By the time my own alarm went off at 05:30 she was long gone. Although I always preferred sticking to my morning routine whenever possible, I found it very difficult to keep to my regime at Charlie's that morning. It all began to go wrong when I stumbled down to the kitchen, only to discover that she didn't own any kind of real coffee. She had some decaffeinated instant crap, but that was it. After desperately searching all the cupboards for something else, and reading the same label of the decaffeinated stuff over and over, hoping I had been mistaken. I eventually accepted my fate. I boiled the kettle and poured myself a cup hoping it would have a placebo effect on me (it didn't). The huge television was very difficult to switch on, but after pressing a thousand different buttons on five different remote controls it eventually flickered to life. Charlie's Brekkie Time didn't start until 07:30, making it impossible for me to watch without arriving late to the office. On that particular day, I had a very strong desire to watch Charlie's show and decided to throw caution to the wind and remain a little longer. While I was waiting for the show to start, I decided to ready myself so as to be able to slip out of the door at a moment's notice. I ironed my shirt, soiled from the previous day's antics. I hadn't packed any spare clothes as I hadn't realised that I would be staying the night with Charlie; the mere suggestion of such a feat would have been incomprehensible the day before. In a misguided attempt to make myself look presentable, I used one of Charlie's unused disposable razors to shave and cut my face to shreds.

At around 07:00 AM I received a text message from her:

"I wanted 2 speak 2 you this AM but didn't know what to say. Can I cum 2 urs 2night? I enjoyed last night-thanks for being a gent."

I typed out a response:

"But for the grace of God Charlie... Trust me, I wouldn't have chosen to be a gentleman."

Grace of God? Pah, the curse of Scarlett more like.

Suited and booted for work, and with a face that resembled a cheese grater, I sat and watched *Charlie's Brekkie Time*. Nothing out of the ordinary happened, she looked completely unaffected. You wouldn't have been able to tell that she was hung-over and filled with inner turmoil; doubting her faith, all for the love of a disease ridden penis. I had to leave after the first half hour though, so I forced myself to switch off the television and meet the rain-sodden English summer morning.

The day itself was unremarkable; I had two offers placed on a property, both rejected by extremely-nervous vendors. Still, despite not getting accepted, I had begun to try and convince myself that simply getting offers on a property was a good sign. I had to force myself to believe that the property market was on the mend; otherwise I may very well have jumped off of the top of Battersea Power Station.

People all around me were talking about a 10% drop in house prices since the beginning of this sorry tale. We hadn't seen anywhere near that much of a drop in Chelsea, it was just that people were too scared to either make a serious offer, or accept one. Still, the state of the market meant that I wasn't able to devote any time to considering the Charlie situation that day, so I slogged away on me telephone as usual. By the time I left the office it was dark outside, and I had nothing to show for it. It was only as I stepped into the night air that I remembered that Charlie was going to be coming round, and a smile threatened to appear beneath my miserable care-worn countenance. I sent her a quick text and battled my way through the traffic. When I arrived, she was already waiting for me outside.

For a moment I grew concerned, I hadn't exactly left my place in a fit state for company – there had been a huge pile of dirty dishes, clothes strewn over the floor, and a bin that smelt like toxic waste. Thankfully, in my absence, my cleaner had resolved the issue and it was sparkling. When I opened the door to be greeted with the smell of lavender as opposed to a stench worse than death, I breathed a sigh of relief. I walked through my front door, Charlie's hand grasped my own, and again, my heart went out to her.

Once sat down, cup of tea in hand, Charlie struggled to come to terms with what she wanted to say. She looked pale; I guess the drinking the previous evening was finally catching up with her. I thought that I would begin, to help out a little bit.

"I enjoyed last night." I said.

"I know." she said, smiling.

That sounded like something I would say. Cocksure and confident, although I knew that she was feeling quite the opposite.

"I think I've got a drinking problem," she said.

I couldn't help but laugh at this, and she looked a little bit hurt.

"You've been drunk twice the whole time I've met you, I think you're ok."

"But it's not that I drink lots, it's the way I act when I'm drunk. I become a different person."

I could have kissed her for that.

"Everyone does that!" I said, still smiling.

"Not me. I don't like the person I become when I'm drunk."

"What? because you had a go at Edward?"

"No, because of what I'm like with you."

"What do you mean?" I replied, more than a little defensive.

"This isn't to say I didn't enjoy last night, I did! It's just important to me not to do anything stupid until the right time."

"We didn't even do anything!"

Charlie shuddered and rolled her eyes – she was an open book. I could see her wondering what kind of man calls what we did the previous night *nothing.*

"We did, and we would have done a lot more if it hadn't been for... if it hadn't have been for..."

"Me!" I said.

At that moment in time, I was genuinely wounded. I wondered at the audacity of that woman suggesting that I would have taken advantage of her in her drunken state. I actually believed that I was wronged here. Somehow I had conveniently forgotten that it was only the Gonorrhoea that had stopped me. I often get like that when I have my back up against the wall; as a result, I am incredibly good at arguing my corner.

Charlie took a deep breath; I could see that this chat wasn't quite going to plan.

"Corinthians One, Six, 18-20" she whispered to herself like a mad woman. I really couldn't abide that stupid habit. I never knew whether she knew the bible that well inside out (if so, that was just weird) or whether she looked up the passages before speaking to me just to piss me off. For all I knew, they were just words and numbers and didn't mean anything.

"Look, I really like you," she said softly, her eyes meek and framed with dark lashes. My spirits soared high, my thoughts of injured pride dissipated swiftly, and the argument died on my lips.

"I need you in my life, you've been a solid friend and a real hero," she continued as I pretended to blush.

"We're so different though, and before we talk about relationships I *need* you to understand that nothing like last night will ever happen again, unless..." my balls shrunk by 300% as I realised she was going to say "we get married". I stood up, held her in my arms and kissed her on the forehead, distracting her from the sentence she was about to say.

"I know," I said in hushed tones.

Her eyes met mine.

"It won't be easy for you," she said smiling. She couldn't work out whether I was being sincere or not, but something inside her didn't care, she wanted this, and was willing to throw caution to the wind. I don't know what came over me that evening, but I found myself agreeing to all her terms and conditions – alcohol and sexual relations were to be a taboo subject unless we ever wed. While giving my acceptance speech to her demands, I don't think I really considered how difficult being celibate would be for me.

It wasn't just hard, it was nigh on impossible. In some ways, I didn't think she could be serious, I had some hopes that I would manage to break her resolve – that she would eventually give into my wiles. After all, I could have had it ALL on that previous night. Unfortunately this turned out not to be the case; from that day forwards, she refused any sexual relations beyond heavy petting – something that might be considered risqué in a public swimming pool – but ultimately leading to a rather unsatisfying relationship on my side. Not a drop of drink touched her lips either, so I was unable to awake that passionate harpy that she kept locked deep within her.

The first few weeks of our relationship I was able to fain a respect for her decision. I had been placed on a course of antibiotics to rid me of my STD and was forced to abstain from all alcohol. Charlie had never seen me go for two weeks straight without alcohol, and I could tell that she was impressed with how sensitive I was to her plight. Although I do have a degree of self-control, two weeks of absolute sobriety and celibacy is enough to drive anyone insane. At the end of the two-weeks I celebrated my clean bill of health with a turbulent descent from saintliness into true debauchery. I must have blown close to £2000 on tits, arse and vintage Champagne in the local strip-club. Stupidly, I had told Charlie that I would meet her for lunch the following day. I walked through her door with bags under my eyes, a furry tongue, and the stench of whiskey emanating from my pores – A look of fierce disappointment swept across Charlie's face when she saw me.

Although my night on the town gave me some respite, it was a matter of days before the gut-wrenching sexual frustration was on me again. Charlie's expectations on what a man should abstain from before marriage were completely unacceptable – here is the complete compendium:

1. Anal sex.
2. Full Penetration.
3. Golden showers.
4. Cunnilingus.
5. Blow-jobs.
6. Tit wanks.
7. Pornography.
8. Masturbation while in each other's presence.
9. Mutual masturbation.
10. Nipple Twisting (although a certain degree of groping was acceptable).
11. Sensual massages (I suspect this was a result of my wandering hands after the last massage I gave her).
12. Nudity in front of each other.
13. Phone sex.
14. Touching her naked breasts, or slipping my hand under her bra.
15. Infidelity.

I know for a fact that most Christians will allow one or more of the above into their bedroom before their wedding night, but Charlie's Church were a bunch of arseholes and forced their flock to be devoid of all sense in their devoutness to the Lord.

Although I dearly tried to accept some of these rules, I have to admit that I found it a completely impractical way of life. Celibacy is enough to turn anyone into a complete animal. After only a few weeks of frustration, I found that Charlie could dress in the most frumpy and boring of outfits, but still be unrelentingly arousing to me – the sight of her uncrossing her legs in a tight skirt or the hint of an erect nipple beneath a blouse would send me into spasms of desire. I became depraved; although there was a complete ban on phone sex, I found myself having a one-sided type of phone sex in which she was speaking to me about her day, and I was masturbating furiously at the sound of her voice. On other occasions, I would sit in her bed in the morning, smelling the perfume on her sheets, watching her on television and ejaculate onto her pillow. How can it be appropriate to abstain from sex if it turns you into a sexual deviant like that? It's not as if I could easily head out and sleep with a random anymore either. Although I was not in the public eye, I was spending enough time with Charlie that it was entirely possible for the tabloids to begin to take an interest. I was paranoid that the story of our relationship would break into the news accompanied by several stories about me cheating on her. Eventually I came crawling back on my hands and knees to Scarlett knowing that she would be completely discreet. It had taken three months of torture before I was desperate enough to swallow my pride and beg for her forgiveness. Begrudgingly, she accepted me into her bed. I found it rather grating that she insisted I wore a condom; trust me, there was no way I was going anywhere near that vacuum of a vagina without a strong layer of latex armour. Despite my extra-thick rubber shield I came in about five seconds on our first ride. However, so bunged up was I with litres of sperm and kilowatts of sexual tension that I nailed the living Christ out of her. We fucked over and over again, and then again and again and again. By the end of the day we were both sore and exhausted, and I was surprised that Scarlett's legs hadn't cramped permanently open.

I never found out first-hand what went on between Edward and Charlie on the night of Charlie's dinner party, though I was curious. I raised the subject with Scarlett one afternoon after one of our weekend "gym" sessions. As it turned out, it wasn't all that interesting a story. She and Edward had never been in an exclusive relationship while he had a wife. Although he was understandably upset by contracting an STD from his fiancé, it wasn't all that difficult to explain away with a legitimate affair prior to their engagement. Still, I don't think he liked the idea of her sleeping with someone else even if it was technically allowed. For a few days he had refused to forgive her, he had slept at his office and threatened to call off the wedding. He had even threatened to go back to his former wife. Un-phased, Scarlett had managed to convince Edward of her version of events with the use of a Red-riding Hood costume and a surprise visit to his office in the dead of night. Predictably, Charlie had attempted to talk sense into Edward that night, but by then it was too late, Edward was once again entranced. Since her relationship with Edward had sprouted, Scarlett had grown to hate Charlie. She despised her with every ounce of her being; she was taking Charlie's (justified) fears about how faithful Scarlett may or may not be to heart.

"I always found her annoying...." she said to me one day, puffing hard on a post-coital cigarette and exhaling as if it were venom "...such a bloody goody-two-shoes."

It was rare that Scarlett talked to me about anything honestly. Typically she was a bundle of lies and secrets all hidden behind each other, impossible to unravel. On this occasion, I could tell that Charlie's constant meddling into Edward's life was really getting to her. She stood up naked, and strolled over to my bedroom window looking through the raindrops clinging to the double-glazing, watching the grey world beyond. I wondered whether any of my neighbours could see her, this blond bombshell with perfect tits gazing out to the sky. I hoped not, I was sure that some of them suspected I was in a relationship with Charlie and I didn't want any stories getting around.

"It's the only reason I'm still fucking you."

As she said this, she stubbed out her cigarette on my window sill burning a dark hole in the white paint. "I hate that bitch. I want her to give up her virginity to a cunt like you. It's worth it just to have the satisfaction she's so stupid."

I didn't react to this, I didn't care. In fact, I fucked Scarlett all the harder for it, she was being honest with me and I loved it.

<u>August-November 2008</u>

For a while, I thought my journey was over. Although my scheme hadn't gone entirely to plan, my manipulations had given me a celebrity (of sorts). She wasn't a superstar, but still, she was kind, gentle and beautiful. It was quite nice walking down the street with her, people would do a double take and realise that it was Charlie Ekells beside me. They never seemed all that star-struck, but I knew that at some point someone would have something close to the following conversation:

"Oh, guess who I saw today."

"Who?"

"That girl from the breakfast show."

"Who?"

"You know, that fit one that does Sunday Sermon."

"Oh, you mean urrr, what's her name, you mean Charlie Ekells?"

"Yes that's the one."

"What was she doing?"

"Walking down the street"

"Oh."

*** *Conversation About Charlie Ends* ***

Not exactly the naked excitement that was engendered when someone saw Elisha hanging off my arm, but still, it was nice to know that she was in the public eye.

It's funny how quickly your life passes by once you are in a regular pattern: Work, Charlie three nights a week, and Scarlett at the weekends. Summer and Autumn quickly disappeared in a haze of work. Huge news stories – The Beijing Olympics, Lehman brothers filing for bankruptcy – it all washed over me barely noticed. I wouldn't call myself particularly happy over this point in time, nor was I particularly unhappy. I plodded on through my routine and my life ebbed along with complete indifference.

All things considered, my relationship with Charlie was a slow-burner. She dared not tell her family about her relationship with me – Edward and Abz had both indicated to her that they didn't like me – and Charlie, who was trying to make amends with Edward, was petrified of rocking the boat. Scarlett knew what was going on, of course, but as far as Charlie was concerned, Scarlett knew as much as Edward. Her brother, the famous Damien Woland was nowhere to be seen. He never visited, he didn't call; he seemingly made no effort at all to keep in touch with his sister. I think that this worried Charlie more than she let on.

"He's such a free spirit…" she said to me once of her brother "… he'll speak to me when he wants to."

I wasn't sure whether this hands-off attitude to his sister could fit into my own definition of someone who is a free spirit, but I could tell that Charlie didn't want to go into detail. Their relationship was clearly dysfunctional, and it's hardly surprising considering their family history. I guess the word '*family*', which in a normal household has so many positive connotations attached to it, becomes the opposite in their situation. Charlie never spoke about her real mother and father, and it would have been easy to assume Edward was her real brother, and his parents, her natural born parents.

Gone were the days when Damien and Charlie would show up to a film premier together arm in arm. Damien, whose stardom had long surpassed his sisters, would show up on the red carpet with a different skank clambering at his chest. I respected the man; he knew what he wanted, and he was famous and wealthy enough to get it. Why hold back? Charlie would never comment on his choice of girlfriend – porn-stars, models, ex call-girls – but whenever I commented on a story concerning him in *A-List*, her lips would press tightly together, she would frown, and be in ill-spirits for the rest of the day.

Meanwhile, my own family were excited to find out that I was close friends with Charlie, and I even took her down to visit my parents and sisters one weekend. Surprisingly, my dad was completely star-struck, and even deigned to ask her for an autograph. He told her that he was going to donate it as a prize at the local fete, but I knew that it was so that he could show off to his mates down the pub. Charlie was so worried about her reputation being soiled, and didn't want to be seen with more than one man on her arm in the public eye, that she wouldn't even let me hold her hand if we were walking along a quiet road with nobody else in sight. So, although I wanted to tell everyone about us, Charlie wouldn't let me (regardless, I think my mum figured it out). Behind closed doors, she gave her heart to me, and I gave some of mine back. If it wasn't for this whole 'no sex' thing, I truly believe that I would have stayed 100% faithful to Charlie.

After some time I even stopped checking for news on Elisha, who had dropped out of the public eye during her pregnancy. After months of my routine, I was feeling comfortable in my situation, and was even toying with the idea of breaking off everything with Scarlett, to truly devote myself to Charlie. I was, after all, rather fond of Charlie, and the guilt and shame were beginning to weigh upon my conscience. It seemed inevitable that my life would be tied to hers, and I had finally begun to acknowledge this. My life would have probably continued down this apathetic route, were it not for one cold weekend morning in late November:

I spent the Friday night with Charlie. Clearly, this didn't mean what one may hope to happen, happened; instead, we shared the bed while I wore some blue stripy pyjamas she had bought me. I usually sleep naked, and the sexual frustration coupled with the unusual and uncomfortable feeling of wearing pyjamas resulted in a very poor night's sleep. The trousers would get caught around my enormous erection, they would ride up and cut my ball sack in two and I would feel hopelessly trapped. You'd think that I would get used to it, but I never did. The claustrophobia inducing garments were always waiting for me, folded up on the pillow of her bed, and despite feeling completely emasculated, I always put them on. This pyjama issue (and the sex thing) was probably why I was only 'toying' with the idea of giving up Scarlett. I couldn't think of anything more pointlessly harrowing than a lifetime of wearing pyjamas in bed.

At some point in the early hours of morning, the door-bell must have sounded, but I was deep in my duvet cocoon, in my pyjama-ridden uneasy sleep. Either I didn't hear it, or I ignored it, but Charlie rose before me (presumably to answer the doorbell). I had grown so used to her rising before me, due to her working hours, that I didn't even notice her absence. I carried on trying in vain to get some proper sleep, but at some point, I cracked and realised that the pyjamas had won the most recent skirmish in our on-going war, and successfully robbed me of a decent night's kip, again. On that particular morning, I had been rather stubborn and put up a pretty strong fight, so by the time I emerged from the combat zone it was getting close to midday. As I rose, a small piece of paper fell off the empty pillow next to me. I assumed that it was some inane message from Charlie telling me something boring about love, or God, or where she had gone; and considering how far the pyjamas had ridden up my crotch, I couldn't be bothered to bend down to pick it up. I ignored the message, and pattered down to the kitchen, yawning and looking down at my feet. Still stretching and wiping the sleep from my eyes, I walked over to the fridge to grab a bite to eat – it was here that I noticed a wedding invitation pinned to Charlie's fridge door with a "*Jesus Loves You*" fridge magnet.

"We have the pleasure of inviting Miss Charlie Ekells & guest to the wedding of Mr Edward Subran and Miss Scarlett Smith on May 30th 2009"

I pondered why Charlie had not discussed this invitation with me the night before, and reread the message, wondering whether she would deign to let me accompany her as her plus one.

"Do you think that you could find it in your heart to forgive me for not inviting you?" Scarlett's voice purred playfully behind me. I jumped in surprise, the invitation dropped to the floor.

"Scarlett! What are you doing here?" I said.

Scarlett was resting nonchalantly on the sofa, her feet up on a foot-rest, toes pointing forwards. Her taut calf-muscles looked so smooth, so soft, and brown and enticing that when I walked over to her I couldn't help but crouch down to give them a little squeeze.

"I popped round to bring the wedding invite in person, Edward thought it would help," she said.

"Have you two made up then?" I said, looking around. Charlie was nowhere to be seen.

"Of sorts."

"What do you mean?"

"Edward's forgiven her, and she's given us her blessing, but I still think she's a bitch."

"So, where is she?"

"She's gone out to get some bacon and milk."

I smiled and moved my hand up to her inner thigh.

"Stop being an idiot Shaun, she'll be back in a couple of minutes."

"I was only joking," I lied. I took my hand away and placed it in my pocket in an attempt at simultaneously hiding my erection and making room for it in my tight pyjama trousers. I felt a little stupid standing in front of her wearing them; but she didn't bother to comment.

"So you're not inviting me then?" I bleated stupidly, needing further affirmation that she was serious.

"No, Edward's taken a bit of a dislike to you. And besides, you're not exactly someone I'd want there either."

I was about to add a rebuttal, but at this point, the faint sound of keys jangling outside could be heard, the door opened and Charlie appeared with two carrier bags packed full of breakfast supplies. She looked at me, and then at Scarlett.

"Oh!" she said and turned bright red. "Shaun, you're up, didn't you get my message?"

I thought back to the small slip of paper that had fallen off the bedside table when I got out of bed. I shrugged my shoulders, I could imagine it now "*Hi Darling, don't come downstairs! Scarlett's come round for breakfast!*"

"Scarlett, I err I ummm," stammered Charlie.

"Relax babe, your secret's safe with me." In reality, Scarlett had already known about my relationship with Charlie and seemed a little bored by Charlie's reaction.

"Scarlett, I think you should know that me and Shaun are really happy together, it's beginning to get quite serious and…"

"Look, I said your secret's safe" snapped Scarlett, cutting Charlie off short. I knew she was uninterested in Charlie's explanations, and didn't make any kind of attempt to feign surprise. Really, the only emotion she showed was contempt and disinterest. Charlie looked a little shell-shocked, and didn't bother continuing.

"Oh, OK." She replied, a little taken aback. She began to rifle through the blue shopping bags putting the breakfast ingredients onto the table-top. In the meantime, I sauntered away from them both and switched on the television. Flicking through the different channels, I couldn't find anything on except adverts. I sighed in frustration, thinking back to my childhood where we only had 4 channels. We had adverts back then too, but they didn't insert five minutes of adverts into every 30 seconds of viewing. Modern television, if one doesn't have the ability to fast-forward through the constant tirade of irritating songs and hype about gadgets nobody would ever use, is a thoroughly frustrating experience.

The two women in my life nattered away behind me, initially in forced and awkward sentences, but after a while, in fluid friendly monologues. Scarlett put on a whole song and dance, expressing the intention to rekindle their lost friendship. Charlie, the naïve fool, seemed to be lapping it all up and promised the same in return. I found myself wondering whether the two of them had ever truly been friends, or whether Scarlett had been putting on this show right from the start. Wealthy, naïve, and famous – no wonder Scarlett was able to wrap Charlie around her little finger.

Then all of a sudden, I heard something that set my heart racing:

"You'll also have a chance to catch up with that elusive brother of yours..." said Scarlett, glowing, "I posted his invite yesterday.

With that, something inside me cracked, and my dream of a lifetime with Charlie was buried beneath the sand. Why was I settling for a banal life? Why not reach for the stars?

Damien Woland was coming to the wedding.

God Damn, what was I doing wasting my time with Charlie?

God Damn, I needed to be rid of her.

God Damn, I still had a shot at Elisha.

Step 5: Damien Woland

<u>December 2008</u>

Emotionally, I had finally decided Charlie was not my journey's end, and one day soon, I would need to leave her. Therefore, I began to prepare myself for the inevitable. I was too fond of Charlie to make such a cold and calculating decision easily, more than anyone on my journey, I cared for her the most. I cursed myself for being such a fool; I shouldn't have allowed this to happen. The plan would have worked so much better if we had only remained friends. I *should* have been able to remain friends with her, but now that was impossible.

I find it hard to explain how I knew I was making the right decision – I had no logical reason to think I would actually end up married to Elisha. I had something good(ish) going with Charlie, and at the time I felt a little bit of an idiot to want her gone, but I was obsessed. Elisha was my goal, and that clawing, itching feeling I got in my stomach was nagging away at me. I don't like giving up on any of the challenges I set myself, and Elisha was the direst of those challenges – nigh on impossible, but with the heftiest reward. With my career in the gutter, I couldn't resist.

Rendering myself impervious to Charlie's charm was difficult; but over time, I was relatively successful in that endeavour. Initially, I found it heart-breaking; Charlie would reach out to me over and over again and I would not allow myself reach back. I forced myself to concentrate on the negatives of our relationship: the chastity, the church, the teetotalism, the mundane life we lived. Over time, it was all I could think about, and I wondered how I could ever have part-convinced myself that I might love her. Strategically, it was important that I continued to play the part of the devoted boyfriend, but inside, I grew empty.

Once I had peeled my affections away, rinsed them off my skin and down a black hole, I began to find our relationship a little vexing. It's a difficult thing – being affectionate to someone you don't want to be with. I hadn't technically accomplished my next step up the social ladder yet. Damien Woland was still untouchable, and if I ever wanted to meet him, I needed to stay glued to Charlie. I was obliged to pretend that I still felt something for her. I was ready to move on, but was stuck and drowning somewhere I didn't want to be. Charlie was such a gentle soul, so sensitive to my feelings, I was sure she'd pick up on it, but she didn't. Perhaps she didn't want to see me for who I was. She was in love with me, and was blind to the fact that I was planning to break her heart.

We spent Christmas together. Charlie made such an effort over me – and it was embarrassing how little effort I put in. We spent it at my place, as it was closer to the church. She forced me to go to midnight mass on Christmas Eve. I don't know what she expected from me, but I do know that she didn't expect me to turn up drunk. Personally, I wonder how anyone can be expected to turn up anywhere sober on Christmas Eve, even if it is to a Church. I think she was particularly irritated at me for eating some Dolly Mixtures stuck on cocktail sticks, which, for some unfathomable reason, were inserted into a load of oranges she was handing out to children as they entered. I stood with her, swaying from side to side, nibbling away and groping her bottom in front of that wanker of a priest. The last few children to collect the Oranges from her began to cry when they realised that their dolly mixtures had been eaten by somebody else. Charlie didn't say anything, but her lips grew tight, like they usually did when Scarlett was around.

The following morning wasn't much better. I knew that she had high hopes for us that Christmas morning. She wanted us to wake up early and exchange gifts, have a Champagne breakfast, to attend the early church service together, and possibly go on a small walk. I didn't go to the church service. I was so hung-over that I had trouble just standing, let alone making my way to that God forsaken house of God. Breakfast was also out of the question, my stomach was too unsettled. So I stayed in bed, and she, looking extremely hurt by my indifference, went to the church on her own.

I had recovered by the time she got back, and cringed as I looked at the vast array of presents underneath the Christmas tree, all for me. So many gifts, with so much thought and detail into each and every one of them. She gave me some cufflinks with my initials engraved in them, a pair of loafers, a bottle of *Jura*, a waistcoat, a new tie, a pedometer, and a monthly subscription to *A-List* magazine (to start when my previous subscription ran out). Worst of all though, she bought me a whole DVD collection of Elisha Cicero films – she smiled when I opened them and said "I know you have a bit of a thing for her!" I had not thought I had ever even mentioned Elisha Cicero in front of Charlie, but I must have, and on more than one occasion. In contrast to this, I got Charlie a clock for her kitchen wall and a £50 M&S Gift Voucher. She pretended not to be disappointed, but I knew that she was.

Damien rang her in the afternoon after months of silence. She smiled when she saw his name appear on her phone, and walked into another room to speak with him. Curious, I pressed my ear against the door to listen. What I heard was not the standard conversation one may expect to hear on Christmas Day:

"Merry Christmas D! How are you?" She answered the phone so cheerfully, but then there was a moment of silence, and all the Christmas cheer was sucked from her. I couldn't hear what he said to her, but all of a sudden she was sobbing. She let out an ear piercing scream.

"You're drunk!"

And then she was arguing with him.

"What's wrong with you?... No...No...Don't be so rude...NO!...If you say that one more time I'm putting the phone down!...I said once more!.... now apologise or I'm going...ok...ok...ok... now what's happened then?...She what?...that doesn't surprise me...so what have you done?...no don't worry, you know how I feel about you and Bianca....Yes I have!...I've told you what I thought of her before and it doesn't surprise me... What have you done to her?...Where is she now?... Is she ok?...that was stupid of you...No.. listen to me D you have to leave her alone...No, you need to leave her alone now...Calm down...No...Calm down.. Ok..Please don't say that D, I love you. You know I love you...No my boyfriend's here, I wouldn't be able to leave him alone on Christmas day...No, I can't....Sorry sweetheart I can't...Drink some water, and please calm down....Please, I love you....Don't say that, I know you don't mean it...Please...ok...are you going to be ok?...ok, sleep well...Merry Christmas."

It was the closest I had ever gotten to a superstar, and I was on the wrong end of an argument. I didn't find out what Damien had been so angry about until months later, but it was my first opportunity to observe his life from afar – I observed that he was most likely a selfish, immature, idiot.

January 2009

Since she had set off for her travels in July, Polly had been sending me the worst conceivable emails. She copied in everyone she had ever met and always began her email with the following phrase:

"*TO ALL MY LOVELY BRITS!!!!!!!!!!!!!!!!!!*"

Always in capital letters with an overabundance of exclamation marks.

My realisation at how tiresome these emails would be dawned on me the first line of the first email she sent:

"Hey peeps! Missing you already! Stuck in the airport waiting for my plane to leave and can't stop thinking about all the friends I'm leaving behind!"

First of all, I hate anyone who uses the word *'peeps'* without irony, and second of all, she was only going away for a couple of months. It wasn't as if she was never going to be seeing these so called *'lovely people'* ever again. She then went on to recount everything she would miss about life in the UK in excruciating detail – the list was unbelievably formulaic and clichéd, it included everything you'd expect a 'Brit abroad' to say – bacon sandwiches, Primark, pubs, marmite, even Eastenders. Browsing through her moronic prose made me irritable and I grew increasingly frustrated that I'd even bothered opening it. She made a list of everything she was looking forward to, where she was going, and what her itinerary was. I couldn't help but be reminded what a dull and needy person she was, the email went on for over 1000 words

Unfortunately that wasn't the end of it, in fact, it got worse. She would send me pointless updates every couple of weeks, saying exactly what she had done and how much she enjoyed it. I already knew where she was going, because of the initial itinerary sent out, and she *always* enjoyed it. I found myself wishing that once, just once, she would tell us how miserable she was. If the email was late she would apologise for not being in touch. I wondered how she found the time to write such long emails. She must have been spending 90% of her time in internet cafés, the rest of her holiday was just a filler to make her visits to the internet cafés worthwhile. After a short stay in India, she travelled the length and breadth of New Zealand, along the West Coast of Australia and finally the northern cities of the USA.

No matter her location, her emails were long and boring without exception, and I soon began deleting them as soon as they entered my inbox. Finally, on the 15th of

January I received an email with the title: *"HOMECOMING!!!!"*

I breathed a sigh of relief: her world tour of internet cafes was coming to an end. I deleted the email without reading it, hoping that my senses wouldn't be accosted by her drivel again.

Sadly, seven days after her email, she called me at work. This is how the conversation went:

Me: Good morning, *Fisher and Irving* Chelsea, how can I help?"

Polly: "It's me."

Me: "Um?" (I hadn't seen her for 6 months and she thought I'd know who it was, the stupid bitch).

Polly: "It's Polly."

Me: "Oh, it's you." (I tried to sound as unenthusiastic as possible when I said this).

Polly: "I'm back!"

Me: "So I gather, yes."

Polly: "So, do you want to meet up?"

Me: "No."

Polly: "For fuck's sake, I thought you may have grown up now?"

Me: "You've only been gone a few months."

Polly: "Are you not going to even bother talking to me like a human being?"

Me: "No."

Polly: "God, Shaun, do you have to?"

Me: "Yes."

Polly: "Look, I wanted to catch up with you and have a chat about us, but I can see now that it would just be waste of breath."

Me: "Ok, so why are you still on the phone?"

Polly: "God, Shaun! Stop it! I want to know about Terry, how is he?"

Me: "How should I know?"

Polly: "He says he's seen a lot of you?" (This sent a shiver down my spine. Seeing a lot of me? I hadn't seen or heard from him since he threatened my life via voicemail).

Me: "Sorry? What did Terry say?"

Polly: "He won't see me, but he's been emailing me and said that you've seen each other a lot since I left."

Me: "What? Why would he say that?"

Polly: "Are you being deliberately obtuse?"

Me: "No, but it's a lie."

Polly: "What's a lie?"

Me: "Terry, I haven't seen him since you left."

Polly: "Really?"

Me: "Yes, really."

Polly: "I don't know what to do with him. He seems to really have gone off the rails since we broke up. Can you call him?"

Me: "Me? No."

Polly: "Look, I think something's seriously wrong with him. His email says that you're best friends again."

Me: "I don't want to have anything to do with him."

Polly: "Ok, I'm going to forward you his email. Read it at least, something really weird is happening and I think you need to sort it out."

Me: "I don't want anything to do with either of you, but you keep on calling me."

Polly: "For God's sake. He's already tried to kill himself once because of you, and now he's acting weirdly. Can't you just try and sort something out?"

Me: "Why do I always get the blame for these things? He was your fucking boyfriend. You're the one that cheated on him. Not me."

Polly: "Just read the fucking email."

Me: "Only if you stop trying to speak to me all the time."

Polly: "This is going nowhere. Read the email, and get over yourself you prick."

She hung up

When the phone disconnected, the office was so quiet you could hear a pin drop. Everyone had stopped what they were doing in order to listen to my domestic problems. I felt a slight pang of shame, especially when everyone started laughing and applauding.

"You've got such a way with women, Shaun!" Guy shouted across the office.

"Yes, he's a regular Casanova!" jeered some cockney arsehole in the Lettings department.

It eventually died down, and everyone else went back to their work. I on the other hand forced myself to read the email that Polly had forwarded on to me. This is what it said:

From: Terry.Taylor
Sent: 23 January 2009 15:09
To: Polly.Edant19922883
Subject: RE: HOMECOMING!!!!

Polly

Sorry I didn't want to come to your party. I dont want you in my life you walked all over me and you cant expect me to pretend that where friends just because your abroad. I amm busy so busy with work since you went on you travels Ive no time to dwell on us. Why didn't you love me like i loved you? Why did you leave me for Shaun? Shaun doesn;t even want you he hates you Shaun's really good I'm in London so much i see him almost every day. Hes really happy and has a new girlfriend. Charlie Ekells from TV I bet you didnt expect Shaun to move that quickly did you? You cant expect everyone to hang

around waiting for you. Now your back dont come near me i don't want to see you again you hurt me and ruined my life.
Terry

I had always assumed that, being a successful television producer, Terry would have a reasonable grasp of the English language. It made absolutely no sense to me why he wrote like a child with learning difficulties. I knew he was miserable, but, how could someone become successful in business without knowing that the abbreviated form of 'we are' is not 'where'? How can someone who doesn't know how to use an apostrophe be expected to manage anyone older than five years old? Either Terry's form of depression had caused him to forget these basic forms of communication, or I was getting a larger insight into the reason he had been unemployed for so long. The email proved to me beyond reasonable doubt that Terry was an imbecile. Unfortunately, despite his poor grammar, the email didn't fail to have an impact. In Charlie's bed that night, as I lay, suffocating in my pyjamas, Terry's email rattled its' way around my mind. How the hell did Terry know about Charlie?

Saturday 24th January 2009

Charlie woke me up at the crack of dawn with a large cup of coffee. She looked a little uncomfortable perched on the end of the bed, and for one awful moment I thought that she was going to break up with me.

"Shaun..." she said gently, while my heartbeat thundered in my ears."...I'm not going to be able to see you for a couple of weeks."

My relief was palpable as I realised this was something that she was worrying about unnecessarily. It was a strange, but not unappealing habit of hers. She had a way of making herself believe that she was a villain even if whatever she was contemplating doing was completely innocuous.

"Huh? How come?" I replied, happy that I wasn't being given the boot.

"Damien's coming to stay for a while. He's in a spot of bother and he needs me."

"Oh, I don't mind. I'm sure I'll be able to help," I said, excitement mounting.

"That's really sweet of you to offer, honey, but you don't know Damien. When he's out of sorts he can be a real pain in the neck."

"Trust me, I won't mind."

"No, trust me, he will. He's really private about these kinds of things. He hates anybody to know he has any weaknesses."

"But, I could take him out. Show him a good time."

"Trust me, that's not what he needs. Damien has people showing him a good time a bit too much nowadays. He needs rest."

"But I'd really like to meet him."

"Oh honey, I know you would, but Damien's quite a complex individual. When he gets in these dark moods, he doesn't want to meet anyone. He'll end up hating you."

"Really?"

"Yes, and that's the last thing I'd want. You're important to me, and if Damien meets you in one of his dark moods he won't like you. I know what he's like. He doesn't change his mind once he's decided he hates you."

"I don't think he'll..."

"He will. I know him, and he can be so difficult sometimes. I don't want the two men I love to be enemies." She was becoming slightly hysterical, so sure was she that he would hate me if I forced her to introduce me. This wasn't something I wanted either, so decided not to push the matter. Still, I wouldn't let a golden opportunity like this pass me by.

"Fine," I said, attempting to sound hurt and annoyed.

"What is it?" she replied, as always, playing straight into it.

"I don't know why we bother with all this," holding my cards close to my chest now.

"With what? With us?" She was the one sounding hurt now.

"You never want to tell anyone about me. You don't trust me with any of your family."

"Shaun, I do! I do."

"Then introduce me to your brother then."

"I can't. He's so awful when he's like this, you don't understand."

"Well, it's the same thing over and over again. You're so scared to tell anyone about us, you can't see that you're strangling this relationship."

"Shaun, you just don't understand what he's like."

"Ok, fine, it's not the right time to meet him, but will there EVER be a good time to meet him?"

"Of course there will be. We've got our whole lives together."

"It doesn't feel that way."

"Shaun, you know I love you. Please believe I *will* introduce you, but it's got to be at the right time."

"Always excuses! To me it doesn't feel like there will ever be a '*right*' time."

"Please, Shaun. I'll make sure the next time I see him you're invited."

"Well, I know that's a load of bullshit already."

"What? How can you say that?"

"Edward's wedding? I know for a fact that you'll be seeing Damien then and you haven't invited me."

"Oh, Shaun, sweetheart. Edward's wedding isn't a good time, you know what he thinks of you, and things are difficult enough between me and him already."

"It's never a good time! Edward doesn't give a shit that you don't like Scarlett, why should you care what he thinks?"

"Fine, OK, I get your point. I'm sorry. I should have asked you as soon as I got the invite."

"So you're bringing me to the wedding?"

"Yes."

"Ok," I kissed her hand. "Sorry for getting angry."

"It's OK. I shouldn't be keeping you hidden from my family."

"When's Damien coming?"

"Tomorrow night. Sorry it's such short notice. He only called me this morning to tell me."

"What he called you already? It's six AM?"

"He needs me Shaun."

"OK, no problem. Maybe I'll see you tonight?"

"Yes, that would be nice."

"I'm supposed to be going out for Guy's birthday, but I'll see what I can do to get out of it for you." It was a lie – I couldn't be bothered to commit to another night with her. I kissed her on the cheek and got ready for work. I could wait another couple of months to meet Damien if it meant catching him in a good mood and on friendly terms.

On my way to work, my mind drifted back to Terry, and the fact that it seemed that he might be stalking me. I decided that I would need to confront him. The problem was that I had no idea where he was currently living, and when I called the number 'Terry (Mental Don't Answer)', I was given a recorded voice telling me that the number I had dialled had not been recognised – I can only guess that his phone had been disconnected. Without any other options available to me, I emailed him:

From: Shaun.Valfierno
Sent: 24 January 2009 09:13
To: Terry.Taylor
Subject: RE: HOMECOMING!!!!

Terry, Call me. We need to talk.
Shaun.

I was working that Saturday, so there was very little I could do beyond that until 17:30, which arrived without any response from Terry. I decided that it would not be wise to dwell on him for too long, and made a conscious effort to arrange nefarious night-time activities to keep me occupied. I began to dial Charlie's number, but paused halfway through; I couldn't cope with another dull night in with her in front of the TV, and I couldn't face being pressured into going to the church the following morning. Instead, I called Scarlett. Thankfully Edward was out that evening. She had been planning on having some drinks with the girls, but I persuaded her that it would be much more fun to spend the night with me.

On my way home, I popped into the supermarket to grab some drinks for myself and Scarlett. I browsed the magazine and newspaper section for a while. Something utterly depressing headlined the majority of the tabloids – Elisha had given birth to a healthy baby boy. I purchased a copy of all the newspapers that made reference to the story, and read each of them in my car. I didn't let it bother me too much, I had known that it was coming for quite some time, but I was disappointed that she seemed so happy in her current situation. If she had appeared at all uneasy, or discontent, I would have felt a lot more confident in my plan. As it stood, the only way to get her into my bed would be to convince her to leave the father of her child – not an easy task. Most of the reports were the same; Benedict-Junior Latterburn-Cicero had been born at 23:27, weighing in at 8lbs on the dot. Both mother and son were said to be healthy, the father (Benedict Senior) was quoted as being '*the happiest man alive*'. He was seen posing for the cameras, both thumbs up, grinning like an idiot. I hated the smarmy git. I hated his stupid face, and his stupid thumbs, his stupid legs, and his stupid sunglasses. I hated absolutely everything about him.

Scarlett visited me that evening, but it did nothing to improve my mood. She was a selfish and vain person, and I realised that she, much like Charlie, meant nothing to me. She too was now a weight dragging me back down and keeping me from reaching my ultimate goal. She stayed until 21:00, at which point, she made her usual hasty departure, back home to her make-believe life as a happily engaged woman. I was sick with myself for running back to her over and over again. I needed to cast her off along with Polly, Terry and Charlie. I was frustrated that I didn't have the strength just to move on from these annoying people. Hopefully, once I had managed to meet Damien, I could cast them all off once and for all.

Terry didn't get back to me for a long time, and by the time he did, it didn't matter that he'd been stalking me. By that time, he had become a danger only to himself.

February 2009

I spent my freedom alternating between the pubs and clubs of the Kings Road, pissing all my hard earned money up the wall. Guy was my usual partner in crime; he was very happy (to put it in his own words) that I had finally emerged from under whatever rock I had been hiding. It was absolute bliss, and I can't say that I missed Charlie in the slightest; it was nice to get away from her.

Damien stayed with Charlie for over two weeks. She called me in the morning every day telling me that she loved me and missed me, a confidence booster if there ever was one. She would always whisper, as if she felt guilty for even being on the phone to me. I really couldn't understand what all the secrecy was all about. The relationship between brother and sister seemed so strange it was bordering on sinister.

However, the greatest benefit that came about from Damien's visit was that when it was over, Charlie felt so guilty about our fight on the night preceding his arrival that not only did she invite me to Scarlett's wedding, she also procured some tickets to a film prémiere of the blockbuster action film 'Undeniable'. Unfortunately, it wasn't something that starred either Damien or Elisha, but still, it was better than a kick in the teeth, and, God bless her, naïve misguided fool, she was trying.

Charlie met me in the afternoon of Sunday the 8th of February. She came to my flat following church. Immediately, I could tell that something had seriously unsettled her mind. When she saw me, she burst into tears and the force of her running into my arms knocked the wind out of me. Sobs racked through her body, and within no time at all, my shoulder was wet through with her tears.

"What's up, honey?"

She shook her head.

"It's OK, you can tell me"

She shook her head again; it seemed that she was unable to speak.

"Is it Damien?"

"Shaun, please, it's so awful, I don't want to talk about it."

"You know you can talk to me."

"Yes, I know. But, I can't, I promised." she sniffled.

"Shaun?"

"Yes?"

"Please tell me I can trust you?" she begged, and I knew that she wasn't talking about her secret.

"You can trust me." I lied.

Wednesday March 11th 2009

Charlie remained permanently on the verge of tears following her brother's departure back to the USA. She grew overly sensitive, and, if I'm honest, it became a complete chore to be around her. She was unusually selfish and introverted. Our conversations became almost exclusively one-sided, her only responses being a series of uncaring and vacant nonsenses. Every now and then, out of sheer irritation, I would ask her a direct question, and she would be forced to admit that she hadn't listened to a word of what I was saying. I always knew when she was doing it: mouth set, brows furrowed, eyes glazed, and the simple act of blinking became a process that she seemed incapable of conducting without great effort. A less confident individual may have attributed this sudden disinterest in my daily affairs as an indication of increasing disinterest in me. I, on the other hand, knew beyond a shade of doubt, that her brother had said or done something that had forced Charlie into this permanent reverie. It had nothing to do with me, though I made it my personal mission to find out what it was. Unfortunately, much like my many ill-fated attempts at initiating intercourse, Charlie was unresponsive.

The tickets to the premiére arrived in the post. On the night in question, we both glammed ourselves up – me in a tux and she in a violet silk dress. Her dress showed off all the curves she usually made such an effort to keep hidden from me. It was painful to watch her, knowing that I could never have her. We caught a taxi to Leicester Square, where the film premiére was being held. Charlie didn't want to be seen beside me on the red carpet in front of so many cameras and spectators; consequently, well before we reached the cinema, we separated: she in front, me trailing one hundred metres behind. As one would expect in mid-March, the weather was awful. A cold and bitter wind swept across the square, my shirt and suit were useless against the chill, and my teeth were chattering. Looking at Charlie, you couldn't tell the weather was so bad, despite her ultra-thin garment. Like a true professional, she didn't react at all. It could have been a summer's day were it not for the condensation rising from her mouth into the stratosphere. She strutted along the carpet looking exceptionally glamorous. Surrounded by a throng of photographers all shouting her name, she posed and pouted, hand on hip, but still somehow retained her infallible projection of modesty and virtue. Only I knew how shy and vulnerable she was. From the outside looking in, she was a confident, sexy, alpha-female in her element.

I handed my ticket over to the burly man at the entrance, and he let me through. As I approached the red carpet, I was filled with a feeling of melancholy. Nobody cared that I was there. Nobody shouted my name. I was a non-entity. The photographers were bored by the sight of me, and used the precious few moments that I walked on the red carpet to check that their lenses were clean, and their cameras in focus. They chattered to each-other and ignored me completely. Although I hate to admit it, I was inordinately disappointed with my reception. There wasn't the slightest reason for any of them to pay any attention to me, but for some reason it got under my skin, especially after the reception that Charlie had received. She wasn't anything special, but they had clamoured over a picture of her looking like that. Perhaps something inside me had hoped that there would at least be some kind of speculation as to who I was. Perhaps somebody would cotton onto the fact that both Charlie and myself had walked down the red carpet alone, and within spitting distance of each other, but there was nothing. I made a solemn promise to myself that the next time my feet touched the red carpet, they would all want to take my picture.

Entering the cinema did nothing to improve my mood. Other than the fact that the top billing actors, director, and producers all appeared on stage to introduce the film and that we were all given a free bottle of water and a bar of chocolate, there wasn't anything to differentiate it from any other trip to the cinema. I had been expecting canapés and Champagne, and some mingling with the stars of the film. Unfortunately there was none of that. I was surrounded by a bunch of nobodies; I didn't recognise any of them. The vast majority of big name celebrities were keeping themselves to themselves, well away from me. Some part of me had hoped that this would be the exact kind of social situation in which to introduce myself to somebody within Elisha's inner-circle. In fact, it was the opposite; there was nothing within this environment to encourage conversation of any kind, let alone introducing myself to complete strangers. So I sat in silence next to Charlie, watching the awful film, pretending to be impressed.

Following the film, we were herded out of the Cinema like sheep. We had no invitations to stick around, and nobody made any attempt at striking up a conversation with anybody else, it felt as if we were exiting any old cinema, watching any old film. We had a taxi waiting for us, and headed straight home, ending our night cuddled in front of the television. I'm sure somebody somewhere was celebrating at an after-party and having a great deal of fun, but not us. As usual, we remained at home, sober, celibate and without sin.

May 28th 2009

About an hour North West of Lisbon, Portugal, is a small and picturesque medieval town called Obidos. It looks like a toy castle town, something that would appear in a *Disney* film. The buildings are old and sun-beaten, painted white with red terracotta roofing. Olive and fig trees grow in abundance amidst narrow and cobbled streets which, wind arbitrarily through the town centre. All of this is surrounded by imposing ancient stone walls and a castle fortress. A blue lagoon, which, according to local cuisine, seems to have an excess of sea-bass and sea-bream, is situated a few miles north-west to the town. It is a town famously known to the Portuguese as *The Wedding City*. It is a perfect setting for a fairy-tale wedding; unfortunately sullied by the fact that Scarlett and Edward decided to hold their wedding there.

We caught an afternoon flight to Lisbon, and hailed a taxi from the airport directly to Obidos. Charlie was unknown in Portugal – unlike her brother, her fame had not reached beyond British borders. The taxi driver showed not a flicker of recognition when we got in. Charlie felt anonymous enough to hold my hand in front of him, and after a time, she even cuddled up to me. She had been out of sorts for the entire journey, barely speaking to me on the plane, but now she relaxed into my arms. We had hired a private villa near the lagoon, which we were going to be sharing with Abz, Damien, and his girlfriend Bianca.

When Charlie had told me of the plan to share with Damien, I could barely contain my excitement. This really would give me an opportunity to talk man to man with him, to unwind late at night over a whiskey, and to sunbathe with cocktails next to the swimming pool. It was the perfect opportunity to become friends. The only problem was Charlie's mood, which seemed to get worse with each passing day, but no matter how much I pressed, she kept her thoughts to herself. I hoped that her dampened spirits wouldn't ruin my plans.

We were first to arrive at the villa; Abz was lunching with her father and future step-mother, and Damien was still travelling on a long-haul flight from JFK airport. The sun beat down on the back of our necks, it was warm and dry. Damien had requested that we stock up the house with food and drink, so when we arrived I poured myself a gin and tonic. Charlie didn't feel the need to comment on my sinful consumption of alcohol. As soon as we arrived, she climbed the stairs to our room and went straight to bed.

Without much else to do, I lay in the sunshine next to the pool, and grew ever more anxious – worrying and wondering how to best come across to someone like Damien. I considered for a moment about what I knew about the man, and once again reviewed his profile on the *A-List* website:

Damien Woland

	Damien Woland
Born	*Damien James Hastings* *06 June 1982* *Hammersmith, London*
Occupation	*Actor*
Years active	*2002–present*

Damien Woland *(born 06 June 1982) is a <u>British</u> actor. He shot to fame after successfully landing a role in <u>Film 4's</u> critically acclaimed film <u>Son of the Dawn</u>.*

Woland subsequently starred in two blockbusting American thrillers, <u>Black Park</u> and <u>Inferno</u> (both 2003). However, it was his turn as the lovesick police officer in 2004's <u>Rom-com</u> <u>Pig in a Blanket</u> that highlighted his versatility and cemented his international box office bankability.

He achieved an _Academy Award_ as _Best Supporting Actor_ in February 2007 for his portrayal of a schizophrenic billionaire, the antagonist in _A Better Class of Enemy_ (2006). The film was a commercial and critical success, winning 7 _Academy Awards_ in total, including _Best Actress_, _Best Adapted Screenplay_, and _Best Original Score._

Early life

Woland was born in _Hammersmith_, _London_, _England_. The biological younger brother of television presenter _Charlie Ekells_.

After his father was convicted of the death of his mother, Woland was taken into foster care at the age of 6 and, with his father's consent, was eventually adopted at the age of 12. He remained in constant contact with his sister throughout childhood.

Woland's upbringing was troubled, and he left school aged 16 without any qualifications. Before landing his breakthrough role in _Son of the Dawn_ he claims to have earned a living as a labourer, although rumours continue to circulate about his involvement in drug dealership and gang related crime.

Personal Life

Woland has amassed a reputation as being the _bad-boy_ of _Hollywood_ with allegations of drug abuse surrounding him, and a string of controversial courtships ranging from his romance with former prostitute turned author _Sharon Adler_, to former _Playboy playmate_ _Bianca Noir_.

Woland has been criticised by the English press for his aggression towards photographers, and rumours persist of drug abuse. Despite all of this, Woland continues to please the crowds, and in 2005, he was named number 6 in _A-List_ magazine's _100 Sexiest Bachelors_.

This helped a little, but didn't really teach me anything I didn't already know. I made a list in my head of things that we might have in common, or that might come in useful as leverage.

1. He was built like a brick-shit-house – discussing my own exercise routine may be a good conversation starter.

2. He was known amongst celebrity circles as a bit of a loose cannon – was this reputation for good reason? How could I use this to achieve my aim?

3. Despite the 'bad boy' image he was emotionally dependent upon his sister – could I use Charlie against him in order to get to him to do my bidding?

4. He had a penchant for dating 'unsuitable women', his current girlfriend Bianca, who he had been with for a year, was no exception to this rule – if all else failed, could I use Bianca?

5. He was a close and personal friend of Elisha Cicero, and had even attended her 'secret' wedding.

I paced around the house for hours, looking at the clock, wondering when he would arrive. His plane was due in at around 20:00, which meant that he should arrive at the villa at around 21:30. By 21:00, I couldn't sit still, so anxious was I to meet him. At 21:15, somebody knocked on the door; I jumped up and ran to meet them. As I opened it, the warm night air hit my face; it was a bit of a shock after so many hours sitting in an air conditioned room. Unfortunately, it wasn't Damien – Abz and Edward were standing in the driveway unpacking an enormous suitcase from the back of Edward's black Mercedes. Abz was wearing a pink bikini top that was far too small to cover her large plastic breasts, and a pair of tight denim shorts that left nothing to the imagination. Edward was, as usual, wearing a white shirt and chinos. He greeted me coolly with a firm handshake and a scowl.

"Good to see you, Shaun," he lied.

"Ready for the big day tomorrow?" I replied.

"Where's Charlie?" he ignored my comment, like he ignored almost everything I said. I couldn't deal with all of this right now, so slunk upstairs to get her. Charlie had broken the news to Edward about our relationship over the phone, and demanded that I be allowed to accompany her as her plus one. Edward had not reacted at all, and accepted his foster-sister's choice in a man with reasonably good grace. Perhaps behind my back he was still trying to warn her off me, but to my face, he pretended to be amicable, although Edward wasn't particularly good at pretending to like someone he clearly hated. When Scarlett found out that I was coming to her wedding, she had only shrugged – she was unthreatened by my attendance. She knew she could trust me to keep our dirty little secret.

"Charlie," I shook her.

"Charlie, wake up!" I shook her again.

She had gone to sleep crying, and her mascara had smeared all over her face. After a time she sat up, blinking in the light.

"Edward and Abz are here," I said.

Before she had a chance to reply, they had both barged into the room uninvited. Charlie feigned a smile, stood up in her nightie and hugged them both.

"Shaun, be a dear and get some drinks sorted," she said, "Edward, go down with Shaun and I'll be with you in a minute."

I led them back down the stairs and poured them both a gin and tonic, while Charlie sorted out her face. She seemed to take an eternity, and every time I tried to start a conversation, either Edward or Abz would roll their eyes. Eventually, she did come down, and it wasn't any less awkward. Charlie didn't attempt to talk, and didn't seem to notice the frosty atmosphere. We all sat in silence, sipping our drinks, until, finally, a car horn sounded outside and Damien Woland himself was standing in the doorway. He breezed into the room carrying a black holdall. He was wearing a tight black t-shirt, black jeans, and black desert boots. His black hair was cropped short, and his beard was trimmed short into designer stubble. Edward, who had known Damien since he was a young boy, grasped his hand with all the warmth he had failed to show me.

"Damien, it's been too long."

Damien smiled, his dark eyes shot around the room.

"Scarlett not here then?" he grunted.

"She's with her mother and sister" replied Edward.

I found myself wondering about Scarlett's mother: what kind of person could have spawned a woman like that?

"You must remember my daughter, Abigail," said Edward gesturing at the spoilt brat in the corner.

"You've grown, Little One," said Damien, hugging Abz. She kissed him on both cheeks and blushed. Charlie stood up and gave him a hug, but something was off key in the greeting. She didn't smile, or even speak. He looked into her face, searching for a sign that she had forgiven him for whatever it was that he had done; it was clear looking at them both, that she hadn't.

"Where's Bianca?" asked Edward.

Nobody had introduced me, and Damien was making no effort to introduce himself.

"She's gone." said Damien.

"Gone?" said Abz.

"We've broken up."

"Oh, that's a shame." said Abz with zero sincerity.

"Any chance I can get a God-damned drink? I'm spitting feathers here." said Damien, clearly wishing to change the subject. He pushed past me, still unintroduced and walked directly into the kitchen, looking in the cupboards for glasses. I followed him.

"What's your tipple then, Damien?" I said, reaching into the correct shelf.

"Uh? Oh, scotch and ginger."

"No problem." I pulled the ice from the freezer, the ginger beer from the fridge, and the whiskey from the liqueur cabinet.

"Say 'when'..." I said while pouring.

"When," said Damien when the glass was half full. I poured in the ginger, and made myself another gin and tonic.

"I'm Shaun by the way," I said while handing him his glass, "cheers."

Damien ignored me, and pushed past me again, walking back into the lounge. My annoyance at being disregarded began to grow, but I followed him back into the living room, where the others had once again taken their seats. I couldn't quite work him out, was he deliberately snubbing me, or was he naturally aloof? Charlie had warned me that he could be difficult, but I had fully expected to be able to work my way around it. I perched atop the arm of one of the sofas, and tried to relax. There were a few more moments of awkward silence until finally Edward tried to enter into a conversation with Damien.

"D, are you working in anything special at the moment?"

"Yeah,"

Damien didn't seem to feel the need to elaborate. I remained beside them all, a complete outsider and felt the urge to scream in frustration. Yet again I was trapped, completely reliant on this fucking arsehole to make my plan work.

"I'm really tired. I think I'm going to hit the hay," said Charlie in an attempt to save us all from an evening of Chinese water torture.

"Don't you want to say something to me?" Damien responded petulantly.

"Not now, Damien. I need to get some sleep." said Charlie

Damien folded his arms and stared out of the window away from everyone. Abz and Edward looked at each other meaningfully; they were as much in the dark about this as I was. Eventually, Edward stood up and pulled Abz over to him, kissing her on the cheek.

"Charlie's right, it's a big day tomorrow, I should head back and get some sleep too."

For some reason, although she tried to hide it, Edward's comment had a big effect on Charlie; all the life in her face was sucked out of her, her pallor became ghostly pale. She didn't say anything, but something was seriously upsetting her. Mechanically, robotically, she stood up and kissed her foster brother goodbye. Edward shook Damien's hand, nodded at me, and left the room. A short while later, we heard Edward drive off into the distance.

"Erm, so, now my dad's gone, shall we, like, have some proper fun?" smiled Abz, sitting up close to the film star. She was star struck in his presence.

"Who the fuck are you anyway? Who do you think you are? Go to bed, you little brat," Damien spat back at Abz.

This unwarranted response came as a complete shock to all of us. It came from nowhere and was so comically over the top that I had to smile. I doubt Abz had ever been spoken to like that before.

"You can't talk to me like that!" she shouted, her voice shaking.

"Argue with me again, fucktard, and you'll fucking regret it. Get the fuck away from me, you cunt." He pushed her away from him, like some vile creature.

"Charlie, you can't let him speak like that to me. I'm calling my dad!" She pulled out her mobile phone, but Damien snatched it off her, threw it to the ground and stamped on it repeatedly. I couldn't quite get my head around what was going on. This was a wedding, and Damien was being overly hateful to the daughter of the groom. It was like an awful joke.

"Damien, you've got to stop this," said Charlie sharply.

"I've always hated this little twat," Damien said again, pushing Abz to the floor for good measure, ensuring that she was well and truly terrified. Abz was sobbing.

"Don't hit me!" she screamed.

"Why don't you get your daddy to protect you?"

"Please," pleaded Abz again.

Damien grabbed her hair and clenched his hand into a fist. I stepped away from the fight, deciding to stay out of it all. Meanwhile, Charlie took two deliberate steps forwards.

"You're on self-destruct mode again Damien, control yourself." Charlie's voice was stern, it wouldn't take any bullshit. This was enough to draw his attention away from Abz.

"You're the one acting like you hate me," he replied.

"You've got nothing to worry about."

"You hate me."

"Damien, you know I love you."

"You fucking hate me."

"You know I don't."

"Your eyes hated me when I walked in."

"We've discussed this. You've got nothing to worry about."

"You're still angry at me."

"You're drunk."

"I'm not."

"You are."

There was silence for a moment, and then Damien appeared to regroup.

"I need to go to bed."

Once again, the atmosphere changed completely, the storm had passed, but what a storm! I half expected there to be flames and wrecked cars and people screaming in the streets. His face looked tired and sad, he appeared to be genuinely apologetic for what he had said and done, but I was given the impression that this wasn't a standalone event; Charlie had known exactly how to handle him. He withdrew from everyone, knowing instinctively that his presence was unwanted, and still, he didn't acknowledge me.

Abz was crying, Charlie was comforting her, Damien grabbed his bags and walked up the stairs to bed. I stood alone in the aftermath, wondering what tempest would strike us next.

May 29th 2009

The next day, as the sun rose, I couldn't help but wonder whether the weirdness of the previous evening had only been a dream. Something didn't sit right – the famous, wealthy, outwardly confident actor had turned into a raving lunatic for no reason at all. I slept on my own in Abz's room. Meanwhile, Abz was sleeping next to Charlie – too afraid to be left alone. I had forgotten to shut the curtains or switch on the air-con so the morning sun beat relentlessly down upon my face and I was uncomfortably hot. My mouth was dry and I was desperate for a piss. I stood up, coughed groggily, and fumbled through my suitcase for my wash-bag. In the spirit of 'being on holiday' I decided to forego my exercise and headed to the *en suite* shower to wash my sweat-soaked body. Downstairs, I heard signs of life, plates clattering, and breakfast being cooked – I wondered how awkward it must be for them all down there, but decided not to worry as I switched on the water and fiddled with the taps to get the temperature right. Ten minutes later, emerging from a steamy shower-room, I was greeted by Charlie lying on my bed in her silk-nightie. She looked divine, the outlined shape of her bra-less perfectly formed breasts torturing me. I walked over to her and gave her a kiss.

"Morning, gorgeous, sleep well?" I said.

"Not really, no" Charlie sighed, seemingly oblivious of my arousal at her unexpected appearance in my bed.

"What's the shizzle then? Has your brother sorted his head out?" I said, absent-mindedly checking myself in the mirror and moisturising my face with after-shave balm.

"Oh it's awful, Shaun. He's ruined everything and I don't know how to fix it."

"Ruined what?"

"I can't say."

"Charlie, you've got to tell someone sometime; it's eating you alive." I picked up a pair of tweezers and plucked a couple of stray hairs from my eyebrows.

"Oh Shaun, I really should, I know I should, but he'd hate me forever."

"You can tell me if you want."

"I can't."

"There's nothing stopping you."

"Please, Shaun. Can you be quiet for a moment and just give me a hug,"

Putting the tweezers down, I strolled over to Charlie and embraced her. I was only wearing a towel, and the crimson blush that spread across her cheeks was indicative of her excitement at my grasp. Suddenly, we were kissing, we were deep in the bed together, and I was groping for the spot between her legs. She moaned quietly as my finger entered her wet vagina. She kissed me harder.

"I love you Shaun." She said

"I *ahem*" I mumbled.

"I want to be with you forever. You make me feel so safe."

She didn't tell me to stop. She let me continue. She removed my towel and, gently, and quietly, she asked me make love to her. Never in my life have I been so surprised. Charlie, sober, naked and begging me to have sex. I was so shocked that the unmentionable happened and I went flaccid.

Such a horrific situation had not happened to me before – I rarely have trouble in that department, but for some reason, the pressure of the moment, coupled with the unforeseen willingness from Charlie had blown my brain away. I couldn't help but ponder on what had driven her to this – why that day, of all days, had she decided to spit in the face of all of her beliefs? Eventually, it didn't matter; for no reason at all, my chap started functioning again. True, as I donned the condom, there was another hair-raising moment from which I thought I wouldn't recover, but thank the Lord I did. Once able-bodied, and back into the swing of things, very soon, it became breathtakingly intense. I became lost in the moment, the sweltering sun beating on my back, the sweat glistening on her cleavage and neck. She was so deliciously wet, and tight, and perfect and she whimpered over and over again as she felt cock inside her for the first time in her life.

Then, when it ended, the horror of what she had done – soiling herself with premarital fornication – dawned upon her. She wept bitter tears while I held her in my arms. I didn't know what to say; I was the one that had systematically corrupted her. I was the one that had tempted her away from the Lord. There was nothing that I could say that wouldn't be a lie. So I let her sob into my chest, with her warm tears pooling into my belly button.

If I'm honest, I was rather relived that it had happened when she was sober. If she had been drunk, I wouldn't have been able to resist; I would have opened up her legs regardless of her state of mind. With Charlie though, sleeping with her while she was drunk would have weighed upon my conscience. It would have been too close to actual rape and would have made me think a little less of myself. This way, though, despite the fact that she was howling in misery, blubbering into my pectorals, I felt strangely relieved. After ten minutes she showed no signs of stopping and I grew a little bored. I wanted to know what had happened to Damien, and was itching to find out.

I pondered on what Scarlett was up to, and whether she would be pleased to know I had finally bedded Charlie. I even thought about Abz downstairs, probably feeling vulnerable and alone – I couldn't help but smile at the thought of her stuck speaking to Damien. In time, not even my own thoughts could save me from the tedium of Charlie's mortification, and I decided to get up.

"Charlie, what time is it? Shouldn't we start getting ready?" I steadfastly wanted to avoid any discussions about why she was crying. She didn't respond – she just clung on to me in silence.

"Charlie," I shook her gently, I'm not sure why, perhaps I was pretending that I thought she was asleep and I was trying to wake her up.

"Charlie, I'm going to have a shower and get ready."

I brushed her off and got into the shower again. I didn't know whether she thought it strange that I was so desperate to wash myself so soon. When I emerged from the bathroom for the second time, she was still there, curled up into a ball. Now I had extricated myself, I felt a little warmer towards her. I walked over and touched her on the cheek.

"Hey babe, are you OK?"

"Yes."

"Are you sure? That was something pretty crazy we just did."

She put her hands over her eyes, and exhaled slowly.

"I know," she was cringing as she said this.

"You're okay then?" I repeated.

"Yes. I wanted it."

"It feels good, doesn't it?" I smiled, and tickled her.

"I don't want it to feel good," she replied seriously.

"Oh dear, I'll be sure to try a little less hard next time."

"Oh, Shaun, please take me seriously for once. I'm really pissed off with myself."

"You shouldn't be."

"Well, I've got a lot to think about."

"Charlie, you've done nothing wrong, just relax. Just enjoy the day. It's your brother's wedding!"

At this, she sat bolt upright.

"You've got nothing to worry about." I said quickly, trying to soothe her mood. Something had gotten her agitated all over again, and the tears began to roll down her cheeks.

It took another half hour before I was able to break free from Charlie's misery. My saviour came in the form of Abz, wonderful Abz, paranoid about our absence. She knocked on the door, and entered without waiting for a response.

"If you two are finished talking about me behind my back, in case you hadn't noticed we've got a wedding to go to."

As usual, she had managed to misinterpret the situation so that it entirely revolved around her. Charlie was naked in bed with me, eyes red raw from crying, and

Abz thought we were talking about her. Still, it forced Charlie out of bed and into the shower.

We only had an hour before the service, and I was famished. I fixed my hair and donned my suit. I walked down the stairs, slightly hesitant as to how Damien would react when he saw me. Initially, he didn't even seem to notice my presence; he was sat alone in the corner of the room with his head in his hands. He didn't look up as I sat down on the barstool in the open plan kitchen. Charlie had clearly done all the cooking; there was a full English breakfast ready and waiting for me. The food had grown cold over the hour or so since she had cooked it, the fat had congealed slightly; the fried egg solidified into rubber. I ate it anyway. As I began chomping down on a second sausage, Damien spoke to me.

"Hey, Shaun, can you do me a favour?"

At this, I made a mental note of the kind of man Damien was – no "good morning", no apology about his actions the night before, just a request that I do something for him – I had him pegged: Damien was quite clearly a complete arsehole. I weighed up my options, and found myself asking what it was that he needed; I wanted to get on his good side after all. I expected that Damien's life was one whole parade of people trying to get on his good side. Damien didn't need to apologise for his actions; people would always be there to grovel before him and do his bidding.

"Tell Charlie that I'll meet you guys there." He stood up, walked out of the front door, jumped into a Lamborghini Diablo, and with a screech of wheels, was gone. I'm ashamed to say it, but after his departure, I felt a little sad and missed him. He had been able to make the hair stand up on the back of my neck just looking at me. He had such presence; he made the room seem fuller and the world a little more exciting. He was wild, selfish, violent and temperamental, but I desperately wanted him to like me. Seconds after his departure, Abz emerged.

"Has he gone?" she murmured nervously.

"Yes, he'll meet us there."

"Good."

"How are you feeling this morning, after, uh, after the *incident* last night?" I cringed inwardly at using a term that wholly and completely reminded me of Terry.

"OMG, how do you think I feel?"

"Did he speak to you this morning?"

"I doubt he can even remember it. He was off his head last night."

In other words, he had pretended that it never happened and both Charlie and Abz had acted the same.

"Does he do that very often?"

"I don't know. I haven't seen him since I was little. He's not really part of my family."

"Why not?"

"I don't know. I guess he had his own family. He like, got adopted by somebody else or something. He used to come to Christmas a lot when I was little though."

"What are you going to do?"

"Like what?"

"Tell your old man?"

"No way! Me and my friends are staying with him in Vegas this summer. I think he'd just drunk too much."

What a fucking retard. Even now she wanted to show him off to her friends. She was going to subject her 'bezzies' to his *warm* and *friendly* temperament. She didn't seem to understand that he clearly hated her with every ounce of his being. Further proof that Damien could do whatever he wanted, whenever he wanted, and suffer no consequences. Everything had been brushed under the carpet and forgotten. I wondered how many times Charlie had forgiven her brother for these indiscretions? I wondered whether he had ever hurt her? Strangely, I began to feel rather protective over the girlfriend I didn't love. Had she spent her whole life dealing with her monster of a brother? Or then again, maybe he was just drunk, and this was just a once in a lifetime event? Somehow, I didn't think that was the case. In preparation for the long day ahead, I poured us all a glass of *Veuve Clicquot*. Even Charlie, now knowing she had already fallen in the eyes of the Lord, also partook. After a couple of glasses, the mood lightened, and I was able to convince myself, for a brief moment, that I was enjoying myself.

We ordered a taxi to take us into the town of Obidos itself. It was a strange old town, seemingly stuck in the 15th Century. The streets were so narrow it became impossible to drive through. Eventually, we stepped out of the taxi and walked the rest of the way. Being Edward's second marriage, they had not hired a church. Instead, the service was to be held on the lawn of a castle that had been converted into a hotel, situated at the peak of the hill on which the town had been built. As we arrived, we were handed small chocolate cups filled with cherry liqueur – a local delicacy, apparently. Not as refreshing as one might want after a walk up a hill in the blazing heat, but it was a friendly welcome regardless. I pondered briefly on where Damien had left his Lamborghini, he was nowhere to be seen.

Edward's best-man, a balding beast of a man, greeted us as we arrived. He shook my hand with sweaty, greasy palms. He was apparently a partner in Edward's Global Macro Hedge Fund business. Being a close friend of the family, he knew Charlie intimately, and made a fuss over her and showed us to our seats. We sat in with Edward's family, right at the front. Edward's parents had died a number of years ago, so there was to be no introduction to Charlie's foster father (thank goodness), but we did meet her foster uncle – a frail old man sat in a wheelchair. He didn't seem to be quite with it, and I don't think he registered anything at all when Charlie introduced me as her boyfriend. In fact, I'm not convinced he even knew who Charlie was.

Scarlett's side was filled to the brim. There must have been 150 guests compared to Edward's 50. You could recognise Scarlett's mother a mile off. She wore a bright red fascinator with matching lipstick. She must have been pushing 65, and although no one could claim that she had aged gracefully, she had at least aged in vogue. Like her daughter, she had bleached blond hair and wonderful long legs. She hid her age behind a façade of fur capelets, off the shoulder bat wing tops, knee high boots, clunky jewellery and a cropped bob. No doubt she was mutton dressed as lamb, but on Scarlett's wedding day, you wouldn't have known it, especially with those alluring lamb's legs she was flaunting around. Her chin was what gave away her true level of decrepitude; it was grizzled and revolting with a long turkey gobble neck hanging below. Scarlett would do well to avoid a neck like that when she was older. Eventually, I found where Damien was sitting – right behind Scarlett's mother on Scarlett's side of the congregation. I was surprised that I had missed him. His huge shoulders weren't exactly hard to miss.

When Scarlett walked out in her white dress, I couldn't help but let out an inward chuckle. Walking down the aisle wearing a bloated corpse would be more fitting. Her mother was welling up at the sight of her. It was a picturesque and perfect wedding, faultless to the last detail. The service was short and sweet. It was too hot for us to all sit out in the sun, and I was happy when we were ushered onto a shaded terrace overflowing with bottles of cool Champagne. I was surprised when Charlie let go of my hand and made a bee-line towards a jug of Pimms. I supposed that she was probably still worrying about our fornications in the morning. Still, by the time I'd finished my fist glass of bubbles, she had downed three – for Charlie, this really was going hell for leather. I grabbed her by the arm.

"Charlie, don't you think you should slow down a bit?"

She gazed back at me with eyes I didn't recognise, the veil had come down, and she had become someone else already.

"You're one to talk!" she snarled at me snatching her arm away and storming back to the waiter to get another drink. I sighed inwardly, perhaps she had been right after all; maybe she did have a problem.

In the meantime, Damien appeared a changed man, and was truly playing up to his film star role. People were queuing up to have their photo taken with him, and he obliged. He had a constant circle of young women fawning over him. He was showing no signs of his true nature; he charmed them all, regaling them with witty anecdotes that had happened on the film set.

In time, a gong sounded and the best man requested that we move into the dining area for the wedding breakfast. Most tables sat ten, our table on the other hand only sat nine; an empty space remained next to Damien where Bianca should have been. We had been placed next to Damien and a number of Scarlett's friends who I knew vaguely from the club-scene. A few of them had even been at Terry's party. I didn't remember their names at all, but they seemed to remember me quite well. One girl with an upturned nose, accompanied by a Neanderthal with enormous forearms even asked me about him.

"I don't know," I replied, "I haven't seen him since he lost his job at *Oops*."

"Really? You both seemed so close?"

"No, not really." I didn't want to discuss Terry, but the pig-nosed bitch continued.

"What's he doing now?"

"I guess he's still looking for another job as a producer."

"What? Oh good, I'm glad he's doing well. Where else was he working?"

"*Oops!*"

"What?" she replied.

"*Oops! TV*"

"No, I mean where else was he working as a producer?" This conversation seemed to be going round in circles.

"He was working at *Oops! TV.*"

"What?" What was wrong with this woman?

"He was working at *Oops! TV* as a producer."

"No, he wasn't." I grew suddenly angry at the futility of talking with this pinheaded woman about a topic I didn't care about.

"If you say so."

I indicated that as far as I was concerned, the conversation was over – by leaving the table with the intention of finding the toilet. I winked at Scarlett as I walked by, and went about my business. Unfortunately, when I returned to the table, the woman started up where we had left off.

"Terry Taylor wasn't a producer at *Oops!*" I rolled my eyes and turned to Charlie, hoping that she'd help me get out of the conversation, but she wasn't any use and the awful woman was determined to see this agonizing exchange through until the bitter end.

"No, I'm still friends with everyone in his team."

"What? You used to work at *Oops*?" I must admit that I was drawn in by this previous statement.

"Yes."

"Didn't he work at *Oops* at all then?"

"Yes, he was a runner. Then they let him go."

Suddenly, it all made sense to me. At least it explained why he appeared to be so useless. He had certainly spent money like a successful businessman, but had earned little more than a waiter. No wonder he ended up having a breakdown, he must have been in a serious amount of debt. I don't think that even Polly knew what he actually did for a living. Good grief, the man was a freak.

After we all agreed how weird it was that Terry had been going around telling people that he was a producer, we were able (finally) to move onto better topics of conversation. During the meal, Damien continued to remain on good form, but Charlie was acting erratically, and I began to feel embarrassed that these women knew that she was my girlfriend. Her eyes had grown bloodshot, and she seemed to have lost the ability to talk without shouting. Most of what she said was nonsensical; half of it didn't even appear to be a sentence, just a random string of words put together. Although I had initially been happy that Charlie had finally fallen off the wagon, it had quickly become a little too excessive for my liking. She hadn't just fallen off the wagon – she'd rolled into a ditch, been swept out to sea and drowned in an ocean of vodka. Her outbursts grew even louder, and everyone around the table became silent and awkward. She shouted at all of us, about – I know not what – it was indecipherable. The only person she refused to acknowledge was Damien; it was as if he didn't exist to her. Then, it was time for the speeches, and this is when the shit really did hit the fan.

There was no *Father of the Bride*; in fact, Scarlett had never even met her real father, so the first person to speak was her Uncle Jory. It was a formal, traditional speech, and very early on he betrayed himself to not truly know Scarlett; describing her as an 'immaculate angel'. Throughout, Charlie was babbling, she even stood up a couple of times so that Damien had to pull her back down and tell her to be quiet. After a few minutes, Uncle Jory's speech was over, and it was time for Edward to step up to the mark. Even before he had begun his speech, Charlie broke free of Damien's grasp and ran towards Edward.

"Stop! I've heard enough of this crap!" she shouted, and I was surprised that the English language had finally returned to her.

Edward turned white as he realised how drunk she was. Knowing Charlie's track record, he may have guessed that she was going to speak about Scarlett in an incredibly offensive manner. However, I doubt he could have guessed what would actually pass her lips next.

"She's been sleeping with Damien. She's been sleeping with my brother."

Silence gripped the room as Charlie continued running, right until the moment where she punched Scarlett in the face. Scarlett fell off her chair backwards, and Charlie straddled her, striking her over and over again with a savage ferocity nobody imagined she could possibly possess.

"You've ruined everything, Scarlett!" she shouted.

Scarlett could do nothing but scream and cry; I'd never seen her look so pathetic and helpless before. Edward, who was closest to the fight, had gone limp. He seemed incapable of pulling Charlie away. He must have believed her. He must have seen that Charlie was telling the truth. Slowly, he stepped towards the fight, and for a moment, I thought he would pull Charlie off; his hands were raised to do just that, but then he paused and turned away. He left his wife in the hands of a vicious assailant in order to pursue Damien.

"You son of a bitch," he screamed, as he ran towards Damien. Apparently, Edward's father had spent more time teaching Charlie how to fight than him: as Edward ran towards Damien, Damien calmly stepped out of the way and used Edward's own weight against him, sending him crashing against the table. Edward lay on the floor senseless, while Damien coolly walked over to the pathetic old man, and with a savage force, kicked him square in the face. He stood back for a second, then kicked him again. Fire raged in his eyes, and I could see that he didn't want to stop. The madness that had enveloped him the night before had returned. As he stood back to kick Edward a third time, someone crashed into him from behind – it was one of Edward's more obscure family members that I'd not noticed before. Damien turned to face his new assailant, but someone else (presumably another family member) grabbed him from behind. Yet another wannabe hero entered the foray and kicked Damien's feet away from him. For a fraction of a second, my loyalties were divided – Charlie (the real Charlie, not the maniac beating up Scarlett) – would want me to stay out of this, but I knew if I helped Damien, he would owe me one.

"Damien, this is why you don't beat up the Groom at his own wedding!" I shouted as I jumped into the three men, holding one of them down. It allowed Damien the precious seconds he needed to get back onto his feet, but unfortunately, it meant that I was now entangled with three people who wanted nothing else but to hurt me. I punched one in the jaw, but another grabbed me from behind. All of a sudden I heard an almighty crash. Damien had smashed a wine bottle against the table and was threatening my opponents with grievous bodily harm.

"Let him go," he wheezed, and I knew my plan had worked, Damien now felt some kind of loyalty towards me. Blood was trickling down from his nose and dark crimson spots were forming on his pristine white collar. His eyes bulged wildly, and I knew that he wouldn't hesitate to stab someone if the mood took him there; he was fearless. Nobody made a move, nobody wanted to end up dead. Even I, who had helped him, held up my hands showing that I meant no harm as I edged away from the angry mob silently forming behind me.

"Let's get out of here," said Damien patting me on the back, my brother in arms.

Still too shocked to speak, I nodded my head and followed him. Edward's family looked like they wanted to lynch us. Scarlett's family had finally managed to pull Charlie off. She was pinned to the ground, arms behind her back, and howling. I wanted to help her, but it would have meant crossing the sea of angry faces, and so I left her. Charlie called to me for help as I slammed the door behind me. I could still hear her shrieking my name as we walked down the hill towards the ancient killing-ground, but I didn't look back. At Damien's side, I followed him down, and down and down, until finally we found his Lamborghini Diablo on the west side of the murder holes that marked the exit to the ancient town.

He fired up his car and we fled Scarlett's wedding. It was only when we were driving under the amber glow of sunset that I was able to take stock of Charlie's revelation. I wondered at my partner in crime, and made an effort at piecing it all together. Who was this lunatic beside me? What made him so awful, yet so exciting to be around? Why had he been fucking someone else's fiancé? For that first part of the evening we didn't say anything to each other. I, for one, remained in silence contemplating all the people we had left behind in Obidos. I wondered about Edward, surely he was going to hospital? The force of the kicks could have even killed him, not that Damien seemed the least bit concerned.

I didn't know where he was taking me, and neither, it seemed, did he. He didn't switch on the Satnav, he didn't stop to think, he didn't even stop to indicate, he simply drove, faster and faster until, eventually we hit the coastline. He drove the car onto the sand, jumped out, and ran into the sea, while I remained on my own, wondering what kind of madness would happen next. He was fully clothed, and doing breast-stoke with a very serious look on his face. He was fighting against an incoming tide, but he was nevertheless, slowly pushing his way out quite deep while the huge waves crashed down on his head.

"Damien!" I screamed "What are you doing?"

"Swimming!" he screamed back as if it was a real explanation.

I sat down in the sand and reluctantly took off my shoes, rolled up my trousers, and waded in a little. The sea was incredibly rough with a strong tidal pull, and it made me a little nervous. After about fifteen minutes he returned. He walked past me dripping and bent over into the doorway of the car. With his back facing me, I wondered at what he was doing. I heard him take a long strong inward breath, sniffing, before he fumbled around under his car seat, and presented me with a large bottle of *Gentleman Jack* Bourbon.

"I think it's time we had a talk." He said.

This put me on the spot a little bit, and I really couldn't think of anything to talk to him about. I sipped the whiskey, and waited for him to start.

"I know you've been sleeping with Scarlett," he said, and I reeled in shock.

"What? Of course not," I replied, quickly passing him the whiskey back.

"There's no point in lying. She told me."

"What? And that's supposed to be proof, is it?" I pulled the whiskey back off him and took a long hard swig. After all the booze at the wedding, I was really beginning to feel it.

"If you lie to me again, I'm going to hit you."

"I'm not lying."

Without hesitating, he punched me square in the face. My nose erupted with blood, and my eyes watered. I was stuck on a beach with a madman who knew I was cheating on his sister. I had no idea where I was, and if he left me, I'd have no idea how to get back.

"I can see that you're not ready to talk about it yet." After such sudden and unnecessary violence, I hadn't expected his voice to be so calm.

"Have some more whiskey," he said.

It was so awkward, so surreal, he didn't even seem to notice that I was bleeding. Feeling somewhat sheepish, I put the bottle back to my lips and took another long hard swig. He watched me with his intense frown.

"More," he said, when I finished, gasping and gagging and feeling a little ill.

This was beginning to feel really weird now – two grown men on a beach, watching the sunset. I looked to see if anyone else was around, but there wasn't a soul to be seen, so I drank again. He kept watching.

When I finished, he looked like he was going to ask me to drink more, but I stopped him.

"Yes, OK, I've been sleeping with Scarlett." I coughed as I said this, and I braced myself for another punch to the face.

"Good, at least we're being honest with each other."

I breathed a small sigh of relief; I had been wondering whether he was going to actually murder me. Damien made another trip back to his car, and I contemplated running away. I heard him snorting again, and it dawned on me what he was doing. Damien was hopelessly addicted to cocaine. I have, of course, spent a few nights talking, and plotting, and pumped on a gram of coke, but I have never, in my life, known someone who uses it more frequently than Damien Woland. He never talks about it, and but for his constant trips to the bathroom, or to his car, or to his bedroom, one would never even suspect. Damien is not the kind of man to share his cocaine with anyone, in fact, I've never seen it happen; he hoards it like a miser, and sucks it up like a crack-whore.

Once the topic of my infidelity had been covered, we were able to discuss other things. Although most of the evening was a bit of a blur, here's a list of some of the things we spoke about:

1. His most recent film – "*Robespierre*" in which he plays the leader of the French revolution

2. His ex-girlfriend Bianca and why they broke up. The problems had started with each blaming the other for giving them Gonorrhoea on Christmas day (I presume this was the reason for the panicked call to Charlie on Christmas day), after which, their relationship slowly deteriorated until Bianca's recent trip into hospital with two black eyes and a fractured wrist. This, by the way, was not something he regretted, and wasn't something he was likely to get into trouble for: a £20,000 pay out saw to that.

3. The moment when he realised his father had killed his mother.

4. How much he loves being able to buy anyone or anything.

5. Charlie.

The conversation about Charlie occurred at around sunrise, after we had polished off two bottles of Gentleman Jack between us. Damien was still alert, while I was hopelessly lost and kept on drifting off to sleep. Every time I shut my eyes, Damien slapped me in the face.

"Damien, mate, I need some sleep," I begged, but he slapped me again.

"Get up, Shaun. I need to speak with you," he said.

"We can talk about it in the morning."

"It *is* the morning." Who can argue with logic like that? I sat up and rubbed my eyes, yawning. Sometimes Damien was like a child: an incredibly rich and strong, petulant child.

"I need to talk to you about what we're going to do about my bitch sister."

I didn't truly believe that Damien hated Charlie. He seemed obsessed with seeking her approval: something which, he feared he would never obtain. I hadn't the guts to point this out to him at the time though.

"What's wrong?"

"I'm sick of her judging me."

Urg, he actually wanted to speak about his feelings?

"Damien, are you sure you don't want to talk about this in the morning?"

"I want you to fuck my sister and leave her."

Spending time with Damien was like being trapped in a cage with a sleeping lion – I knew that there was something dormant and dangerous and completely fucked up waiting to lash out at me. His mind was so unhealthy, so obsessed with proving to his older sister that he wasn't as bad as she thought he was. It didn't matter if I ruined his sister in the process, as long as she could finally concede that he wasn't all that bad. That was his entire motivation. I think he hated himself completely when he said those words. It was one last desperate attempt at redemption, twisted and distorted beyond recognition.

I was initially sickened by his suggestion, until I realised that this was exactly what I had been intending to do all along. Thankfully, even my addled brain saw it for the golden goose that it was. I could carry on doing exactly what I wanted to do, and all the time, make him think I was doing it all for him. I finally had some leverage. I didn't want to just agree, I wanted a deal. Seeing this opportunity sobered up my mind in a flash; and by some miracle I was able to do exactly what comes naturally to me, I was able to pitch him.

"What makes you think I'd ever do such a thing?" I asked. This could become the deal of a lifetime so I needed to qualify the living Christ out of the man.

"You don't love her."

"What? Yes, I do. What makes you think I don't love her?"

"You've been sleeping with Scarlett."

"Ok, I may not love her, but I really do like her. This could seriously fuck her up. Why would I ever want to hurt her like that?" Remember, open questions. Get the applicant to talk. Find out their motivations and their desires.

"I can make it worth your while."

"How?"

"I can pay you." Damien was not a good salesman; he had no idea what I wanted; he was just praying that I was entirely motivated by money (which if I'm honest, would usually be a fair assumption to make).

"I don't want your money. What else can you offer me?" Stay in control of the conversation – don't let them dictate the terms.

"My car?" He was desperate, didn't he realise that I could buy his car twice over with the money I'd need from him in order to make this worthwhile. Besides, it was a rental, and they didn't even make Diablos anymore. Time to throw in a bit of market chat:

"Damien, there are many ways to make money, but not very many famous and attractive women out there like your sister. I'm pretty much set for life with your sister. If I don't marry her, what other major celebrities do you think would be willing to hook up with me?" It's the standard supply and demand argument – available celebrities who were likely to fall in love with me were most definitely in short supply.

"What do you want then?"

"I need you to set me up with another celebrity."

"Who? How?"

"I need you to set me up with Elisha Cicero."

He snorted.

"Mate, she's the elite and she's already married," he replied.

"You just need to get us in the same room together. I know I could get into her pants."

"You're delusional. You seriously think she'd look twice at a little twat like you?"

"Fuck that, Damien, I'm offering you a good deal here. What does it matter to you? I'll still shag your bitch of a sister."

"Don't talk about her like that!" The fire in his eyes made me realise I had gone too far.

"Deal or no deal?"

"You're not worthy to lick Charlie's boots, you little shit."

"Deal or no deal?" I repeated, instinctively feeling a threat.

Damien seemed to be in two minds – it could have gone either way. As I saw it, there were two outcomes that Damien was contemplating:

1. Ultra-violence (they may never find my body).

2. Forgiving my unforgivable rudeness about Charlie, and finally finding a way to knock her down a peg or two.

It was a tense moment, and my life hung in the balance.

"You'll leave Charlie straight after, and you won't mention that I had anything to do with it?" He finally said, after what seemed like a lifetime.

"Whatever you want, as long as I get to meet Elisha," I attempted to sound calm and cool, but my hands were shaking.

"Well, I suppose if nothing else, it'll be a laugh." He began to chuckle, genuinely finding mirth in the idea of ruining Elisha's marriage. Damien shook my hand and allowed me to try and get some sleep. Before I shut my eyes, I smiled at the rising sun as the stars disappeared out of the morning sky. Everything was coming together.

Step 6: Elisha Cicero

The aftermath of the wedding greeted me in a disjointed haze. I had lain unconscious on the sand while the blistering sun beat down upon my face, burning my bloodied nose to a crisp. There had been a gentle sea breeze keeping me cool throughout the early morning, and it had tricked me into thinking the sun was less intense than it actually was. When the swash from the sea wet my back, I woke up with a start. I looked around in a panic, fully expecting Damien to have driven off without me. He was asleep in the driver's seat of his car, the door open; water surrounded the wheels. The car was set so low that already water was threatening to pour in through the doors. I stood up and began to run across the water to warn Damien, but in my sorry state I tripped and fell headfirst into the backwash. While I floundered in the water against the heavy current, Damien awoke (possibly as a consequence of my yelp as I fell), revved his engine, and successfully manoeuvred his way out of the water. Coughing up half a gallon of seawater, I ambled over to the car.

"You're not getting in here in those wet clothes" he said.

Considering the type of car, if Damien hadn't just spent the night sleeping in his sodden clothes, I would have understood. As it was, I knew he just wanted to get on my nerves. This was only a hire car, he didn't care about it. Although I was irritated, I felt so nauseous that I complied with his request immediately. As there were no spare clothes or towels, I stripped off to my boxers and began to get in.

"You're not getting in this car in those wet pants" he grinned wickedly.

"Are you serious?" I said.

"Deeply serious," his mouth frothed when he said this and I felt a little sick. Damien wasn't gay; he took no sexual pleasure in my naked body, but I'm pretty sure he got a hard-on from degrading and humiliating his fellow man. I knew that if I didn't agree to it, he would simply drive off without me, so I sighed and took off my underpants. Even then, he wouldn't let me in until I'd thrown all of them away, leaving them on the beach in the sand. My head was pounding, and I had a thirst that was threatening to make me gag. Damien seemed impervious to the pain, but he must surely have been suffering too. Using his Satnav we found our way back to the villa. As I reached for the door to get out, he pulled me back.

"Are we still on?"

It took me a few seconds to remember our conversation from the night before, but when I did, I had to smile. He had been serious!

"Uh, yeah, I suppose so," I croaked.

"So how is it going to happen?"

"What?"

"How are you going to persuade her to fuck you?"

Oh shit, I hadn't wanted to deal with this right away. I wanted a few weeks to consider whether I could actually do this to her.

"Are you sure you want me to do this, Damien? It's going to mess her up."

"Don't you dare back out now you prick. I've already set the wheels in motion." He picked up his phone, as if to indicate he had been using it.

"What wheels?"

"Elisha, it's who you want isn't it?"

"Oh, er, yes. Yes. You know it is."

"Then how are you going to do it?"

I hadn't wanted to tell him, but he hadn't given me much of a choice.

"The deed is done." I said, and he beamed an enormous film-star smile with his pearly white teeth.

"Really?"

"Yes."

"Fucking hell, you *are* good. Nobody's managed that before."

"Thanks." I made to leave again.

"So are you going to leave her then?"

"Yes, at some point." I said this half-heartedly, as I knew what was coming.

"Do it now."

"Damien, I think I need to do this properly. She's already going to be pretty upset."

"If you don't go in there now, the deal's off."

I couldn't say why I was getting cold feet. It all just seemed so sudden, and I couldn't help but feel sorry for poor Charlie.

"Fine."

Damien smiled again and ushered me to get out.

I got out of his car bollock naked, and furtively made my way into the house. Thankfully nobody was around. I snuck into Abz's room where I had left all of my clothes. Without showering, I packed everything into a small suitcase and headed down the stairs. I couldn't face leaving Charlie face to face, so I wrote a quick note. I had intended to write something nice, and passionate, and with a very real meaning, but I was incredibly hung-over and couldn't think of anything appropriate to say. In the end I settled for a short few words, which would made her understand that our relationship was truly over:

Charlie
I'm leaving you. Like your brother, I've been sleeping with Scarlett.
Shaun

Red with shame, I tiptoed out of the house. I was a single man again.

<u>June 2009</u>

I soon got over my guilt about Charlie, after all, it marked a very dramatic change in my fortunes. As if from nowhere, the property market rose from the dead. The newspapers continued to print their usual stories of double dip recessions and low mortgage approvals, but, for me, the credit crunch had effectively ended. A shift had occurred in my applicants' attitudes. There didn't seem to be any real reason for it, but personally, I think they all had just had enough of sitting around and feeling sorry for themselves. We're talking about wealthy people here, these aren't the kind of people who had been forced onto a diet of soup over the past year; they were as fat and as wealthy as ever, and now, they were fed up with everyone telling them that they shouldn't buy London property. I couldn't say that I was particularly happy in the job, much of its sparkle had worn off, and it still wasn't anywhere as easy as it had been before the credit crunch, but at least I was making some money again.

I received several very teary voicemail messages from Charlie over the next few weeks, but really, I was much too busy with work and catching up with *Soma Holiday* to take much notice. Scarlett came to visit me two weeks after her wedding. I couldn't put my finger on what was wrong, but all of a sudden she looked a little less sexy, and a little more drab than I'd ever seen her before. She hadn't bothered to call me, she had just turned up on my doorstep. When I opened my door to let her in, she jumped into my arms and started sobbing. It reminded me a little of how Polly had been in the beginning; it was sickening seeing such raw and pathetic emotions coming from Scarlett.

"Have you heard from Edward at all?" she said.

"No," I responded.

"Shit."

"Why don't you stick around for a bit?" I said, unbuttoning her blouse.

"What? Oh OK, if you like."

She lay down on my sofa, and let me fuck her. It was like having sex with a dead person, she didn't really do anything. I think she enjoyed it. I even think she may have come with a gentle shudder; but there was no sign of the passion or excitement that usually lit up our copulations. Silently, she completely succumbed to my bidding. I must say that, surprisingly, there was something about it that made me feel really good about myself; I was able to convince myself while pounding away against her that I had managed to break her spirit: I'd finally tamed the beast. When it was over, she spoke to me.

"What am I going to do, Shaun?"

"About what?"

"About my life. It's gone to shit."

"Scarlett, did you actually love Edward?"

"Yes." I didn't believe her.

"Then why bother with all this crap with me and Damien?"

"What's wrong with wanting a bit of passion now and again? "

"Why would you ever love a man who couldn't satisfy you?"

"Edward looked after me."

"You mean Edward had money."

"I suppose that was part of it."

"I don't think I'll ever understand you, Scarlett. What is it you need from life?"

"I want to be happy, Shaun. Is that too much to ask?"

"No, I suppose not." I replied, kissing her on the forehead.

Despite being knocked down a few pegs, Scarlett was still the same shallow human being. Her happiness was all that mattered to her, regardless of whether achieving her happiness hurt the people that she supposedly loved.

I didn't know whether our chat that night helped, but over the coming weeks, Scarlett began to show signs of the confidence that had always overwhelmed her entire personality, but she still struggled to come to terms with the realisation she wasn't infallible. Her life had been brutally unravelled in front of all of her family and friends, and I'm certain that for a time, I was truly the only person she was sleeping with. I had become a boyfriend of sorts to her. I think she found it comforting that I knew all about her dark side but didn't care, and for that reason she became dependent upon my affections. She even began to confide, something that would have been unheard of prior to her wedding day.

After a few days in hospital, Edward had decided not to press charges against Damien; after all, it was Edward who had attacked first. He had, however, filed for an annulment to the marriage on the basis that the marriage wasn't ever consummated. From what I gathered, he had cut off all communication with Charlie; he wasn't willing to forgive her for waiting until the wedding day to tell him, which in fairness, seemed a reasonable justification. I guess that there had been a certain element of threatening behaviour from Damien that may have led to Charlie's late decision to reveal the truth.

Damien seemed very happy with the results of our bargain. He had renewed his relationship with Charlie, and apparently, she had been very apologetic over revealing his secret. She had broken down in tears telling him what she had done, and that she was sorry for judging him for all those years. This was all related to me on the telephone by Damien, before throwing in a comment that made my day: "Oh, and I'm having a party in Vegas next month. I'm inviting a few select friends; you need to come".

Everything seemed to be going my way, and but for the event that caused me to miss the *Soma Holiday* Grand Finale, my life would have been perfect.

I arrived home early that night, excited to get in and watch my favourite show. I had no idea that someone had any sinister intentions against me. I did not suspect that someone had been waiting for me to get home. It happened in a flash – as I retrieved my key from my blazer pocket to enter my building, someone rushed me from behind and knocked me to the floor. I tried to rise, but they forced me to the ground and wrenched the key from my grasp. With my head on the concrete steps, I had no idea who my assailant was. For several moments, I thought I was in mortal peril, and braced myself for further pain – would he stamp on my head? Stab me with a knife? Kick me in the face?

"You can take whatever you want!" I screamed "I've got £50 in my wallet, you can have it."

He didn't take my money, and he didn't hurt me, instead, he began to cry and I realised it was Terry. Fucking Terry! The moron I wanted nothing to do with.

"Terry, what are you doing?" I began to get up off the ground, but surprisingly, he kicked me in my stomach, winding me. I felt a little ashamed that he had somehow gotten the better of me.

"You want to speak to me?" he said. He stood over me brandishing my keys as if they were a knife.

"I'm getting up." I felt I needed to offer an explanation as to what I was doing, he looked unhinged and I didn't know what he'd do if I made any more sudden movements. This time I stood up slowly, and attempted to keep my cool; inside I was seething.

"Yes, why have you been following me?" I grunted, still a little out of breath.

"I haven't been following you." A lie if I ever heard one; I don't know what I expected really; after all, I was dealing with a lunatic.

He clenched his fists. He'd lost a lot of weight since last I saw him; he was pale, and had large dark bags under his eyes. I realised that it probably wasn't the time to argue with him, so kept my cool and accepted his falsehood with as much grace as I could muster.

"OK. Can I have my keys back please?" I spoke slowly, as if to a child. He looked like an animal and I felt that using language like this might get through into his addled brain. Instead of giving me the keys, he opened the door to my building and beckoned me to follow.

"Terry, do you need me to call anyone? Do you need me to call your parents?" I said, wondering where this was all heading.

He shook his head frantically.

"No no no no no no. Stop it," he said while ushering me towards the door of my own flat.

I wasn't certain what his intention was, but he was beginning to unnerve me – the hairs on the back of my neck were standing on end and my heart was pounding in my chest. There was something inhuman about him, the whinging and gormless personality that had plagued me during our early acquaintance had disappeared, wholly consumed by his illness. He fumbled with my keys again, his skeletal wrists twitched at my doorknob struggling to keep steady, but eventually he managed to gain entry. I followed hesitantly, conscious that I should probably be running out into the street screaming, but unable to for fear of what he would do to my flat while I was gone.

He held the door open for me, and as I entered he slammed it shut. Acting as a barrier between myself and the exit, he pulled out a huge meat-cleaver from his coat pocket – it was so surreal and unexpected, that initially I didn't quite register what he was holding. After a few thumping heartbeats reality dawned on me, and my heart rearranged its pace, noticeably jumping and skipping like broken record.

"You've ruined my life," he said.

In my shock, I had lost the power of speech; I wanted to plead, to beg him to leave me alone, but I couldn't. I held my breath and backed away.

"You've emasculated me," he said.

Still I held my breath and stepped backwards into the kitchen.

"Why couldn't you just be my friend?" he said.

Finally, I found my voice

"We can be friends." I said, feeling dizzy.

"Not now. Not now we can't. I know we can't."

"Yes, we can."

"You stole my girlfriend and didn't want her." He took a step towards me.

"No!" I took a step back.

"You hated me and I spent all my money on you."

"Terry, please."

"You've emasculated me." He took another step forward.

"I haven't." I took another step back, but now my back was against the wall.

"You've emasculated me," he repeated again.

I looked from side to side, searching for some way to escape; I made a furtive step in the direction of the window.

"I want to show you what you've done to me."

He smiled, and unbuttoned his trousers. I must admit I was confused by this action, was he going to rape me after all?

"I want to show you how much you've hurt me."

I felt sick as he pulled down his trousers and hacked at his genitalia. Like gutting a chicken, he pulled sinewy tissue away, and hacked seven or eight times until both testicles and his penis had been separated from his body.

"Take them," he said, deathly pale.

"What?"

"Take them, they're yours."

"No." I said, finally finding my confidence now I knew he was in no fit state to kill or rape me.

"I said TAKE THEM!" he screamed.

Blood was spurting from his wounds, and I began to run towards the window.

In desperation, he threw his genitalia at me; his bloodied testicles squelched against the back of my head, while his limp penis flew over my shoulder into my path. In my panic I slipped on it and fell backwards onto the floor where I vomited. He dropped the knife and lumbered towards me with his trousers still half way down his thighs, blood pouring down his legs.

"Why did you have to be so mean?" he said weakly before passing out.

For a few moments I sat still, surrounded by blood and the amputated genitalia, wanting to cry. Finally I came to my senses, pulled my mobile out of my pocket and dialled '999'.

1st July 2009

Yet again, Terry survived: not that I really wanted him to. His actions had blown my mind, and for a time I must have been in a state of post-traumatic stress. The following day I awoke hungover to hell; having drunk myself into a stupor after the ambulance and police had departed. The first thing I thought about was Terry castrating himself. It played on my mind. Could I have done anything to stop him? Should I have made more of an effort to keep in touch after Cape Town? I asked myself these same questions over and over again. I called in sick, and ambled around my flat in horror, reeling at the havoc wrought upon it. There was a blood stain, a deep dark wretched blood stain on my carpet, flecks of blood on my wall, and one of my favourite suits had been unceremoniously stuffed into the kitchen bin.

I wanted to call someone to help me tidy up, or to speak to, or to help me forget, but nobody came to mind. I looked down at the contacts list on my phone and stopped at Scarlett's name. I couldn't face calling her. Although she had changed, she hadn't changed enough for me to want to confide in her, possibly even cry in front of her. Then I searched for Polly's name, but she would be devastated, and she would blame me, and I would find no comfort there. I didn't want to call my sisters or my parents, they didn't know me. I couldn't call anybody from work, I'd always kept them at arm's length, and I didn't want them knowing about my business. Frantic now, I looked up old friends from university or school, people who I hadn't spoken to for months – I couldn't just call them out of the blue and expect them to come running to my aid. All of a sudden, I felt horribly alone; I had nobody who would care, I had nobody who could possibly make me feel better, except, well, except Charlie. I called her without hesitating. I needed her. No matter what I had done to her – she was still the only good person in my life.

I don't remember exactly how the conversation went, but suffice to say, I wasn't my usual upbeat charming self. I'm ashamed to say that I actually wept. I apologised to her, I told her how much she meant to me, I told her how lonely I was, I told her what Terry had done the night before and I asked if I could see her. This is how she replied:

"Come over, I'll treat you to some pancakes to cheer you up. Despite everything, I…I…still love you." Her voice cracked a little as she said this last bit.

While I spoke to Charlie, I truly meant what I said. I needed her, she was the only person who could make me feel better, I loved her all over again and at that moment would have done anything if only to get her back. I showered, put on my clothes, and left the house in autopilot, eager to see her. I couldn't believe after what I had done, she still loved me. She still wanted me in her life. I took a deep breath of the summer air, and made a promise to myself that I would be different, that I could change my ways, that I didn't want to use anyone any more. I realised that I could be happy with Charlie, I could be a good person too.

On my way to the station, my mobile phone rang, and I answered:

Damien: "Yo S-Dog! It's Damien. How you doing, mate?" he could be so friendly at times, one could almost believe he had human emotions. It was strange how, after just hearing his voice, all my love for Charlie evaporated in an instant.

Me: "D! I'm good mate. You won't believe what happened to me last night."

Damien: "Well, why don't you tell me about it tomorrow night?"

Me: "Are you coming to London?"

Damien: "No, mate, you're coming to see me in Vegas."

Me: (it must be noted that at this point I was being sarcastic.) "Ha, yeah I'd love to."

Damien: "I'm serious, Elisha's coming down tomorrow. If you want to meet her, you better get on a plane."

Me: "D, I've got work."

Damien: "Get on that plane, Shaun, this is your chance."

Me: "Ummm."

Damien: "Have you ever been to Vegas?"

Me: "No."

Damien: "Trust me, you'll love it."

Me: "OK, fuck it, I'll come."

Damien: "Don't bullshit me. If you're not going to come, let me know now."

Me: "I'll be there. When should I book my return flight back?"

Damien: "I'm here for another month, but you can stay as long as you need."

Me: "I need to work. I guess I can stay a week though"

Damien: "No problem. Let me know what flight you're getting and I'll have someone pick you up."

Me: "OK."

Damien: "See you tomorrow."

Me: "Yes, OK."

I hung up and turned for home. Within 45 minutes, I was £2100 lighter, and in a taxi to Heathrow for a 1400 flight. After sending my flight details to Damien I called my boss. I told him in detail what had happened with Terry, and that I had decided to take a week off work to recover (using holiday time as opposed to sick leave). With that, I switched off my phone. I didn't want to speak with Charlie; I couldn't face telling her I wasn't coming, and with that, our life together that had so fleetingly been within our grasp, crumbled into dust.

Vegas is an amazing place. My wildest dreams couldn't have imagined such a rich and endless source of debauchery. Forget the Nevada desert, forget downtown Vegas, forget the Grand Canyon – Las Vegas Strip is all you need. A black man in a stretched hummer picked me up from the airport, carried my bags for me, and dropped me off at the MGM Grand casino where Damien had set up semi-permanent residence. Upon my arrival, I was sent directly to his room. He had hired out a lavish apartment with, enough room for me and several concubines. The extravagance of it all was beyond me; I couldn't comprehend how much money Damien was spending. He had told me he was drinking in Caesars Palace, and that I should meet him there. The alleged party with Elisha wasn't supposed to be happening until the following evening, but I was eager to soak in the sights and sounds, and as ever, was very keen to meet him. It didn't seem far to Caesar's, so I walked – something that struck Damien as incredibly funny when I eventually caught up with him. I must admit, it wasn't an experience I wanted again, I was drenched in sweat. Getting into any nightclub in Vegas is like getting into Fort Knox, there are queues for queues sake, and you need photo ID regardless of how old you look – unless, of course, you are part of Damien Woland's crowd. The doors fly open and like royalty, you breeze past the crowds, and with all heads turned, bikini clad women show you to your seat.

We were sat in a VIP area at a rooftop bar, overlooking the Vegas strip, a clear sky awesome above our heads. That first night Elisha wasn't there; that first night, it was Damien, myself and Elisha's husband. Damien found it hilarious when I recognised him for who he was.

"What the fuck is he doing here?" I whispered into Damien's ear.

"Relax! It's part of the plan."

God, I hoped that he wasn't going to deliberately embarrass me.

"How?"

"You'll see. Let me introduce you."

At that moment I felt many things: I felt tired, I felt excited, I felt overwhelmed by the extravagance, but most of all I felt like I didn't want to speak to the goon who had knocked-up Elisha. I'd flown the best part of 5000 miles to meet Elisha, only to end up being greeted by fucking Benedict fucking Latterburn.

It's not even as if he was an interesting person. He was utterly devoid of a personality, an empty husk of a human being. His very presence sucked the atmosphere or joy out of any conversation. He was six foot three, and classically handsome. He could have been the prototype for a renaissance marble sculpture – the body, the banter, and the brains.

After careful observation of friends and celebrities, I've come to realise an undeniable fact about people who play too much sport – they're all incomprehensibly dull. It seems to happen somewhere between giving up drink during the 'sports season' and the point at which they spend more time training for a game than living their actual lives. True, a little bit of exercise, or a regular kick about on a Saturday afternoon helps build confidence and team skills, but ultimately, if you spend your whole life thinking about a game and exercising to improve a game, it quickly becomes the only thing that you are qualified to talk about – a game – something that most people enjoy, but could get by without. This banality seeps through the core of their being, and the worst part of it is, that they are completely oblivious to that fact. They live their lives as if they are in a secret little gang, as if only they truly know the limits of the universe, and despite the lack of any individual or interesting trait, they are horrendously self-assured and arrogant. In light of all of this, the fact that he was married to Elisha had little consequence – I would have always despised him.

Needless to say, in Vegas, in Damien's element, Benedict's Yin was completely unable to temper Damien's Yang. Benedict was such a perfect specimen of the empty-husk personality type, he didn't even realise that he was out of kilter with the rest of group – in his make-believe world, he was showing us how to have a good time in his home country, despite not uttering a single syllable that anyone bothered to take note of.

That evening, with two celebrities and several magnums of Vintage on our table, we were the target of pretty much every girl within the confines of the Nevada desert. But I was able to resist any advances that came my way. I wanted to be introduced to Elisha with a glowing recommendation from the man she would leave for me. With girls fawning over Damien in every direction, I was often left alone with Benedict (he being so devoid of charm that girls were actively repelled by him, despite his status). By 04:00 AM I was more than a little frustrated at the effort it took to speak with that gormless waste of space. My annoyance was clearly evident on my face, as Damien broke away from his harem and whispered in my ear:

"I know he's fucking annoying. Keep your eye on the goal; it's all part of the plan."

He really had taken our agreement to heart and seemed to be genuinely enjoying the challenge. Ultimately when it comes down to social predators like Damien, everyone else is lower down in the food-chain, regardless of whether he considers them friends or not. He seemed to have spun a thousand devious little threads, creating a nasty little web, and I was caught somewhere in it – thankfully, for the time being, it didn't seem like I was the fly.

Damien's plan ended up being far more simplistic than any of the outlandish ideas that had been running through my head. His plan (if indeed it could be called a plan at all) was to get Benedict horrendously drunk. That was the extent of it – no undercover prostitutes, no photographers lurking in the shadows, just drink, drink, and more drink. This plan meant nothing to me. I didn't know Benedict and whether getting him drunk had any significance whatsoever, so was initially a little bemused by the whole affair. I found myself hoping that he had a hidden personality like Charlie, that he would turn into an abusive arsehole when he had a few too many. I found myself watching him, wondering when he would flip out, hoping it would be sooner rather than later, watching for signs of erratic behaviour. Damien ordered round after round of drinks, each round getting slightly more hardcore – wine, Champagne, Vodka, Pernod, Jagermeister – in truth, Damien's plan didn't revolve solely around getting Benedict drunk, it seemed to actually be: get *everyone* as drunk as possible. The end of the night became a complete blur, I have hazy memories of being in a limo with four topless girls, and at another point being at the Blackjack tables, but I couldn't say for certain whether we won or lost. I do know that I found myself in McDonald's at 08:30am, arguing with the management that I didn't want the breakfast menu – I wanted a Big Mac. In Vegas you can get what you want when you want, you can have a roast dinner for breakfast, or a bottle of vodka delivered to your room; everything gets distorted and time eventually loses all meaning – apart from the unmoveable McDonalds. I left in disgust, munching grudgingly on my Triple Sausage and Egg Mcmuffin, still unsure on the mechanics of Damien's, staggering slightly from alcohol and exhaustion.

July 2nd 2009

This was the day that I finally met Elisha Cicero, when, what had started out as a pipedream suddenly became very real. I had watched all her films, read and recorded all of her interviews. I knew her. Well, I knew as much about her as anyone who didn't belong to her elite celeb clique could possibly hope for – but in reality, all this painstakingly acquired knowledge didn't even scratch the surface of who the *real* Elisha was. I remember that moment as if it were yesterday. I stumbled out of bed in my pants, straight into the bathroom. I vomited once, twice, and a third time. I vomited so hard that I was forced to my knees. Once the vomit stopped, I shat diarrhoea all over my vomit. That's how my day started – by vomiting and then shitting on it.

It did not in any shape or form feel like the kind of day in which destinies were to be fulfilled.

Despite Damien's revelation that he had invited her, and that she would be arriving in the morning, it didn't seem to click that it would actually happen. It was so unreal, so unbelievable. Still, I prepared for it: I rose at 10:00AM sharp, and after half an hour spent expelling liquid from my orifices, I showered, dressed, preened, and generally made myself as presentable as possible considering the circumstances. Finally, I made my way down to the impressive lobby and wandered over to the all-you-can eat buffet for a steak. There was no sign of Damien or Benedict. I checked my phone – 57 missed calls from Charlie, about a 100 text messages too, which I deleted, one by one, trying not to read them.

When I arrived back at the room, Damien, Elisha, and Elisha's entourage were unpacking and ready to greet me. It soon became evident that Damien's plan had worked perfectly – there was no sign of Benedict. The plan had been a lot more subtle than I would have given him credit for. I should have known – Damien got his kicks from messing with people's lives; he knew how to work the long-game. Elisha had arrived at the airport at 09:00 that morning. Hilariously, Benedict had promised to meet her there in a car. Elisha had also arranged to go to the *Wet Republic* pool party at around midday. Hilariously, Benedict had been planning on going with her. Elisha had also been planning on spending the night with Damien, myself and a few other friends. Hilariously, Benedict had promised to stay in, and look after Benedict Junior. Benedict was in no fit state to manage any of these things; his hangover surpassed both mine and Damien's put together. Apparently, Benedict was well known to suffer from bad hangovers. It was not uncommon for him to be confined to his bed for a whole day, vomiting into a bucket. You would have thought that he would have declined some of the drinks that Damien was forcing down his throat, but Damien is a very difficult man to say "No" to, and his own perceived infallibility had spurred him on to throw caution to the wind. I guessed that the final nail in his coffin had probably been the Jager shots; Damien had given Benedict more than his fair share (possibly twice the amount that I drank).

The upshot of this was that when Elisha arrived at McCarren International Airport, her husband had been otherwise engaged. Damien's plan wouldn't have won any awards for devious genius, but at least it highlighted how utterly useless and unreliable Elisha's husband was on a day she would spend drinking with me.

I felt a flush creep up the back of my head and along my face when I shook her hand and kissed her on the cheek. Initially, she barely registered my presence, greeting me cordially with a pleasant "pleased to meet you," before turning to Damien and entering an in depth conversation with him about her son. Watching their interchange, it was amusing to see Damien on such good behaviour. It became apparent that Damien was not his usual unbearable self when around people on an equal social standing to him. It was only anyone he considered inferior that got to understand who he actually was. Elisha was blissfully unaware of the demon lurking underneath her friend's skin.

At this stage, I was happy to stand back and let Damien take the lead. Elisha trusted him. She trusted him enough to invite him to her secret wedding. To me, this became a clear cut example of Elisha's relationships with all of her friends in the industry. They were all so concerned with impressing each other that they don't really get to know each other. While she spoke to Damien, voicing her irritation at her husband's idiocy, my gaze lingered on her. Initially she was too wrapped up in speaking to Damien, but after a few minutes, I'm sure she could feel me watching. She pretended that she hadn't noticed me staring, but I knew, it was clear as day – a furtive movement of her eyes to the left and then flattered bemusement. Following this she looked anywhere but in my direction. Although she tried to hide it, I sensed raw excitement. Even then, there was something between us.

It was only after our journey to the pool party, where we lay, safely ensconced on two parallel sun-loungers, margaritas in hand, surrounded by hundreds of beautiful bronzed women bopping away in their bikini's that she finally dared speak to me directly.

"So Shaun, I can't quite work out where you fit in. What are you doing here?" It was blunt, but not unkind; she seemed genuinely curious.

"I've been wondering the same about you," I replied coolly. The sweltering Nevada sun beat down upon her chest, her sun-tan oil had turned to a glossy sheen and her breasts were exquisite. I wondered at her slender figure, you wouldn't have known that she had an eight month old son by looking at her. She was abnormal in that way; her beauty had not been tarnished by her pregnancy.

She stopped for a second, unsure whether I was serious. Did I really not know who she was?

"I'm joking. I obviously know who you are, Elisha. I'm a friend of Damien's from London," I smiled.

She pretended to laugh, probably out of politeness – sarcasm was not something she understood.

"God, I love the British sense of humour." She put her warm hand on my shoulder. She had the kind of confidence that can only come to those on top of their game; I knew for a fact that she earned $30 million in 2009. Despite the huge wealth, she didn't seem as detached from reality as Damien; on first impressions, she seemed grounded.

After this little interchange, our awkwardness was gone. She sat beside me and we spoke until sunset. As it turned out, we had very little in common. She persistently and continually spoke about her baby who had been left in the capable arms of one of her bodyguards back at the hotel. Still, I was transfixed. I don't really know how I feigned interest for seven hours, (I imagine the rum, tequila and vodka helped) listening to every insignificant word that she said. On discovering that her personality was not her most valuable asset, I have to admit, my heart sank. I had been so convinced she would be something new, something different. But she was bland. She was sexy and beautiful, but somehow, still a bit boring and un-alluring.

Maybe I was being unfair, I was sure at one point she must have been fun and interesting; she just had a baby on her brain. This just goes to show that no matter what exercise routine or diet women go on following their pregnancy, even if they keep their body in pristine condition, their brain is still fucked – they won't be able to stop mentioning their child in every sentence. In spite of all this bullshit and my own misgivings, she seemed to genuinely enjoy my conversation; she forced a laugh at most of my jokes, she smiled when I smiled, and she flirted with me. There was a steady stream of buff, tanned alpha males trying to chat up Elisha in earnest – but they didn't have a chance – they were outsiders. Elisha was only willing to speak longer than a few seconds with those in the inner-sanctum, namely, Damien, and yours truly. My plan had worked. I had known from the start that if I could only approach her as an equal, I would be able to charm her like I charm everyone else.

The drinks flowed throughout the day, and then the night. It was the same as before – people stopping and gawping in amazement at the film stars, the same idiotic antics from Damien, the hordes of women clamouring for him, even the conversation was the same. Elisha contributed as much to the life and soul of the party as her godforsaken husband, who did not put in an appearance. By the end of the night, the novelty of meeting the one and only Elisha Cicero had completely worn off, and I found myself gazing wistfully at some of the girls surrounding Damien. At one point, I even picked up my phone and listened to some of the messages Charlie had left me following my hasty departure. It hadn't been perfect with Charlie, but at least I had enjoyed listening to her. Charlie had had such a gentle way with words, such a soft and tender voice; I could have listened to her talk for hours. The recorded sound of her sobbing did nothing to lift my spirits, so I switched off my phone in revulsion. With grim and steely determination I accepted my fate. I had made my choice, Elisha was going to do her duty and oblige all my hard effort by rewarding me with fame, her wealth, her lifestyle, and hopefully even her love – there was no point in crying over spilt milk.

Elisha, Benedict, and Benedict Junior left the following morning, straight back to Illinois, where Benedict was due for pre-season training. Benedict lingered over his farewell for an age, he was mildly embarrassed about his absolute failure to function while we were enjoying ourselves. I almost felt sorry for him; he had done exactly what we wanted him to do. Consequently, my send-off was a lot warmer than it would have been otherwise. Although I didn't manage to get into Elisha's pants, nor even manage to kiss her, I felt that the night out had been a tremendous success. I had flirted with her and she had gone away with my business card clasped resolutely in her hand. I had firmly wedged myself a place within her thoughts, and perhaps even her hopes. I was certain that she would eventually come clambering into my bed. The seeds had been sown and Elisha would inevitably become mine.

The rest of my time in Vegas, although equally booze fuelled, was not as pleasant as it could have been. Damien had fulfilled his part of our bargain and built me up in front of Elisha. Consequently, he spent the rest of the week systematically putting me down in front of everyone else. Some of his hilarious antics involved: forcing me to drink until I vomited, pissing on me as I lay asleep by the pool, locking me out of the apartment, and even throwing an empty bottle of beer at my face (resulting in a chipped tooth). By dint of my gratitude, and the knowledge that I would likely need further support from him in the coming months, I was able to restrain my anger, and pretended I was amused by it all. By the end of the holiday, something had shifted in Damien's attitude towards me, and although he still enjoyed asserting his authority, he did so in a more amicable way. His actions weren't laced with the true venom that they were previously; the threat of madness in his eyes, although not completely gone, had at least been tarnished. He didn't treat me with anything like real respect, but I believe that he thought of me as – if not a friend – a pet, or a plaything, or something of that ilk.

July 10th 2009

I returned home a broken man, the depravity of Vegas leaving me well and truly destroyed. After a horrendous flight sat next to a sweaty fat man with halitosis, I was ready for a rest. Unfortunately, as I walked through my door, reality rushed up and slammed me in the face – I dry heaved when I saw the awful blood stain on my carpet. Vegas hadn't completely wiped Terry's new incident from my mind, but it had helped me to pretend that I was less fucked up about it than I actually was. I hadn't expected such a huge surge of fear and disgust to overpower my senses, but I could barely face being alone in my apartment. With shaking legs and a booming heart, I locked myself in my room and attempted to push the memory away again. I looked at my phone, and felt a flood of longing for Charlie's embrace. I had decided that I couldn't call her again, there was no telling what Damien would do to me if I got back with her, and the thought of that maniacal look in his eyes made me fear for my life. I was exhausted; I shouldn't have done it, but with the blood stain on my carpet playing on my mind, I found myself calling Polly to find out what had become of Terry. It was all very different from his first *incident* when I had been holistically involved in the recovery process.

Polly: "Shaun?" (She must still have my number saved on her phone)

Shaun: "Polly, sorry it's a bit late, but I'm just back from holiday and wanted to check on Terry, see how he is."

Polly: "Why? What's happened to Terry?"

Me: "Shit, I thought you knew."

Polly: "Knew what? What have you done to him now?" (I let this pass).

Me: "Ok, before I tell you, please can you stay calm?"

Polly: "Stop being so pretentious and just tell me."

Me: "You're not going to like this, and I'm sorry it's ended up this way."

Polly: "What's happened?"

Me: "He's castrated himself."

Polly: "WHAT?? WHAT DO YOU MEAN HE'S CASTRATED HIMSELF?"

Me: "Polly, there's no way to sugar-coat this, he's cut his nuts and dick off."

Polly: "Are you being serious?"

Me: "Unfortunately, yes. Sorry."

Polly: "How? When? "

Me: "With a meat-cleaver last week."

Polly: "WHAT? WHY ARE YOU ONLY TELLING ME NOW?"

Me: "I've been on holiday."

Polly: "So how did you know about it if you've been on holiday?"

Me: "He did it in my flat."

Polly: "What, and then you just went on holiday like nothing happened?"

Me: "No, I needed to get away from it all after what I'd seen."

Polly: "I've never in my life known such a selfish prick. Why didn't you call me? Have you spoken to him at least?"

Me: "I called the hospital to check if he was alive, and they said he seemed to be doing ok."

Polly: "So you just left him there? Did you tell anyone else what had happened?"

Me: "Like who?"

Polly: "Like his family, or someone who actually cares about someone else apart from themselves!"

Me: "Well I was the one who called the fucking ambulance. I assumed that they would be able to sort everything else out."

Polly: "I can't believe you just fucking sent him to the hospital and haven't called."

Me: "Well, I was hoping that you'd know."

Polly: "How was I supposed to know? Divination? You didn't tell me, you prick."

Me: "Calm down, he's OK."

Polly: "He's chopped his fucking balls off. Of course he's not OK."

Me: "And his cock."

Polly: "What?"

Me: "He chopped off his cock too."

Polly: "And that's supposed to make me feel better is it? Oh! You're right. He MUST be okay if he's chopped off his cock as well. Thanks SO MUCH for reminding me."

Me: "Polly, I'm too tired to do this now. Can't you just find out if he's ok?"

Polly: "Just do me a favour and fuck off out of both our lives Shaun."

Me: "I'd love to thanks. It's you two who keep drawing me back in."

As usual, she hung up on me. I went to sleep almost immediately after our interchange. Conversations with Polly were always exhausting, but this one took the biscuit. I shook away these unpleasant thoughts, and went to sleep imagining what Elisha would be like in bed.

July 11th – November 30th 2009

I had the foresight to ensure I had the whole weekend to recover. I pretty much slept and did nothing else. I don't know when a really long, really deep sleep clinically becomes a coma, but I'm pretty sure my sleep that weekend came fairly close. I didn't even cook for myself. I lay in bed and got takeaway curry delivered to the door (for lunch and dinner), and ate it in my underpants in my bedroom.

Despite festering among my own filth for 48 hours, rising for work was a real struggle. I really wanted to call a sicky for one more day. My head felt heavy and my eyes hurt in the daylight, but I forced my way through the dismal grey summer morning and with my head bowed low, I walked into the office to face my job. I was greeted with 842 emails in my Inbox. After arranging for a new carpet to be fitted, I diligently made my way through them all, not having the motivation to actually respond to anything. Instead, I sorted them into two folders: *Money Men* and *Waste Men*. Apart from a few diamonds in the rough, unfortunately, the majority of them were *Waste Men*. The 409th email that I checked was from someone called Violet Gently. With a sigh, I opened it, subconsciously getting ready to move it to my *Waste Men* folder.

From: Violet.Gently
Sent: 5 July 2009 22:30
To: Shaun.Valfierno

Shaun,

Sorry about the alter-ego but I'm sure you understand! I wanted to tell you how much fun I had with you guys the other night. You were a perfect gentleman, and definitely know how to show a girl a good time. Let me know if you're ever in the neighbourhood and I'll be sure to return the favour.

Elisha

X

As I read the signature, kiss and all, I felt that there was nothing else to do but grin moronically and salute the screen. I read the email again, and then again and then at least another ten times, attempting to uncover what she really meant. Did it have a genuine "nice to meet you" sentiment, or was it only a polite American custom? Was there a whiff of "I want to fuck your brains out", or did she somehow think that I was only interested in her friendship? Did she always use that pseudonym because of her celebrity status, or had she created a new account in order to keep everything a secret from her husband? I thought long and hard on how to reply, and finally came up with this:

From: Shaun.Valfierno
Sent: 13 July 2009 11:14
To: Violet.Gently

Hey Babe.

Great to hear from you! Yes, it was fantastic wasn't it? Me and Terry were a little lonely after you'd gone. I've got to tell you, I haven't met anyone as charismatic, or interesting as you for a long time. I had so much fun! It really was like a shadow was cast over the Nevada desert after your plane had flown away. Chicago is a very lucky town indeed.

If I'm honest, I doubt that I'll be able to make it out there any time soon (but I suppose I could be persuaded, wink wink) In the mean-time, are you likely to be travelling to London? It would be great to pick up where we left off.

Love

Shaun

P.S Violet Gently?

After I sent the message, I looked over what I had said and was initially pleased. I felt that it had the right amount of charm, mixed in with a playful goofiness that would be sure to attract her; it hinted that I wanted something more, but was not overstated so as to scare her (a married woman) away. Most importantly, there was no mention in either her, or my email about her husband. Then, with a jolt, I realised: Terry?? What the fuck?? I had accidentally used Terry's name instead of Damien's. What the fuck was wrong with me? It's so Goddamned irritating when you're trying to be smooth and you do something like that. It might be a small mistake, but it can speak volumes to the person you're trying to impress If she doesn't know who Terry is, she won't understand the rest of the sentence, and then all the compliments following it might come across as a little weird or desperate.

It's not even like I'd be able to send an email to correct the mistake – if I did that, it would look like I was trying too hard. Fucking Terry, still messing with my mind from his sick bed.

Thankfully, she didn't mention my faux pas and responded before the day was over:

From: Violet.Gently
Sent: 13 July 2009 16:23
To: Shaun.Valfierno

Shaun!

I was beginning to wonder whether your Vegas hangover had killed you! You can't leave us Prima Donnas hanging around like that ya know? Soooooooo pleased you finally emailed me ;) Well….Violet Gently! OMG it's a bit embarrassing, but you asked so I'm gonna tell you! Have you ever heard of a porno name? Violet is what my cat was called and my mom's name before she married daddy was Gently. Put them together and what do you get??

Love

Violet (lol) xx

Once again, I found the email intriguing and difficult to read into. Certainly it seemed to hint at a fun personality that had been repressed by her baby brain when I met her. It was good to hear her referencing something sexual in an email, albeit limited to the single word 'porno' in a sentence. If she had created this porno email just for me, that would speak volumes, but if she always used it, then it was simply a quirk of her personality and I was reading too much into it.

Frustratingly, the only question she asked me was whether I'd heard of a porno name. This wasn't the kind of question that needed answering, nor did she really invite me to continue our correspondence. Unnervingly, I got the distinct impression that she would have preferred to have ceased contact then and there. I tried to convince myself that it was because she was feeling guilty about finding me attractive; unfortunately, when dealing with someone as beautiful and successful as Elisha, you need more confidence than sense and I couldn't quite manage it. Regardless of her reasons, I wasn't going to end it there; if I had to force her into my life – I would.

From: Shaun.Valfierno
Sent: 13 July 2009 18:45
To: Violet.Gently

Violet, My name is Fluffy Jonson, I'm pleased to make your acquaintance.
Kindest Regards
Lord Fluffy Jonson IV

Thankfully, it had the desired effect:

From: Violet.Gently
Sent: 13July 2009 19:13
To: Shaun.Valfierno
LOL! That's made my day! Why hello Mr. Fluffy, I'm pleased to meet you too. Now, with a name like Fluffy Jonson I was wondering what you might do for a living?

From: Shaun.Valfierno
Sent: 13 July 2009 19:22
To: Violet.Gently
Dear Violet,
That's the million dollar question. Come to London and I'll show you.
P.S. It may be pertinent to bring a video camera, that way you'll be able to capture my career in its entirety.

It was all very tongue-in-cheek, but was a genuine invite nonetheless, and I hoped that she would either accept it at face value or shrug it off as another joke. If the whim took her, she could come and see me almost any time she wanted to. Unfortunately, I didn't get a response that night, nor did she tell me she was jumping on a plane when I got her response the following afternoon, though her tone remained playful.

I continued my correspondence with Elisha, emailing her at least three times a day, and always received a response. Usually the emails were of a very light-hearted nature – I wanted to show her my fun side. Her emails were of a very similar nature also, and I began to hope that the personality which had been suffocated by her baby-brain might still be showing some signs of life. That's not to say that she didn't mention her son at all. In fact, there was usually some kind of off-hand comment about something that Junior had done that made her laugh or feel particularly motherly feelings. Although I couldn't have given a crap whether Junior was Jesus Christ reincarnated, I dutifully responded with comments I thought Elisha would appreciate – things like: "WOW! He's really growing up!" or "My God that's so cute! – comments that made me gag as I wrote them. After a few weeks of very regular contact, she even allowed me intimate glimpses into her domestic life – things like how she was struggling balancing her duties as a mother with her career, or her concerns as to how much having a baby had affected her figure.

Best of all though, she started to complain about her husband to me whenever they had a fight. The great thing about her frustrations at Benedict was that they were about normal everyday issues, and I was easily able to fan the flames: "What?!! He's almost 30 and a father, you'd think he'd have learnt how to clean up after himself by now!" or: "How can he think that's acceptable? You're not his mother too!" and best of all: "If he can't be bothered to spend time with his son, he's just a bad father, simple as that."

I was very happy to find out that no matter how much money you earn, your wife still expects you to tidy up your own plate and change your own son's nappy. Her moron of a husband seemed incapable of doing any of this after a long hard day of egg-chasing.

Some of my comments may seem quite bold, but I felt our relationship had grown strong enough for me to be able to say whatever I wanted. Apparently, I wasn't quite there yet – her response to my last comment clearly demonstrated where her loyalties lay:

From: Violet.Gently
Sent: 23 October 2009 15:37
To: Shaun.Valfierno
Listen!
Benedict is not a bad father. How DARE you presume to judge him?????

From: Shaun.Valfierno
Sent: 23 October 2009 15:51
To: Violet.Gently
Hi Babe
Sorry, I got a little carried away there. I didn't mean to upset you, but sometimes I feel like all you do is complain about him. Over these past few months I've grown to realise how strong and beautiful you are, inside and out. I sometimes worry that Benedict doesn't treat you like you should be treated. But I guess, in my eyes at least, nobody is good enough for you.
Sorry again, hope you find it in your heart to forgive me.
Love Fluffy
xx

Thankfully, flattery gets you everywhere:

From: Violet.Gently
Sent: 23 October 2009 16:46
To: Shaun.Valfierno
It's OK, I can never stay mad at you for long ;)
You're just too darned cute! I'm not everything you
think I am though, you only get to hear one side of
the story, you might give Benedict a break if you
heard his side.
Xx

From: Shaun.Valfierno
Sent: 23 October 2009 17:15
To: Violet.Gently
Don't ever put yourself down. You are everything
I think you are and much much more. Your heart
beats and the world listens. You only deserve the
best in life.
x

It was around this time that Charlie Ekells fell from grace. It started out as something seemingly innocuous – she missed a couple of *Brekkie Time* shows due to illness. To someone who knew her though, this simple fact spoke volumes about something being seriously wrong in her life. Charlie never missed work. Come hell or high water she always made it into her presenter's chair. One weekend prior to our breakup, she had been bed-ridden with a pretty serious stomach bug, but still, on Monday morning, she forced herself into the studio. Nobody watching her would have been able to tell that she had a bucket beneath her desk and was vomiting into it during the ad-breaks. As a consequence, in October 2009, when I noticed that she had been temporarily replaced by the winner of the previous year's Soma Holiday, I grew concerned for her well-being.

It was only a few days later, when her picture appeared in *A-List* magazine, that I discovered what had been going on. She hadn't made the front page at this point – those stories would come later – but she had been snapped in a very compromising position for someone with her outspoken views on religion. I was at home when I saw it, drinking a cup of coffee and eating some toast. She was in a nightclub, holding a bottle of wine to her lips and guzzling it as if it were water. She was wearing a mini-skirt, and a greasy looking man – clearly a play-boy of some description – was grinding her backside. His hand, his sleazy little hand, was placed between her thighs massaging her cunt. Worst of all though, was her hand. She held it behind her back, groping his crotch like a common slut. He was smiling in that knowing way that certain men smile, ready to take her home and fuck her brains out. I threw the magazine across the room in disgust. I didn't feel any pity for Charlie, just red hot anger. How had she reduced herself to this? How had she become something that she had always pertained to hate? Had it all been a lie – her belief in God? her chastity?

What a fucking bitch, to pretend to have beliefs and then give them up as soon as her life got a little bumpy. I immediately lost any guilt over leaving Charlie in favour of Elisha; Charlie had grown into something much worse than her brother – she had become tabloid fodder. According to the article that accompanied the image, she called in sick just a few hours after that photo had been taken, and now her whole career had been compromised.

Over the weeks and months that followed, Charlie became a joke. Each new headline took her down further and further until, quite frankly, the nation got bored with her antics. It was as if the press relished it. In her previous life she had been so chaste, so immaculate, and so saintly, that it was as if she had painted a big red target on herself. If it had been someone else, someone who hadn't been so outspoken about alcohol, about drugs, someone who hadn't been on the television, then nobody would have noticed. Nobody would have cared that she was caught on camera giving fellatio, that she snorted cocaine, or that she was thrown out of a night-club for punching a bar-girl in the face. Scarlett, whose own life had not been left unaffected by Charlie's outburst at her wedding, revelled in Charlie's demise. Like all of the other cynics in the country, Scarlett felt that it was all poetically just. For me however, each new low fuelled my anger at her. She had become a different person; she had become someone that I despised.

December 2009

Frustrations and boredom plagued me over the coming weeks. I was so close to my goal, I was so close to being able to hold Elisha that I struggled to get anything done at work. I lost my appetite. I lost my motivation in my job. Just picking up the phone to speak with an applicant became a chore, and the sheer ordinariness of my life threatened to suffocate me. I was itching to ask her to come to London again. This time though, I would be sure to be clear that it wasn't a joke. The problem was that if I mistimed it and scared her away, I wouldn't get a second chance. So I continued flirting from afar, forcing my way into her thoughts through cyberspace and bearing the tediousness of my existence with as much sophistication as I could muster. Scarlett's tits, at least, helped dull the pain.

Then, after months of talking, and waiting, and hoping, I finally got the email from Elisha that I'd been itching for:

From: <u>Violet.Gently</u>
Sent: 2nd December 2009 12:22
To: <u>Shaun.Valfierno</u>

Fluffy!

How are you feeling today? A bit better I hope? You know what I think? Tell your boss where to shove it where the sun don't shine and find yourself a different job. Real estate isn't important enough to get this upset about. Anyway, I've got something that will cheer you up: I'm coming to London next week! I'm plugging 'Elfish Days' on a few shows. Do you think we could meet?

Love

Violet

From: <u>Shaun.Valfierno</u>
Sent: 2nd December 2009 12:28
To: <u>Violet.Gently</u>

Violet,

I'm so excited to see you I can barely concentrate on my work! When is your flight in? I can pick you up if you want? Is Junior coming too?

Love

Fluffy

From: <u>Violet.Gently</u>
Sent: 2nd December 2009 12:46
To: <u>Shaun.Valfierno</u>

Fluffy

It's just me I'm afraid, you'll have to wait until next time to see the little monster. It's so nice of you to offer to pick me up, but Eyeall has arranged everything for me. I fly in on Monday night, I've

*promised to meet up with Damien on Tuesday and
I've got to work on Wednesday, but I should be
available for lunch on Thursday?*

Lots of love
Violet xx

On reading these last few emails, I was struck by a nasty thought: had I become a *nice* friend called Fluffy who ate *Eggs* bloody *Benedict* at brunch? Did this mean she didn't consider me to be the kind of friend who would take her out and show her a good time? Our emails over the months had become ever more flirtatious, but I was concerned that my nickname and all my stupid statements about her son hadn't contributed to my alpha-male image. I tried to allay my concerns by considering my situation logically, and decided that it shouldn't really matter; I was, after all, supposed to be playing the long-game. I had done my best to win her affections, and if the best I could do for now was to be a trusted friend, then so be it. I could push into the boundaries of her heart over time. However, following these thoughts, I had to face my work for another hour, and although the credit crunch was supposed to be in decline, every measly second that I sat at my desk felt like torture, and my calm decision to bide my time was thrown out of the window. I couldn't live a normal life anymore. I wanted something exceptional. I needed to close the deal ASAP. Elisha's sweet friend Fluffy was going to remind her that he was, after all, Fluffy Jonson, porn-star extraordinaire.

The first port of call was to get in touch with Damien, which was a feat easier set upon than accomplished – he wasn't the kind of person to return messages out of politeness. I bombarded him with SMS, emails, and phone calls, but the arsehole didn't get back to me for two whole days. I doubt he would have even told me he was in the UK but for my relentless persistence. My understanding was that he and his sister had become a lot closer since I broke up with her, and I imagine he had planned to spend most of his time partying with the new Charlie (something to which I would definitely not be welcome). He did, however, oblige me in so much as allowing me to crash his night out with Elisha when he found out that I was intending to close the deal. He wasn't convinced that I had any chance of success, but, it seemed to amuse him that I still hadn't give up the ghost and his devious streak revelled in the possibility of an upcoming scandal. Amongst a few other favours, I asked him not to tell Elisha that I was coming, and to make sure that she was well lubricated before I arrived.

Tuesday 8th December 2009

The days preceding the big night out felt painfully drawn out; I spent them sitting at my desk doing the absolute minimum amount of work possible. For the first time in my career, I arrived at the office as late as possible (08:45 – before the daily morning meetings), and departed as early as possible (19:00 – the time that my contract stated was the end of my working day.) I don't know what the rest of the office thought of my attitude change, but Lance took me aside one day to express his own concerns.

"Shaun, can I have a word?" he said as I arrived one morning at 08:50 (five minutes late for the morning meeting). He took me into the little office that was usually reserved for *Dead Men Walking*, and for a moment I thought he might be handing me my P45. To my utter surprise, rather than being worried or upset by the notion of leaving my job, I was overcome with excitement.

"Take a seat," he said to me, and I wondered how many other people had taken the same seat as I had before having all their belongings handed to them in a box. Shrugging my shoulders, I sat down in the seat that had a window behind my back. Sitting opposite me,

Lance would have the sun in his eyes. I felt that this would give me some kind of psychological advantage over him in the power struggle that was to follow.

"Shaun," he said, "Do you know why I wanted to speak with you today?" he said, squinting slightly into the bright sunrays.

"I'm guessing that you felt it was something important." I replied.

"Yes, I need to know where your head is at. Your figures have been in steady decline for the past six months. Have you got anything to say about that?"

"It's the economy," I replied, without hesitation.

"You know as well as I, that's not an excuse in this office. You're supposed to be a Senior Sales Consultant, but you're not acting like one. I need some assurances from you about your figures. What are you going to do to turn them around?"

"Lance, I've worked in this office for six years. Have I ever let you down before?"

"Shaun, there's only so much time your experience can buy you. I need to start seeing some results. What's in your pipeline for this week?"

"I've got viewings lined up every night this week."

"Are they first or second viewings? Are any of these actually going to turn into business or are you just going through the motions?"

"Ok, they're first viewings, and realistically, I'm not going to get any serious offers before next week. As of next week, you'll see my figures increase dramatically."

"What about banking some money? Have you got anything close to exchange?"

"Mallord Street has had an issue with the survey, and the first-time buyers in Nell Gwynn House have had their mortgage rejected, so nothing this week, no."

"Have you referred either of them to Woolsten Marks?"

"Not yet, no."

He was silent for a moment, perhaps wondering how to continue, and then sighed:

"Shaun, I can't have a senior team member fucking up now; it's difficult enough as it is. How can you suggest that you're doing everything you can, if you haven't even referred your applicants to our own mortgage broker?"

"OK, good point, I'll refer them today."

"I can't have any more empty promises from you. You're going to finish on doughnuts again, aren't you? I need you to tell me what actions you're taking to sort yourself out?"

God, I was bored by this, I knew what he wanted me to say, but was really struggling to give a fuck. It wasn't that I hated my job, but somehow my priorities had shifted so that it was no longer the most important thing in my life. My obsession with winning Elisha had become frenzied; it had become an all-consuming drain on my mind and energy. Still, frustratingly, I couldn't just abandon my job on the off-chance I would be successful with Elisha, so I swallowed my pride and gave Lance what he wanted:

"Ok, write this down, Lance. By next week you'll be eating your words," I smiled, building up some fake camaraderie.

"Really?" His eyes glistened hopefully and he was suddenly looking a little less sceptical. Lance was a true believer in arrogant swagger as proof of confidence and motivation. This was exactly the kind of thing I would have said before I started my crusade for Elisha.

"Yes, first of all, I accept that my head's not been in the game recently, but I promise that as of tomorrow morning I will once again be first in and last to leave. I will have the highest talk time on the phone, and I will pledge to you that I will get a minimum of one million pounds worth of property under offer over the next fortnight."

It was fairly strong talk, but if I could get my focus on the job back to what it once was, it wouldn't be impossible. After all, the following day I would know one way or another whether Elisha was attracted to me. For now though, Lance seemed to be satisfied.

Damien had taken Elisha to a member's club, so when I arrived that night, I needed him to come down and sign me in. I was pleased to notice that he already stank of whiskey; he had clearly taken my instructions about making sure that they were well lubricated to heart. She too was looking a little worse for wear.

"FLUFFY! I didn't know you were coming!" she screamed as I walked through the door. She took a running leap into my arms and kissed me on the cheek. A couple of people smirked into their glasses as they heard my nickname.

"Fluffy???" Damien grimaced in distaste.

"It's a long story. I'll explain later," I whispered back at him, still locked in a delicious Cicero embrace.

"I hadn't expected to see you until Thursday, Fluffs! Why didn't you tell me you were coming tonight?" she slurred, before kissing me wetly on the cheek again.

"I wanted to surprise you, Vi. Seems like you're having a good night?"

"Yes! So much fun! Do you fancy a dance?"

"Give me a chance to get a drink, but yes, sounds good."

I walked to the bar and ordered an *Old Fashioned*. Elisha followed me smiling from ear to ear. While the barman was making my drink – stirring furiously and making a great show of his barman flair– Elisha chattered away. She seemed so enormously pleased to see me, and didn't mention Benedict Junior once. After a couple of cocktails, I risked my skills on the dance-floor. Elisha didn't mind my clumsy confidence; in fact, she giggled into her hands and copied my idiotic moves before showing what she could really do. Presumably she had learnt how to dance during her drama tuition because she was amazing. As usual, I found myself threatened by her success – people were watching her out of the corner or their eyes. After a time, people's attention also moved to me, and although I've always said I didn't care that I was technically inept on the dance-floor, on this occasion, I found it difficult to remain self-assured and my movements became awkward and ungainly. Thankfully, Elisha realised how difficult I was finding it, and put me out of my misery by taking my hand and leading me back towards the bar, where we stood chatting for several hours.

Despite having Elisha's undivided attention, I was finding it difficult to make my move with so many eyes watching. It began to get very late, and I was starting to worry that I had missed my chance. Thankfully, Damien came to the rescue:

"My place is five minutes away in a taxi, I suggest we all head back there to finish what we've started?"

Elisha grimaced and looked at her watch:

"I've gotta work tomorrow, D. I should probably get some sleep."

"Hey, what do you take me for? I've had a room made up for you. What hotel are you staying at?"

"The *Shermalt.*"

"Yeah, you'll get a much better sleep than if you head back to that shit-hole. It's all the way across town too. I tell you what, I'll even make you breakfast in bed."

Elisha smiled and put her hand on his chest, fondly.

"You're always so sweet. Of course I'll stay."

It was always a shock to see Damien act this way, so out of character; he must have found it a real chore. I found myself feeling extremely grateful towards him – he seemed to have a real soft-spot for me and my objective.

It had all been part of the plan (I could hardly have hoped to seduce her from my own hovel), but he was going out of his way to make it seem both easy and natural to head back to his enormous bachelor pad. Even so, he really was going beyond the call of duty to be offering her breakfast in bed.

The taxi was waiting outside for us. I found myself drifting off to sleep on the short journey home. Damien pinched me hard on my arm, so hard, that I think he may have drawn blood. The sharp pain dug into my brain, and I was soon wide awake.

"I've spent many fucking hours helping you out on this fucking futile endeavour of yours. Don't insult me by falling asleep now, or I promise you'll fucking regret it." He whispered venomously in my ear. There he was again, the real Damien peeking through the cracks. I touched him on the shoulder.

"D, don't think I don't appreciate everything you've done for me. Trust me! I will seal the deal tonight if it kills me."

"Don't do it again."

I saluted in response.

He smiled at me then, a dangerous sort of smile, and I knew that he would destroy me if I offended him with such stupidity again. I knew I was playing with fire asking a favour of Damien; this time clearly, was no exception. I kept my hand on his shoulder as if to reassure him. Elisha in the meantime, was completely oblivious to our discussion in the corner; she was too busy soaking in the sights of London Town.

We arrived back at Damien's purpose-built apartment block, recently designed and constructed by the multi-millionaire developer Alaweed Al-Sawiris. It overlooked the river and was made almost entirely of glass. I would have given my right hand to get a viewing in there, but they were almost always sold privately for disgusting prices. I assumed that Damien rented this place on a short-term lease when in town, but didn't want to ask him – if he actually owned the place, I was fairly sure that he would take my question as an insult and harbour a grudge until he found a good moment to exact his revenge.

I found myself wondering what kind of relationship he now had with Charlie. Previously, he had usually been on best-behaviour around her, trying his hardest to prove he was worthy of her approval. He had begged her the night before Scarlett's wedding not to ruin Scarlett's marriage. He knew that she would hold the family rift he had caused against him, and for some reason, this had caused him to panic. Now that he had nothing to prove to Charlie, now that he had pulled her down to his own level, I wondered whether he still crept around her with a limp-dick. Somehow I doubted it, and I wondered how Charlie was coping with the relentless abuse.

In the meantime, Elisha jumped onto the sofa, and this time it was she who looked like she was going to fall asleep. Damien looked at me meaningfully.

"Elisha," he said "I'll go and make sure your room is ready, and make us a drink."

"Thanks, dude" she said, putting her thumb in the air. Before leaving the room, he walked over to me and whispered in my ear:

"Time to close the deal I think, Shaun."

I winked at him confidently as he exited up the wide marble stair case. Elisha was drunk, and we were finally alone together. I slipped next to her on the sofa and silently looked at her directly in the eyes. Amidst the cautious fear of betraying her husband, I could tell she was tempted; her eyes were eating me up and begging me to make a move. There was no point in delaying any longer, or checking whether she really wanted to do this – in fact, in her right mind, I was fairly certain that she wouldn't have chosen me over her famous husband. Her husband was more successful, more wealthy, taller and broader, but she was away from him, and I was her chance to try something different. That night, I was a symbol of the unknown, an emblem of excitement. Marriage does that to people – it turns a stimulating and vibrant relationship into something boring and repetitive. I've always felt that to have a successful and lasting marriage, you really have to hate yourself. It's the equivalent of being on the Atkins diet. Over the last few years, metaphorically speaking, Elisha had eaten a hell of a lot of steak, and it had been good for her. However, now she was faced with something a bit naughty and delicious; I guess I was the equivalent of some Special Fried Rice from a Chinese takeaway. Perhaps not quite as good for her as her usual diet, but for the love of God, she must have been sick to death of sirloin.

The room was quiet. A flash storm had started up outside and the rain hammered against the glass. Without saying a word, I moved my hand towards her own, our fingertips touched: it felt electric. I knew she had resolved to move her hand away from mine, but she couldn't, she wanted my touch, and so for a time we sat in silence, fingertips gently touching, eyes locked. My other hand stroked her arm, slowly moving upwards to scoop the back of her neck. I felt fifteen again, butterflies flittered away in my stomach when I realised what was happening. She resisted slightly as I pulled her face towards my own, but it was a half-hearted struggle and she melted to my touch. Her lips parted, and I kissed her long and hard.

Did the ground shake when we kissed? Did music play? Did seraphims look down from on high and write sonnets of beauty and wonder? The answer: unequivocally no. For my part, I was ecstatic at reaching my goal, but as soon as my initial excitement passed, I noticed that her breath stank of stale-booze. Further to this, I couldn't get Charlie out of my mind; was Elisha really worth it? Had this beautiful, sexy, glamorous woman with the breath of a disease-ridden camel really been worth ruining Charlie's life? At that moment, (probably because I was trying not to gag) I felt a wave of shame and remorse. I hadn't just ruined Charlie's life: I had shattered her beliefs, and maimed her self-respect. Perhaps my lack of passion rubbed off on Elisha – she pulled back from me.

"I can't do this to Benedict, I have to go." When she said this, the thrill of the chase returned, and I forgot all my misgivings. I pulled her back, and whispered.

"Come on, nobody's going to know." I began to kiss her neck gently, and she moaned softly, allowing me to continue.

"I'm no good for you, Shaun, I'm married."

"I know" I said, without stopping.

"I've got a son."

"I know." I repeated.

"We have to stop."

"What, and miss out on the good bit?" I put my hand between her legs. She moaned louder than before, but managed to pull herself together, and stopped me.

"God, you wouldn't believe how much I want this. But I really can't," she said, now standing up. She bent down and kissed me on the forehead.

"I know it's clichéd, but in another life-time, it would have been perfect."

"I'll hold you to that." I replied, knowing that her other life would arrive a lot sooner than she expected. Little did she know, that I had anonymously tipped-off a paparazzi photographer who had documented our entire night with a wide-angled lens.

<u>December 2009 – May 2011</u>

The story hit the papers while Elisha was still in the UK. I can only imagine how Benedict reacted to the furore, but I expect he wasn't particularly happy to see a snapshot of my hand on his wife's cunt. It really didn't help matters that Elisha was contractually obliged to remain in the UK until her film hit the cinemas. I didn't feel guilty about it at all, and surprisingly, it was I who had suggested it to Damien (not the other way round). I just felt that I couldn't go on pretending that I cared about my job any longer; I couldn't wait for it to play out naturally. I was easily able to justify it to myself that it would have happened anyway eventually, and if Elisha hadn't kissed me, the pictures wouldn't have been of any public interest whatsoever. It was really Elisha's own fault for giving into temptation, and not my own.

My favourite headline was presented in A-List magazine:

"The *Real* Notting Hill"

I was pleasantly surprised to find that it painted me in a very positive light, beginning with the following line: "*Move over Hugh Grant and Julia Roberts, Shaun and Elisha are in town! Life has been bleak for most estate agents in recent months, all except for one man who has caught the eye of none other than glamourpuss Elisha Cicero! Shaun Valfierno, the stud who has captured Elisha's heart, has so far remained tight-lipped about what really happened on his night out with the stars last week, but sources tell us that he is over the moon...*" Thankfully, in the UK at least, the magazines and tabloids all seemed to be on my side, completely glossing over the usual moral qualms involved with adultery. I suppose it was probably something to do with the fact that on the whole, stories about cuckolded American Footballers do not generally make for interesting reading in Britain. In just a few days, I had become a celebrity of note.

The day the story hit, my colleagues all applauded me as I walked into the office. Lance shrugged his shoulders when I handed in my notice.

"What's the plan now Shaun?" he said.

"I don't know, but there's a lot of easy money to be had. I hope you understand?"

"Of course I do, but is it going to last?"

"If I'm honest, I don't know. But I need a bit of a shake-up anyway. If I play this right, I might be able to set up my own sales-office."

"That's not a bad idea, as long as you don't come sniffing round any of my clients."

"What? In this hellhole? No chance. There's no money to be made here."

Lance laughed at my irony.

Generally speaking, people in sales do not work their notice periods off. Management know that someone who is leaving is unlikely to be motivated enough to actually make any money; as such, I walked out of the office ten minutes later. As usual for someone leaving, there was no card or leaving present. I left silently, without even a farewell to Guy. I left work, and headed straight to Damien's for some drinks to celebrate.

The weeks that followed were a little odd. It was especially strange having to talk my mother through what had happened with Elisha, and how I'd been stupid to allow such graphic pictures to be taken. If my father was star-struck at the notion of Charlie, he positively reeled at the thought of me and Elisha. My whole family were bombarded by a sea of story-mongers hoping to find something of my back-story. Thankfully, I'd always kept my true self at arm's length from them, so even if they had wanted to, they would have very little to tell.

I sent Elisha only one text message, knowing that she would eventually come back:

"Hey, sorry about everything that's happened. Damien's furious and is trying to sue the papers. If I ever find out who it was that took those pictures, someone is going to end up in hospital. I've lost my job because of all the publicity. Call me if you need a shoulder to cry on. Love Fluffy."

I had no response from her for several weeks. I grew accustomed to journalists and photographers stopping me in the street, but as far as possible, I tried to avoid all contact. If I was ever going to win Elisha properly, she had to believe that I wasn't actively looking to sell my story.

It was over this period that I finally managed to sever my ties with Scarlett. I hadn't spoken to her since before the pictures were published, and in fact, she had slipped from my mind what with everything that was happening. She arrived at my place one evening unannounced, carrying a bottle of *Veuve Cliquot* and wearing a fur-coat, stilettos and nothing else. I couldn't help but grimace when I saw her, it was all rather hackneyed, and I had grown to expect a lot more from her. She must have noticed the look on my face – she flushed red and her nostrils flared.

"Are you going to invite me in then, Mr. Cicero?"

"Yes, of course, come in, sexy!" I mumbled awkwardly, kissing her on the cheek.

"That's not quite the reaction I was expecting," she said.

"Sorry babe. I wasn't expecting you."

"I know. It's a surprise."

"Well you're here now."

"Yes."

We stood in my hallway for a few moments. I'm guessing that she had expected me to ravish her the moment she walked through the door, but I really couldn't be bothered with her nonsense.

"Scarlett, this is really nice but I'm not feeling well. I'm just about to head to bed," I lied, hoping that she could take a hint.

"Don't be such a baby, Shaun, I'm horny, I need a fuck," she grabbed my cock through my trousers when she said this.

"I'm serious, babe, I just need some rest."

Tears welled in her eyes, but she fought them back down.

"You'll fuck it all up, you know."

"What?"

"You'll fuck it up somehow, and then you'll have nobody"

I began to feel sorry for her.

"I think it's time for you to leave."

"It's all going to go wrong for you, Shaun, like it has for me"

"Ok." I opened the door and ushered her out.

"When it does, don't come crawling back to me."

"Ok, bye." I closed the door in her face.

As expected, Elisha's relationship with Benedict senior ended just a few days after her return to America, the evidence was too damning, and according to one source in the press, the marriage had become 'untenable'. It wasn't long before I got her response:

"Hi Fluffs, thanks for your message, I know it wasn't your fault (hey! It takes two to Tango!). I'm not sure if you've seen, but me and Benedict have separated ☹, me and Junior are staying with my mom at the moment. I'm so miserable I can't sleep. I feel terrible about you losing your job! What a mess we've got ourselves into! Anyway, I know this is unwise, but I was hoping that I could take you up on that offer of a shoulder to cry on? Benedict has Junior next weekend and I really could use something to cheer me up. Let me know if it's convenient for you, and relax, it's my fault that you've lost your job so dinner is on me. xxx"

It really was as easy as that. I guess she decided that as she had already been punished for sleeping with me, but had not in fact done the deed, she may as well give in to temptation after all. We met in secret, and spent the entire weekend in a hotel room gorging on room-service. I was pleased to note that the bad-breath that had been so shocking when first we kissed appeared to be a one off occurrence; she looked, smelt, and tasted sublime.

Due to the number of unsolicited calls I was receiving, I changed my phone number and made sure that I only gave out my new contact details to people who I had any inclination of staying in touch with. Consequently, I lost touch with Charlie, Terry, and Polly. Though I did often wonder what had become of them all.

Once I had her, it was only a matter of keeping her. In the first few weeks she had a lot of doubts, but over time, I was easily able to put them to rest. Once her initial concerns were forgotten, from Elisha's point of view it was a whirl-wind romance. Within three months she told me that she loved me, and within six months she set up permanent residence in Surrey. It hadn't been difficult. With bugger all else going on in my life, I devoted it entirely to her, buying her presents, cooking her dinner, taking Junior to the park – she lapped it up. Her friendship group was so superficial that I don't think that she was able tell the difference between true affection and the fake caricature of love that I was presenting. I moved into her mansion and let out my own house. I must say, that as much as I enjoyed the glamorous life-style, I resented being wholly dependent upon her. With her blessing, I began giving interviews to the press. I always portrayed myself as a family man, wholly and completely in love with Elisha and her son Junior. The money I made from this, and my brief but lucrative modelling career was a pittance in comparison with Elisha's salary, but still, it was a better income than I had been used to.

To me though, now that my quest was over, I felt a little let down. I didn't know what I had expected, but not the emptiness that was consuming me. Now I had fame, and money, and a stunner to fuck any which way I wanted, but without anything new to strive for, it all felt a little bit of an anti-climax. Further to this, I surprised myself by discovering that I found it so difficult not having a job. I wasn't used to such a lack of structure in my life, and I found myself moping around a lot and watching too much television – I grew bored with it all.

I did enjoy being seen in public with her on my arm – walking down the street, or going to a restaurant with her – but behind closed doors, she wasn't any different to any other girl. My main problem was that I had built up this fake family oriented persona, and was now forced to pretend to be this person 24 hours a day. I wasn't able to be honest with Elisha like I had ultimately been with Scarlett, or have a laugh with her like I did with Charlie. As it turned out, apart from a few quirks, Elisha did not have much of a sense of humour at all – cynicism and sarcasm flew over her head like bullets from a French soldier's gun. Making money became too easy, and all her friends were fake and plastic. They had so much money, and cared so little about what was going on in the world that one of them was surprised when I mentioned working as an estate agent through the recession. To my complete disbelief, she said "What? There's a recession on?" I found myself being embarrassed at the people we hung around – people who had enough money to be shocked that everyone else did not have enough 'artistic integrity' to chase their dreams in show-business without a job on the side. It was like being surrounded by a bunch of self-absorbed drama students, in fact, it was worse than that; these people didn't seem to remember living a normal life at all. I was ashamed that Damien of all people had become my best friend. Damien, a man incapable of altruism, was the only person who I was able to enjoy myself with. It wasn't as bad as it sounds, I rarely saw him without Elisha in tow, meaning that he was usually on best behaviour. However, there were times when I needed to see him on his own; his monster side was always a great reminder of where I had come from, and kept my feet on the ground.

The main problem with our relationship, though, was Benedict Junior. I wasn't ready to be a father, but I had become burdened with someone else's brat. I'll admit that on the odd occasion he did something that made me laugh with genuine affection, but for the most part, Junior was simply annoying. Children at that age are so dependent upon their parents, and with Benedict senior remaining in Illinois, I was the only father the little sod had. It wasn't even like he had a likeable name – Benedict Junior – a constant reminder that his dullard of a father had been inside Elisha's cunt before me. By the time I came on the picture, Junior was already walking and making gurgling sounds with an American accent, which thankfully faded over time. Children are so selfish – having their mothers cater to their every whim, and throwing a tantrum when they don't get their way. It's like having a pet that takes up all your time, causes a shit load of stress, but doesn't give anything back at all.

Despite our last meeting together, I remained in touch with Scarlett throughout. I deliberately avoided meeting her in person, I didn't trust myself to keep my hands off her, so our relationship was entirely telephone based. Over the months that followed, I was surprised to discover that our dysfunctional relationship evolved into a true friendship. I found her to be my one true confidante, and I would rant about my home life to her regularly. She always seemed happy when I called, and listened attentively to everything I said. I always found our telephone conversations to be cathartic in the extreme, and found my evenings with Elisha and Junior much more manageable if I had set half an hour aside to moan about them to Scarlett.

After Elisha's divorce came through, it wasn't a difficult decision to propose to her. Despite my frustration, and general dissatisfaction with the predicament I had put myself in, I knew that the entire male population (and probably a high percentage of the female population) would give their right arm to be me.

Teary eyed, she accepted my proposal, and on the 24th April 2011, we were married in Vegas. As with Elisha's previous marriage, we kept it fairly low key. My parents and sisters were understandably a little upset not to be invited, but it wasn't that kind of affair, and I didn't particularly want them hanging around me and Damien during my stag party. The weirdest thing struck me as I said my wedding vows: they didn't mean anything to me. I knew as I said them that they were all lies, and for a few dangerous seconds the words stuck like sandpaper in my throat. I forced myself to say them, and once I had done that, it was too late to turn back. After all, what did I have to turn back to? A life with Charlie? Not a chance. It's a strange thing, how life makes people strangers. The Charlie I knew was gone, transformed and altered beyond recognition. We hadn't spoken for over a year, and she was lost to me. So I swallowed my soul, and married my wife.

This was it, mission accomplished. My hard work since that fateful meeting with Polly in the summer of 2007 had come to fruition. I wasn't as happy as I thought I would have been, but if I had the chance to do it again, would I? Fuck yeah. My main regret about it all though, was the trail of devastation I had left in my wake. Lives ruined, genitalia lost, all for the sake of a beautiful woman. If only I had been a little more careful with how I handled the people that had helped me on my way. When I started out, I had little idea I would be successful in my endeavour, and even less of an idea of the repercussions that would befall me as a consequence of my actions...

Epilogue

My life had become a whirlwind of red carpets, expensive restaurants and star-studded after-parties, but things took a turn for the worse when Elisha got back to her career in earnest. Until this point, she had been limiting her roles in films to bit-parts, and voice-overs in animations. This had kept her in the public eye, while giving her more time with her son. Now that the little shit had turned two, she was able to regroup and refocus on leading roles again. Consequently, I was left on my own for weeks on end with a two year old. It was at this point it dawned on me that I had set this up all wrong: I had pretended to like her son in order to get into her pants. I had not expected her to dismiss the nanny to allow me more quality time with him. Worse though, his dad would call or Skype from time to time, and as Junior was barely able to string three words together, I was forced to idly sit by and listen to my wife's ex-husband make a complete twat of himself. I even had to make idle chit-chat with him at the beginning and end of every call. It was horrendous.

It was quite fortuitous timing that I received a letter from *Oops! TV* on the very same day that Elisha announced that she would be spending the month of June in Italy filming 'Julius The Musical: The life and times of Julius Caesar in song'. *Oops!* had invited me to be one of their celebrity guest-stars on *Soma Holiday*, and I jumped at the chance to appear on my favourite show. Most celebrities that went into the *Soma House* had no idea how to play the game. They breezed in, obnoxious, loud, and without a clue how to win the public's favour. It was such an honour (and an unbelievably good excuse to get away from Benedict) that I accepted the invitation without a second thought. I was also interested in furthering my public image as much as possible. I didn't just want to be known as Elisha's lapdog, I wanted to be a celebrity in my own right.

Although *Oops! TV* tell everybody to keep your participation on the show a secret, I had no choice but to let Elisha know so that she could make appropriate child-care arrangements. She looked surprised as I said it, and in fairness, according to her view of me, it was quite out of character for me to be so attention seeking as to go on a reality TV show. She wasn't annoyed, or put out, but she was perhaps mildly embarrassed, as if such things were beneath her.

By the time June came round, I was so bored with being in the house with the baby that I was itching to have some fun. Gone were the days that I could ask Guy out for a cheeky pint in the town, and Damien's journeys back to his home country were sporadic at best. Thankfully, the day prior to the contest beginning, I was expected to give some interviews to introduce myself to the viewing public. Following the interviews, *Oops!* had put me up for the night in a hotel. Although I wasn't allowed any friends or family to visit, a number of crew-members were instructed to keep me company and ensure I didn't go wondering into town (in case I bumped into any of the other celebrity guest stars.) I was formally introduced to my entourage in the hotel bar – there were three of them altogether. Two of them met me at the front door, and explained that my third guard was at the bar buying a round of drinks – no expense was spared to ensure the celebrity guests were well cared for, and in the best of spirits when entering the *Soma House*.

I didn't recognise her from behind. She had a slim, petite figure and long luscious dark hair. Even once she turned, it didn't immediately click who it was. Polly was standing before me holding a bottle of white wine and a pint of Guinness. She looked a lot better than when I had last seen her over three years previously – she had unblemished pale skin and her legs had lost the wobble that had so distracted me when we were... (I guess an 'item' is too strong a word), when we were fucking on a regular basis. Weirdly, her face looked younger, and her tits looked more pert; they weren't bigger, they were just standing to attention in a more obvious way. In truth, her appearance struck me like a breath of fresh air; someone from my past, from the good old days of university and normality had just appeared back in my life as if from nowhere. The nasty business of Terry's castration (the last time I spoke to her) did not jump to the forefront of my mind – quite simply, I was very happy to see her.

"Polly?" I said, rather obviously.

"Hi, Shaun." she smiled.

"It's been ages! You look great!" I sucked in the sight of her, and breathed in the familiar scent of her perfume.

"Yeah, I lost a load of weight with my Deli Belly when I was travelling, and I've somehow managed to keep it off since."

"Nobody gets to look *that* good from Deli belly. You look really well."

"Thanks, Shaun. It's been hard work – I swim every day now."

"Well it tells!"

I meant what I was saying, I couldn't keep my eyes off of her. She didn't look like the same girl.

"I got you a Guinness. I suppose you still drink the Black Stuff?"

"Great, thanks."

After getting back from travelling, Polly had taken on a few bar jobs, before finally getting a job at *Oops! TV* (through one of Terry's old work colleagues who had risen through the ranks). As usual, she still didn't seem to have much responsibility in her job – she was after all, supposed to be my stooge for the evening – but she seemed happier, and less care-worn. We spent most of the first thirty minutes catching up on what some of our mutual acquaintances from university were doing. Unlike me, she had kept in regular touch with most of them. During this period, the memory of Terry's groin bleeding on my carpet jumped to my mind. It wasn't without hesitation that I asked:

"How is Terry?"

"Still in Bethlem."

I had a sinking feeling, I thought I knew where she was taking about.

"Bethlem?"

"A hospital for mental illness."

"Ah." I thought about apologising, or expressing sympathy, but I didn't want to dwell for too long on our past problems, I was enjoying myself too much. I wanted to tactfully change the topic of conversation, but struggled to grasp anything that didn't sound too trivial. Thankfully, she seemed to be of like mind, and began speaking to me about a pet cat that she had recently adopted and the conversation meandered away from the horrors I had suffered at the hands of Terry Taylor. It felt as if nothing awkward had ever happened between us; we were friends again. After a time, Polly's workmates got bored of our chatter, and turned in for the night. I think that they had been disappointed not to have had enough interaction with me, Polly and I were inseparable. Being a hotel, no last orders were called, and we drank until the early hours of the morning. I was pretty shit-faced by the time she said:

"Bed time me thinks. We've both got a big day tomorrow."

I looked at my watch and was surprised to see it was nearly 04:00 AM! I was going to be on live TV at midday – what a stupid decision to stay up this late and get this drunk. As one, we stood up and made our way through the lobby into the elevator. We smiled at each other when we noticed that we were on the same floor.

"What room are you in?" I said.

"Three-two-one" she said.

"I'm in three-two-two," I replied, "It looks like we're going to be neighbours."

We walked in silence along the brightly lit hallways, while memories of our past endeavours floated through my mind. I found myself reminiscing about our university days, when our sex had been uncomplicated and passionate. I realised that I missed those carefree days, and what's more, in that moment, I missed Polly. As we reached our rooms, the heat was rising inside me, and I wanted her. We came to a stop outside of her room, and I tried to wish her good night. She stared back at me, and I supposed that she too was remembering how much fun we had at university. Her hand shot out and clasped the back of my neck. She pulled me towards her until our faces met. We kissed, and then, without speaking, she fumbled for her key and pulled me into her room.

As she swooped in to close the curtains, a modicum of sanity returned to me. What in fucks name was I doing? I'd nailed Polly countless times. Gallons and gallons of my semen had already been swallowed up by her hungry cunt. Why risk Elisha exploring old territory?

"I can't do this. I'm married." I said.

She ignored me. She took off her dress and unclasped her bra so that her gorgeous little tits clouded my senses. Even her legs seemed longer than they had been before. How had she done this to herself?

"I'm serious. I love me wife." It was an attempt to convince myself more than her.

"But I've missed you." She gently pushed me back onto the bed and straddled me. Through my trousers, I could feel her warmth enveloping me.

"Polly, we need to stop."

"I've missed your cock too." She stroked my inner thigh and worked her way up to my Chap. It betrayed me and stiffened at her touch – ready for action.

"Jesus, what's got into you tonight?" I moaned.

She didn't respond, instead she unbuttoned my shirt and began to lick my nipples. I couldn't resist her any longer. I pulled her knickers off and decided to fuck her one last time. For a moment or two, I could think of nothing else apart from my raw, all-encompassing lust.

But as I entered her familiar vagina, I was reminded how much I despised her. In spite of her make-over she was the same old Polly, with the same tired moves. Despite her efforts, she still couldn't hold my attention, and the spell was broken. I lost my focus on the task at hand, and realised it was all a horrible mistake. I should have been beyond this.   What the fuck was I doing?

I withdrew.

"What's wrong?" she said

"I need to go" I replied, deciding to use the same tactic Charlie had used in our early acquaintance. I hastily pulled on my trousers and my shirt, grabbed my shoes and ran out of the room without another word. I slammed the door behind me, breathing hard, my penis erect and frustratingly unfulfilled. The booze had now taken its toll – the hall was spinning, and I thought I might vomit – but I snuck into my room with a smile on my face. I had *finally* succeeded in resisting temptation.

June 2011

There is very little to say about my time on Soma Holiday. I thought I had been doing so well, and for ten days I worked hard at proving to everyone that I was a clean-living, kind-hearted, altruistic gentleman. While the other celebrities bickered over every perceived slight, and our 'servants' tried their hardest not to resent their ridiculous demands, I stayed out of the arguments and tried to stay friends with everyone.

I truly thought that I was going to win. Everyone inside seemed to like me, and I was so certain that the viewing public would adore the self-righteous person I was portraying. Unfortunately, on Friday the 10th of June, I was voted out of the Soma House. It really did come as quite a shock, especially when the doors opened and the entire crowd booed at me in unison. The presenter, Mustapha MacRowne, ushered me towards the stage, and attempted to feign delight at my presence. The audience continued to heckle me; one person even threw a bottle of water that sprayed all over my suit. I tried to stay calm, posing in front of the cameras, wondering what Elisha was going to say when she realised that she had married a figure of hate. I couldn't work out why I had come across so poorly, perhaps it was all a misunderstanding? Perhaps I could explain it away.

Nobody greeted me at my exit interview from the show. Not Elisha, not my parents, none of my friends. I must have appeared quite lonely. Nothing in the "Shaun Valfierno Highlights" reel indicated where I had gone wrong. It was only when my interview started that I understood what had happened.

Mustapha: "Shaun, you've been a great housemate, a real pleasure to watch on screen. Not one person in the house has voted you out. I wanted to get your opinion on where you think you've gone wrong?"

Me: "Well, first of all, I wanted to say what a great pleasure it is to be here Mustapha. I've always been a big fan of the show. I'm so excited to be sitting here on the sofa!"

Mustapha: "Thanks Shaun, but do you have any idea why you've been voted out?"

Me: "I guess I've possibly been a bit dull for people to like?"

Mustapha: "Shaun, in the house you had everything going for you, but I'm afraid things outside of the house have been unravelling. Take a look at these headlines in the papers. I think that you've got some explaining to do."

What followed was a rather cruel compilation of news stories and interviews of people discussing my intimate night with Polly. I had been labelled as a love-rat. Polly had been brutally honest about our affair, and had given details about our life story, even mentioning what had happened to Terry. The heart breaking account of deceit and betrayal given from Terry Taylor's padded cell may have been the nail in the coffin for me as far as the public were concerned. I was a disgusting spectre who had pulled the wool over everyone's eyes and deserved to be shunned.

It all clicked into place: Polly had organised this. She had been planning to get her revenge on me for ruining Terry's life. She must have pulled some strings to get me an invite to appear on the show. She had requested to be my chaperone. She had arranged to have our rooms next to each other at the hotel. She had even taken graphic pictures of our copulations on her phone and sold them to the highest bidder. I never knew she had it in her to be so manipulative. I went red with shame as my world came crumbling down. Yet again, there were pictures of me in a compromising position, but this time they were not working to my advantage. I could tell that people were watching my reaction, waiting for me to do something. I decided that I didn't have time for all this shit; I needed to speak to Elisha.

Me: "I've got to go"

Mustapha: "Wait, I…"

I pushed him over on live TV, and ran out of the studio (something that the newspapers would make a spectacle of; something else that I would come to regret.) Everything had gone wrong. Everything had turned to shit.

By the time I arrived home, Elisha had already evicted me. My clothes and all of my belongings had been thrown outside of the house a few days previously, and were consequently ruined as a result of being left out in the rain. Furthermore, all the locks had been changed, so I couldn't gain access. She wasn't home, she had arranged for me to be evicted from Italy, and she refused all my phone calls. I spent the night at a hotel, with the paparazzi camping on my doorstep. Ultimately, Scarlett had been right – I had fucked everything up. My marriage fell apart, Elisha wouldn't forgive me, and the world thought of me as lying scum. It had all gone completely wrong; Polly had her vengeance.

After two weeks of loneliness and misery, and with nobody else to turn to, I found myself calling Scarlett, needing her company.

July 2011

It was always to be expected that I would end up with Scarlett; Elisha and I had had nothing in common, and Charlie was lost to me. I should probably have spent some time alone to get over my marriage, but I had become a social out-cast and needed company. Scarlett understood me; she knew how to comfort me, and how to cheer me up. Besides, it wasn't as if our relationship had ever truly ended, even during our respective short and disastrous marriages.

One summer's day, while Scarlett lay naked and asleep on my chest, I found myself contemplating the future, wondering whether I should attempt to restart my career in estate agency, or try to salvage my life as a celebrity. Now that I had become a public hate-figure, offers to endorse products had dried up. I would need to work long and hard to reinvent myself, and regain the public's trust. If I'm honest, the thought of either choice left a horrible taste in my mouth. I didn't know what I wanted to do.

One thing I did know was that Scarlett made me feel good about myself; she helped me forget how much I had fucked everything up. I wondered whether we could actually make a proper go of it. Perhaps we belonged together? Perhaps we could change our ways and become good for each other? Perhaps we could mend each other? Scarlett broke me from my reverie by getting out of bed to have a shower. As I closed my eyes and listened to the hum of the boiler, and the sound of the water spraying against the tiles, her phone sounded. I sat up and looked over to it, wondering whether she still had the same old pin. Old habits die hard, so I picked it up and successfully gained access to her messages.

This is what I saw:

Damien: *"Hey, I'm in the City tonight, fancy a fuck?"*

Scarlett: *"My pants are wet through in anticipation."*

Damien: *"21:30 in the usual spot."*

I put my head in my hands and sobbed. I wanted the games to end.

19984145R00173

Printed in Great Britain
by Amazon